MID

When Charlie first saw Crystal his mouth suddenly became dry. His eyes moved from her face and hair to the voluptuous semi-spheres of her breasts, which pulsed and strained above the skintight, laced bodice of a minuscule corset. Fashioned from blood-red leather, it clasped her narrow waist in its erotic embrace and ended just above the dark cloud of her pubis. Stretched tight around her bare hips, she wore a suspender belt made from the same soft leather and her legs were encased in super-sheer seamed stockings. On her feet she wore red leather stilettos.

As Charlie entered the room, Crystal spoke to him, her voice low and deadly. 'How dare you enter this room fully clothed. Undress immediately.'

It was then he noticed the narrow, black riding crop held lightly in her right hand . . .

Midnight Music

Erica Boleyn

HEADLINE
DELTA

First published in 1994
by HEADLINE BOOK PUBLISHING

A HEADLINE DELTA paperback

10 9 8 7 6 5 4 3 2 1

ISBN 0 7472 4190 2

Typeset by CBS, Felixstowe, Suffolk

Printed and bound in Great Britain by
Cox & Wyman Ltd, Reading, Berks

HEADLINE BOOK PUBLISHING
A division of Hodder Headline PLC
338 Euston Road
London NW1 3BH

Midnight Music

Chapter One

'Thanks a bunch, pal! I'll do the same for you one day.'
Crystal Clearwater wrapped her long Arran coat around herself with an air of peeved deliberation and a voluble sigh, expelling a plume of warm, breathy vapour into the morning air. With one slim, black-booted foot she kicked a tiny pebble so that it skimmed crazily across the frostbitten bottom of the empty swimming pool. In doing so, she surprised an elderly, ragged-looking blackbird which had unwittingly landed there for a swift breather before continuing its near-hopeless quest for breakfast comestibles in the chill, winter-shrouded gardens of High Links Hall, world-renowned health and beauty spa and exclusive Somerset retreat for the rich and famous members of society's elite.

'Aw, poor little thing! I'm a bad-tempered bitch when I'm roused, aren't I? She fished guiltily in the back pocket of her hip-hugging Levi's and found a small cereal bar which she'd been saving to have with her mid-morning coffee. Extricating it from its plastic wrapper, which she carefully replaced in her pocket, she broke it up into small pieces and lobbed the fragments onto a patch of silvered, frozen grass a few yards away.

Rubbing her ungloved hands together and blowing on

them in an attempt to rekindle some semblance of sensation in her fingers, Crystal gazed knowingly at the ragamuffin bird, a wry smile on her face. Perched on a nearby branch, it ruffled its greying feathers and cocked its head at her, peering back with a beady, yellow-rimmed eye before dropping purposefully to the patch of grass like a silent, malevolent goblin and beginning rapidly to demolish its unexpected treat.

Crystal watched it for a moment or two, then turned to her companion with an indulgent grin. 'Cheeky little beggar! That bird's been sent to haunt me, I swear it. Follows me around like a tiny black spectre whenever I come out here for a stroll, desperate for a quick peek in my pockets to see if I've brought any nosh for it. Must have me down as a soft touch or something. Like some others I could name.' Her eyes not once leaving Frankie de Rosa's pinched features, Crystal bared her teeth at him in mock rage and her grin turned into an evil grimace, comical in its grotesque intensity.

Frankie was well used to the wicked sense of humour of his favourite sparring partner and subject of many a romantic, not to say erotic, fancy. Frankie's rôle was that of chief bodyguard and personal minder to the manageress of High Links, Sadie St George. He was also general overseer, in charge of the smooth running of the place, keeping an eye open at all times for possible hiccoughs in the day-to-day comings and goings. As such, he was in frequent and generally amiable contact with the stunning, albeit formidable, Crystal Clearwater, PR Manager and soother of frayed nerves and injured sensibilities amongst staff and guests alike. At the moment, however, relations between the two of them were not all they might be. Frankie was aware of a distinct frostiness emanating from Crystal's cool demeanour, which had very little to do with the wintry morning and a great deal to do with her obvious displeasure with him.

Guiltily averting his eyes from hers, Frankie wrapped his suit jacket tightly around himself and stamped his feet – unsuitably shod for the time of year in a pair of lightweight leather slip-ons – on the hard ground. Playing for time, he arranged and rearranged the somewhat dapper, paisley-patterned silk scarf – his one and only nod towards the vagaries of the season – around his neck and tucked the fringed ends under his lapels.

'And that's another thing, Frankie. I wish to goodness you'd make a few more concessions to the English winter. You'll catch your death dressed like that. You're not at home in dear old Naples now, you know!'

'More's the pity, Crystal, my love. More's the pity. So help me, if I could scrape together sufficient dosh, I'd snap up a couple of air tickets for Sharon and me and we'd spend the festive season out there, where the climate's a mite softer around the edges, instead of . . .' His voice trailed off lamely and his eyes met Crystal's for the first time since he'd spotted her taking her daily stroll in the High Links grounds that morning, when he'd nervously slipped out to join her in a bid to establish his case for the defence.

Crystal glared at him. 'Instead of sneaking off with her for a mucky couple of nights of Yuletide fun and frolics at that poncey excuse for a coaching inn on the main road. Honestly, Frank, I'd have thought even you had more taste than to subject her to that place. Strip lighting throughout, chips with everything and a bottle of Pomagne on the house for the

3

lucky winner of the plate-throwing contest. Two bottles for the unfortunate runner-up.

'I ask you, Frank, is The Spotted Cow any sort of a place to spend one of the holiest of our Christian festivals? And in the arms of a lover, to boot? And you claiming to be Roman Catholic, too.' Crystal's brow furrowed as she looked at him and she shook her head slowly, clicking her tongue in disapproval.

Frankie was crestfallen, appalled at Crystal's uncannily accurate description of the establishment within which he'd chosen to woo his girlfriend, Sharon Neavis, for the duration of the Christmas period. 'Aw, come on, Crystal. The Cow's not as black as it's painted. Besides, it's good and cheap and there's plenty of scope for the odd knees-up or two. Anyway, Sharon's like me. She likes to let her hair down once in a while and have a bit of a giggle but can't stand the idea of having to put on airs and graces and be on her best behaviour all the time – like you do at some places I could mention . . .' He glanced meaningfully across at the stately, grey stone majesty of High Links Hall – its outline sharp and imposing against the wintry sky – as though to emphasise his point.

'Anyway, personal preferences aside for a moment, I'm sorry to land you with a working Christmas, Crystal. It's just a damn shame that Sadie, in her managerial wisdom, won't let you and I take time off simultaneously. I mean, I know we're the ones who do all the work around here and keep the show on the road but, when all's said and done, the place is crawling with able-bodied staff. You'd think the old girl would be prepared to relax the rules a little for a couple of days over Christmas, wouldn't you?'

Crystal nodded, an expression of weary resignation on her

face. 'You would indeed, Frank. But who knows what weird and wacky notions are circling the inner recesses of our boss's fluffy, peroxide head at the moment. Ever since her latest bit of stuff, Casper the magic-fingered masseur, flew the nest on the end of your esteemed and burly colleague, Nick Knack's, size eleven to seek employment elsewhere, she's become even more eccentric and ga-ga than usual.

'I for one am hoping to God that she finds herself a replacement lover pretty damn quick so that we can all return to some semblance of normality. Did you catch a glimpse of that memo she send round yesterday? "From now on, all staff must seek the permission of their supervisors before paying a call of nature during working hours." And all because a couple of dozy junior kitchen staff decided to take a leak at the same time, leaving a saucepanful of celery soup unattended which chose that moment to boil over and scald the head chef. I ask you! Permission to go for a pee! She'll have us all in knee socks and pigtails next. Compulsory cod-liver oil and lights out by nine-thirty.'

Tickled by Crystal's habitual and merciless sense of humour at their boss's expense, Frankie's shoulders began to shake with silent laughter.

Crystal followed suit and then, regaining her composure, she continued: 'Anyway, I might just as well work over Christmas. There don't seem to be many alternatives, really, the way things have worked out. I was hoping to spend a couple of days with Mum and Dad up in Liverpool. You know, Christmas dinner with all the trimmings and as much Madeira and crème de menthe as I can drink. Nice and casual and homely with the three of us sitting companionably in front of the Magicoal, passing round the Black Magic while our beloved Queen drones on with her usual misplaced optimism from the telly on the sideboard – colour control turned full up, of course.

'Not that the poor old soul's got much to be cheerful about these days. What with the press behaving like a bunch of turbo-charged pit bull terriers and her kids doing *Dallas* impersonations all over the place . . .

'Anyway, the folks have opted to spend Christmas on the Costa del Sol this year, so that's that idea taken care of.' Crystal sighed.

Frankie was sympathetic but realistic. 'Can't say I entirely blame them, love. At their time of life a drop of sunshine and sangria with their Christmas lunch could be just what the doctor ordered. Anyway, what about old lover-boy Isaac? The snake-hipped guitar wizard from the Smoke. How come he's not whipping you off for a fortnight in Bali at the fans' expense?'

Despite the temperature in the garden, Crystal blushed and stared at the shiny toes of her boots, her expression pensive and dreamy. 'Oh . . . he's probably in Australia or New Zealand or somewhere by now, chatting up the sheilas on Bondi Beach armed with a pair of Ray Bans and a four-pack of Fosters.' Crystal rubbed her frostbitten hands together again and stamped her feet on the hard ground at the same time.

Concerned, Frankie looked at her enquiringly. 'Can I take it that the course of true love is not running as smoothly as you'd have hoped?' He had to admit, even if only to himself, that he'd had his doubts about the wisdom of Crystal's hitching her emotional wagon to a pop star – especially one as famous and as universally desired as Isaac Mallory. He was afraid she may end up with nothing to show for it but a broken heart and an untidy mess of shattered dreams. It seemed to him now, more's the pity, that his fears may have been justified.

With a slow smile, Crystal lowered her lashes provocatively and glanced rather fetchingly at Frankie out of the corner of her eye. Despite himself, Frankie experienced the customary restriction in his nether regions at the sight.

'Don't you worry your pretty little head about me, Frankie baby. Relations between Isaac and me are perfectly fine and dandy, thank you very much.' Crystal paused for a moment, thoughtfully, and her face assumed a frustrated frown. 'When he's around and on his own, that is, and not swanning off on world tours, surrounded by a bunch of boozy acolytes and a bevy of assorted adoring beauties.'

Her expression altering once more, this time for the better, Crystal turned to Frankie with an affectionate smile and patted him good-naturedly on the shoulder. 'Anyway, love, I'm sure Christmas at High Links will be absolutely fine. I don't doubt that there'll be plenty to keep me out of mischief – if what they say about the reputation of a certain female VIP, mentioned on the advance guest list and characterised as highly confidential, is anything to go by . . .

'Hey, did I say *out* of mischief? Could turn out to be a case of High Jinks at High Links!' Crystal smiled mysteriously, then bit her lip and giggled at Frankie's bewildered expression before continuing: 'Anyway, must dash. Standing round gassing won't pay the bills, will it?' Tossing back her waist-length, liquorice-dark hair in a businesslike manner, she blew him a quick kiss, turned on her shiny-booted heel and was gone, leaving only the faint whiff of her designer perfume

7

as a potent reminder of her recent presence.

Now, who the hell could this mystery guest be that Crystal was tormenting him with? She sounded like a bit of all right, anyway. Maybe Frankie had been a little hasty when he'd fixed to spend Christmas with Sharon at The Spotted Cow. Oh well, not to worry. It was too late to change the arrangements now. Confused and misty-eyed with emotion, Frankie gazed after Crystal's slim, sassy figure as she walked away from him – hotly pursued by the opportunistic blackbird – and surreptitiously adjusted the front of his straining trousers.

It was criminal the things that woman was capable of doing to him. What with all that hair and those legs which seemed to go on for miles and miles – all the way up to her armpits, in fact. Crystal Clearwater really was one of the most prick-stimulating broads Frankie had ever known. A real instant horn job.

The granddaughter of a native American Indian, she possessed the inscrutable, olive-skinned beauty and the sleek, finely muscled greyhound physique of an athlete – an entirely female and highly voluptuous one. With her high cheekbones, her elegant head held high and that intense, level gaze of hers which was apt to dissolve into a sultry smile or a delightful, wicked chuckle at the least provocation, there wasn't a man alive immune to her considerable charms. And Frankie de Rosa was no exception. He'd well and truly melted under Crystal's spell a good many months before and, despite his affection for and current involvement with the lovely Sharon, the magic Crystal had sown in his heart, not to mention his groin, had yet to evaporate. In fact, he doubted that it ever would.

With an extravagant sigh of thwarted desire, Frankie

shivered and wrapped his lightweight suit jacket around himself in an effort to extract the last meagre vestiges of warmth from it before returning to the relative calm and sanctity of the office he shared with his burly side-kick, Nick Knack, and a steaming mug of Ty-Phoo.

Crystal had first met Isaac Mallory a few months before when he and his rock band, the notorious Steel Dinosaurs, had spent a recuperative few days at High Links Hall at the tail end of a taxing European tour and the recording of their latest album.

For Crystal, Isaac had long been an object of fantasy and romantic speculation, even before she'd set eyes on him in the flesh. But to discover that he was to spend several days under the same roof and finally to encounter him in real life – dark, lanky and impossibly handsome – had been like the momentous culmination of every sensual dream she'd ever had.

When Crystal and Isaac met for the first time, drenched in a summer downpour outside the main entrance to High Links, something magical had happened between them, setting off erotic alarm bells which refused to be quietened until they'd made wild, tender love to each other at three o'clock in the morning beside the outdoor swimming pool in the very garden where Crystal and Frankie had recently stood.

Alive with a shared passion, they'd made love to each other time and time again over the days which followed in any number of risky and imaginative venues in and around the Hall and gardens. But finally it was time for Isaac to leave High Links and return to London with what remained of his band – Frankie de Rosa having succeeded in filching

Sharon from Kevin McGlone, the Steel Dinosaurs' boorish and uncouth drummer, and Barney the bass guitarist leaving to set up a smallholding in Wales, aided and abetted by the pert young Polly, High Links' former receptionist.

Isaac's hectic butterfly lifestyle and Crystal's responsibility and deep involvement in her job had made it virtually impossible for them to meet since that fateful week in July. Late in September, however, just as the fruit hung ripe and luscious in the Somerset hedgerows and the low autumn mists were heavy with the scent of woodsmoke, Isaac telephoned. He'd just returned from a week in Amsterdam, where the Steel Dinosaurs had entertained their Dutch fans with a series of gigs, and was now spending a few days at his house in London's Camden Lock before embarking on what promised to be a mammoth world tour.

To Crystal's utter delight, he invited her to take advantage of this brief respite in his work schedule by spending some time with him before he left for America. Intense excitement and anticipation overcame Crystal's natural reserve like a giant, joyous tidal wave. She accepted his invitation immediately, hugging herself with glee at the prospect and skilfully executing a series of spontaneous cartwheels around her spacious office before collapsing back – dishevelled, with flashing eyes and glowing cheeks – into her silk-draped executive chair.

Crystal spent the journey to London in a state of intense, delicious excitement. Periodically picking up a newspaper or magazine and scanning its contents, she'd suddenly be struck by a vision of her lover, dark-eyed and sensual, and a warm, insidious shiver would spread through her languorous limbs, turning them to jelly and causing her heart to hammer in her breast. After her umpteenth attempt at reading, she carelessly stuffed the newspaper back in her luggage and, eyes closed and lips softened by a wistful little smile, gave herself up to the highly romantic and erotic images and emotions which assailed her mind and body. When the train finally arrived in London, Crystal grabbed her luggage and, wrapping her long purple coat around herself for warmth and comfort, made her way purposefully towards the ticket collector, periodically pushed and jostled by the hurrying hoards of passengers. Finally emerging into the bright, daylight bustle of the concourse outside and putting her cases down on the pavement, Crystal immediately became a source of interest and speculation amongst a group of weary taxi drivers, many of whom stood together in small, convivial groups, propped up against their vehicles, smoking cigarettes and sipping from plastic beakers of watery station-buffet tea, casually passing the time of day in each other's company.

The driver whose cab was parked at the front of the queue nudged his companion and gave him a knowing wink before extinguishing his cigarette on the pavement with the toe of his shoe and turning to Crystal with an expression of appreciative appraisal. 'Afternoon, miss. Can I take you somewhere?'

From a position near the back of the queue came a loud guffaw. 'Blimey, mate! Take her somewhere? I will if you don't!'

The first driver turned to his uncouth colleague with a disapproving glare. Crystal, not unfamiliar with this particular brand of male reaction and apparently untouched by the blatant innuendo inherent in the exchange between the two men, grinned philosophically from one to the other of them.

'Thanks but no thanks. I'm expecting someone, actually.'

Right on cue, a sleek black Porsche with dark, smoked-glass windows swung round into the station forecourt and parked a few yards away from where Crystal was standing, its powerful engine rumbling patiently.

Crystal's heart leapt. Surely that couldn't be Isaac . . . could it? He hadn't mentioned anything about a Porsche. The windows were so dark that she couldn't even begin to see who was inside. As she peered across at it, however, praying for x-ray vision, the headlights flashed at her and she guessed that whoever was driving the car must be signalling to her, since she was the only person paying the slightest attention to it.

Picking up her cases, Crystal made her way serenely, if a trifle hesitantly, across to the Porsche, serenaded by a chorus of muffled wolf whistles and the sound of clearing throats. As she reached the passenger door it opened smoothly and silently to allow her access, at the same time emitting a particular, deliciously familiar masculine aroma which sent a shiver of recognition up her spine. After first allowing herself to be relieved of her luggage by a pair of heart-stoppingly tender male hands, Crystal took a deep breath, bent down and climbed as gracefully as she could under the circumstances into the car's warm, womb-like interior. Eric Clapton's *Layla* was playing quietly on the car's high-tech music system.

'Hi, Isaac . . .' she breathed, turning to her lover with a warm smile, heart pounding with excitement and anticipation. As she did so, Isaac gathered her powerfully into his arms without a moment's hesitation or even a return greeting and almost succeeded in crushing the breath from her lungs with his strong, urgent embrace. With a small, strangled groan he buried his face in her neck, inhaling the very essence of her mingled with her perfume. Then his lips moved up to her eyes and cheeks, covering them with tiny, fiery kisses before finally nuzzling her long hair and greedily nibbling her earlobe.

'Hello, Crystal,' Isaac mumbled against her ear. 'Christ, but I've missed you. I can't tell you how much I've been looking forward to seeing you again.' Struck by a sudden thought, he pulled away from Crystal and, clasping her purple shoulders, gazed into her sparkling, love-struck eyes, exploring her face with an expression of wonder and amazement as though seeing her for the first time.

'I don't believe it,' he whispered hoarsely. 'I wouldn't have thought it possible, but you're even more beautiful and goddamn horny-looking than I remember.' He stroked a tender finger across her flushed cheek, down her fine, aquiline nose and finally let it come to rest against her invitingly full lips.

Gazing back at him, Crystal's mouth dried and her heart began to pound with a delicious urgency as she experienced the familiar, heavy sensation of warmth and fullness at the base of her belly, the muscles of her sex flickering and tingling as though tantalisingly caressed by the fluttering wings of butterflies. Narrowing her eyes with desire, she tilted her head back and slowly parted her lips, allowing Isaac to insinuate his finger between them and into the sultry wetness of her mouth, whereupon she gently nibbled it with her teeth and sucked on it with slow, lascivious abandon.

After a moment or two spent witnessing this highly suggestive oral display, Isaac could bear it no longer. He screwed his eyes tight shut, threw back his head and groaned deep in his throat, at the same time removing his finger from Crystal's mouth and clasping her raven head to his black-leather-jacketed shoulder. 'And all this before we've even left the station forecourt. Good job I opted for smoked windows.' He chuckled and sat back, then cast a smouldering, sidelong glance at the object of his desire, his expression betraying a mixture of longing and mischief.

'Anyway, you gorgeous, witchy woman,' he whispered. 'I think we've both waited long enough for each other, don't you?' Crystal flushed and her heart did a loop-the-loop. She smiled slowly and nodded her agreement. 'Come on, then. Let's not waste any more valuable time . . .' Eyes glittering with desire and with a decidedly determined set to his jaw, Isaac reluctantly tore his eyes away from Crystal and swung round into the driver's position, releasing the car's handbrake and manoeuvring out into the heavy stream of London traffic with the consummate care and skill of the seasoned inner-city driver he was.

Resting her smooth head against the powerful car's soft, luxurious upholstery, Crystal spent the journey back to Isaac's house in a state of mounting sexual longing and internal sensual awareness. Closing her eyes in a bid to banish the images of grey buildings, hurrying pedestrians and other road-users which were unfolding, movie-like, across her field of vision, she sighed deeply, breathing in the intoxicating aroma of good-quality leather and her own subtle perfume. She leant back further into her seat, giving herself up to the sensations of warmth against her face and the feel of her clothing against the highly sensitive skin of her body, the fleeting notion of its imminent removal sending darts of lust from her erect nipples to her warm sex.

'So, was the trip to Holland a success?' she asked, a contented smile on her face. 'Doubtless the Steel Dinosaurs made their usual impact on the local youth, not to mention the parents of the local youth.'

Isaac chuckled, peering simultaneously into his rear-view mirror at the driver of a scarlet BMW who was staring daggers at him and showing every sign of trying to cut him up, nudging him slowly but surely into the innermost reaches of the inside lane. Eyes not once leaving the road in front, Isaac shook his fist at the driver behind and raised two fingers in a silent but unmistakeable V-sign. 'Bloody road hog! I don't know what it is about rich bastards who drive posh cars and ponce around as though they have sole claim to the road, but they bring out the raving Red in me, let me tell you!'

Incredulous, Crystal opened her eyes wide and gasped in amazement at the ironic, barefaced nerve of Isaac's comment. 'You've got to be joking – what about the rich bastard who just happens to be driving this particular posh car? You don't count, I suppose?'

Isaac looked sheepish and rubbed his ear in embarrassment. 'Oh yes, you're right, of course. I keep forgetting about my latest acquisition. I only bought it a fortnight ago and I keep forgetting I've got it. I spend ten minutes on the pavement outside my house every morning looking for my old car, cursing the thieving swine who stole it during the night.' He glanced at Crystal and grinned good-humouredly at her. 'Anyway, in answer to your question about the Dutch jaunt – yes, it was a tremendous success. If anything, the Steel Dinosaurs are even more popular in countries like Holland and Germany and Scandinavia, etcetera, than we are in the good old UK. Foreign kids seem to have an inexhaustible passion for the kind of raucous, heavy metal type stuff that we bash out in a way that seems to be diminishing over here in Britain. Still, let's not knock them – they're our bread and butter. Long may their musical tastes continue to languish in the mid-1970's.'

Crystal turned her head and looked at him, puzzled. 'I had no idea you were so cynical about your music. I always thought you took it dead seriously. Seeing you up there on stage, you seem to throw your heart and soul into it, as though your life depended on it.'

'My life does depend on it in a way. My livelihood at least. The band's popularity pays my mortgage and keeps my car on the road and food in my cupboard. Anyway, I'm a bit of an actor at heart. I love all that posturing and gyrating in front of an auditorium full of adoring kids. And I love my guitar and the things I can make it do. I never stop thinking how lucky I am to be who I am, doing what I love best and making a bloody good living out of it into the bargain. But I sometimes wish the Steel Dinosaurs were a little less mainstream. A bit more adventurous and avant-garde, you know? I've got all these great ideas and plans for the future . . .'

Isaac turned his head and peered at Crystal mysteriously, eyes glittering with excitement as though he were dying to let her into a secret but had suddenly thought better of it, deciding instead to prolong the agony a while longer.

'Anyway, enough of that. It'll keep 'til later.' Before Crystal had time to protest and demand that he tell her what was on his mind, Isaac grinned and clapped a silencing hand over her mouth, eyes still fixed on the road in front, which quickly took the wind out of her sails and caused her to collapse in a fit of muffled giggles. 'Okay, anything you say!'

she said when he finally released her.

Isaac's voice was as soft as silk as he continued, pulling over to the kerb and manoeuvring the Porsche into a space between two cars: 'Besides, we're here now. Let's get this heap of scrap metal parked and then I'll whisk you up and show you my etchings. To start with, at least. Just to get you warmed up . . .' Isaac glanced at her and then back at the road. His smile was slow and lazy.

A sudden shock of tingling excitement flashed like summer lightning through Crystal's limbs, causing them to feel weak with anticipation and her cheeks to flush hotly. In a couple of minutes she'd be right there in Isaac's house. Isaac Mallory . . . the rock star who for so many years had fuelled her horniest and most outrageous erotic fantasies, even more so since they'd become lovers that summer. The notion, dawning as it was in her fevered consciousness, that at last these sexy daydreams were to become a vital, pulsing reality once more was almost more than she could cope with.

Misty-eyed with longing she gazed through the smoked-glass window of the expensive car towards the tall, well-heeled Edwardian houses which lined the gracious, tree-lined avenue. Two prosperous-looking kids whizzed past on state-of-the-art, customised roller skates, whooping and yelling good-naturedly at each other, their healthy, well-nourished faces pink and bright with excitement. Isaac switched off the car's ignition and turned towards her, leaning back casually into his seat, watching her as she in turn watched the children disappear down the road and turn a corner at the end. 'One of the other advantages of belonging to a successful rock band,' he said, gently amused by Crystal's obvious approval of this attractive and salubrious neighbourhood, 'is that I can afford to live in one of the more habitable parts of London. The river's only a couple of streets away, and the market, too. There's some great little pubs, as well. My local does the best meat and potato pie in the northern hemisphere. I'll take you there. But first . . .' Reaching out a hand, he tenderly stroked Crystal's cheek and then, reluctantly, he tore his gaze away and leapt from the car, bounding over to the passenger door and opening it, allowing Crystal to climb out onto the pavement and treating himself to a tantalising glimpse of her unbelievably long, black-booted legs.

Without a word, he grabbed her luggage from the back of the car, locked it and then went ahead of her up the steps to a bright, canary-yellow front door. 'Welcome to my little oasis in the centre of this mad, bad world.' Ushering Crystal into the house with a smile and a grand gesture, he stood aside, silently indicating for her to enter what she assumed to be the main living room. Then he deftly removed her long purple coat, gently slipping it from her shoulders and draping it artfully over the stripped-pine newel post at the foot of the stairs.

Isaac's living room, which was large and welcoming, was lit by generous swathes of warm, autumn sunshine which streamed through the high sash windows with their dove-grey, semi-transparent drapes, glancing off the natural wood, gleaming steel and glass surfaces with which the room was somewhat minimally furnished. A small open fire danced in the cast-iron hearth, thoughtfully lit by Isaac before he'd left for the station.

Crystal was immediately struck by the Scandinavian-like simplicity of the room – clean, uncluttered lines, natural materials in a preponderance of greys and charcoals and unvarnished wood shades, with here and there a splash of colour in the form of a tapestry cushion, a modern sculpture or a vibrant, straight-sided vase. The plain walls were decorated with abstract fabric hangings and various works by contemporary artists, steel or wood-framed and visually commanding without being obtrusive.

Liking what she saw and impressed by what she perceived to be a further insight into the charm and character of her lover, Crystal smiled to herself and moved slowly over to the fire. She removed her tall, elegant boots and dropped to her haunches to gaze into the leaping flames, warming her hands in their radiant heat. Turning to look at Isaac – who was standing watching her in the doorway, removing his leather jacket in a somewhat distracted manner – she flicked a long, raven lock over her shoulder so that it fell, gleaming, down her back and smiled at him. 'Well I have to admit that I'm seriously impressed. This is one of the nicest rooms I've ever had the good fortune to be seduced in. I had no idea you had such stunning taste, Isaac. Although I should have guessed, of course. I mean, look at your taste in women . . .' She giggled, amused by the audacity of her joke.

Isaac laughed softly and, without taking his eyes off Crystal, made his way across the room towards her. Kicking off his shoes, he dropped to his knees on the rug behind her. Rising to greet him, though still with her back to him, Crystal closed her eyes and drew in her breath as she felt his warm body move up against her back. His hands began to stroke her shoulders, before stretching around to cup her full, firm breasts, exerting just the right amount of gentle, tantalising pressure.

Beneath the fine, ivory silk of her blouse Crystal was

braless and a delicious shiver ran through her body as her naked breasts responded to Isaac's touch through the thin fabric. Aware of the warm, sultry weight and pressure of her bosoms against his sensitive palms, her nipples tingled delightfully, rising and hardening like a pair of lush, ripe berries as his fingertips grazed their puckered surface.

Aware of the impact his erotic ministrations were having on the ebony-haired beauty in front of him, Isaac's sex responded in kind, rising and hardening as it filled with dark, pulsing blood, pressing urgently inside his jeans against the curvy ridge between her full, feminine buttocks.

Eyes closed, Crystal's head dropped back against Isaac's, her silky hair mingling with his dark curls, and she let out a low, soft moan of pleasure. She hollowed her back, pushing out her hips and backside, and slowly began to gyrate the lower half of her body in a slow, sensual motion guaranteed to intensify the pressure of his stiffening penis against her quivering bottom.

Isaac's breathing quickened and he began to tremble as a light, warm flush suffused his body. Reaching down he pulled his ever-hardening groin away from Crystal's shapely bum just long enough to quickly unfasten his jeans and pull them down to his knees, along with his underpants. In front of him Crystal turned her head to look into his eyes – her straight, beautiful hair hanging loose and luscious about her face and shoulders like shiny wet liquorice – and treated him to a slow, lazy smile. Wriggling her hips and bottom so that the firm, gleaming flesh jiggled delightfully before his smouldering, lust-filled gaze, Crystal slowly lowered her own jeans to reveal one of the smallest pairs of panties Isaac had ever been fortunate enough to witness. Fashioned, it would appear, from a single scrap of soft, blood-red satin, they stretched like a shiny, gossamer-fine second skin across the uppermost part of her bottom, disappearing in a single, narrow thong between the full, voluptuous *rondeurs* of her cheeks, sinfully scarlet against the rich clotted cream of her velvet-smooth curves.

Lost for words and senses reeling at this unbelievably arousing vision before him, Isaac devoured this gorgeous female with his eyes, tentatively moving his trembling hands over the smooth, warm skin of her back while pushing up her silky blouse to reveal her nakedness beneath. Raising her arms like an obedient child Crystal allowed him to remove the garment and toss it to the floor, where it lay like some exotic bloom, warm and discarded in the glow from the fire.

Parting her knees as far as her dropped jeans would allow Crystal undulated her lithe, newly naked torso like a snake, bare breasts bouncing and swaying with the movement of her body. She pushed her beautiful, scarlet satin-clad arse towards him like a bitch on heat – lewd and sexually demanding. Then she leaned forward so that her elbows and forearms rested on the floor, her heavy, sex-flushed breasts hanging suspended, erect nipples touching the carpet, her loose hair dropping like glossy curtains to the ground. When she turned her head to look at him, the black silky strands which partly obscured one eye did nothing to disguise the hot, smouldering lust Isaac saw written there.

Tearing her eyes away from his, she allowed her gaze to drop to her lover's erect penis and dwell there a while, visually devouring the hard, turgid flesh which pulsed with life and the pink-flushed glans with a single, tiny drop of pre-ejaculatory semen at its tip. Taking her weight once more onto her knees, Crystal reached behind her back with her hands and, still gazing transfixed at Isaac's erect penis, parted the cheeks of her bottom to reveal her own pouting sex, open and flushed in readiness for the inevitable consummation of her erotic desire – fleshy outer labia darkly swollen with pulsing blood and secret inner lips pink and slick with her aromatic, vaginal secretions.

'I can't tell you how I've longed for this moment, Isaac . . .' she said in a half-whisper, her voice husky with emotion. 'Ever since the last time we made love to each other all those weeks ago I've longed to touch you and to feel you touching me; to hear your heartbeat; to feel your lips against my skin and your warm breath on my naked body; your hardness pressing against my pussy, desperate to be inside me . . . Take me, Isaac, I'm all yours . . .' With these words, heavy with lust, Crystal dropped to her elbows once more, presenting her splendid rear end to the object of her desire, desperate to be entered by him and made powerful love to in a way which at long last would slake her overwhelming physical need.

Drunk with his own need for release and driven nearly insane by the scent of Crystal's aroused sex, which was rising like some heady, exotic incense to his nostrils, Isaac began to tremble and a hot sweat broke out over his body. His penis tingled and throbbed, dusky and dark-veined, excited and emboldened by Crystal's lewd invitation and the sweet madness of his desperate desire to comply with her wishes by riding her beautiful, shameless, near-naked body until they reached their longed-for climaxes.

Eyes glittering darkly with arousal, Isaac's breathing quickened and his heart pounded in his chest. Taking his engorged, pulsing stiffness in his right fist he frigged it once or twice before moving as close to Crystal as he could possibly get. Then, with a fevered urgency, he positioned the glowing tip of his cock at the dark, swollen opening to her vagina and stroked it tantalisingly to and fro against her juicy lips until she cried out in joyful, half-crazed anticipation.

'You asked for it, woman. I'm going to fuck you . . . right now!' Isaac's voice was a hoarse whisper as he clasped Crystal's shapely hips in each hand for support and, gathering her to him, plunged his penis inside her, as fully and completely as he possibly could, aware of the tight, muscular walls of her vagina as they squeezed and pulsated around him.

As he moved powerfully back and forth within her, Isaac's mind and senses were alive only to the delicious friction of his throbbing penis inside this stunning, erotic female. Mesmerised at first by the sight of his own and Crystal's genitals – slick and inflamed, joined in urgent copulation – his eyes then travelled along the smooth, glowing skin of her naked back and the milky curves of her gorgeous breasts, almost out of sight but maddeningly revealed to him and bouncing delightfully with each thrust.

Letting go of her hips, he reached round and took her trembling breasts in his hands, feeling their flushed warmth and weight against his palms, squeezing and massaging the tender flesh, thrilled by the sensation of her large, erect nipples and the feel of her strong, rapid heartbeat.

'My God, Isaac . . .' Crystal groaned, 'I think I'm going to explode!' Pushing out her bottom to meet each thrust of Isaac's cock, she was able to further intensify the almost unbearably stimulating sensation of being filled to absolute capacity by this hot, randy male organ. Crystal began to judder uncontrollably in her sexual delirium, throwing back her ebony head so that her hair fell in a wide, shiny black fan across the flushed skin of her back. She whispered sweet, unintelligible words to her lover as her vagina melted in wave after delicious wave of fluttering, butterfly contractions.

With a rush of pleasure Isaac felt the heat and intensity of Crystal's orgasm and rode with it, choosing to prolong the agony of his own climax, however difficult that may prove to be, a while longer. As her shuddering subsided, Isaac's thrusts slowed to a gentle, lazy rhythm and he leaned over her, wrapping her hot, sated body in his strong arms and hugging her to him while whispering his passion and urgent need against her silky, fragrant hair, his breath warm against her damp cheek and his heartbeat fast and regular against her back.

'Ladies first, as they say . . .' he murmured, nuzzling her hair, a note of humour in his voice mixed with simmering desire. 'You really are an incredibly randy woman, aren't you? Like a goddamn she-cat. You drive me wild with lust you crazy, horny angel.' He nibbled her earlobe, moaning softly, his breathing quickening once more. His prick was no longer in Crystal's pussy but rubbing sensually back and forth in the cleft between the cheeks of her curvy, gently undulating arse. 'Fuck me, woman,' he whispered. 'Get on top of me and slide my prick inside you and ride me . . .'

Trembling with lust, eyes dark and glowing, Isaac lay back against the soft carpet, hands behind his head to better enjoy the view. Damp, dark tendrils of hair clung to his flushed, sweat-streaked face. His broad chest, slick with sweat, rose and fell as he breathed and his erect penis pulsed against his flat belly.

Crystal raised herself up onto her knees and turned to look at him, catching her breath at the sight of his powerful, masculine beauty, reclining in the glow from the fire and from the setting sun. A wave of passion flowed through her limbs, leaving her weak with emotion and anticipation at the thought of feeling Isaac's erect penis inside her once more. She turned to face him and, breasts swaying gently, straddled his thighs so that her pubic mound was placed directly above his stiff sex. 'Right now, I can't think of anything I'd rather do . . .' she breathed huskily, taking him in her soft hand and guiding him into her warm, muscular vagina.

Feeling him deep inside her, clasped tightly as though in a velvet glove, Crystal began to move in gentle, sensual undulations, aware only of her genitals which were joined with Isaac's in this most intimate and private of human acts. At this moment she felt that the very core of her being was centred in and around that glowing, pulsing union of turgid flesh.

Breathing easily now and in rhythm with her body, Crystal threw back her head so that her long, blue-black hair tumbled down her back. She closed her eyes and allowed her hands to move to her breasts, gleaming with sweat, and began to stroke her dark, jutting nipples with the tips of her fingers so that thrill upon thrill of erotic sensation coursed through her breasts and belly and vagina, further increasing her sexual rapture by causing her inner muscles to contract even more strongly around Isaac's penis.

In his prone position on the floor, cock fully embedded and stimulated almost beyond endurance in the mobile, sheath-like sex of his gorgeous lover, Isaac's breathing grew ragged and urgent as he felt his orgasm rapidly approach. He watched,

25

fascinated, as with each wanton undulation of Crystal's hips and thighs her dark cloud of pubic hair mingled with his own and her glorious, firm breasts swayed and shuddered with the exertion, her large, erect nipples blackberry-dark with tingling passion.

Crystal was perspiring freely now and her damp skin gleamed like burnished bronze, her body glowing as though with an inner fire. Her hair clung wetly to her flesh and, as her movements became ever freer and more fevered with her mounting passion, it whipped with wild abandon around her flushed face and breasts.

As Isaac felt Crystal reach her climax once more, sighing and moaning amid spasm after spasm, he felt that he could no longer hold on to his own craved-for bodily release. With a cry of joy his body tensed and he ejaculated jet after jet of warm, pulsing semen into her welcoming pussy, the fluttering, wave-like motion of her muscular walls contracting ever more powerfully to receive him.

Finally, the intense eroticism of the moment subsided and Isaac fell back with a smile and a long-drawn-out sigh onto the carpet, limp, exhausted and deliciously sated. His penis, embedded still in Crystal's vagina, remained stiff for a while before slowly beginning to subside, shrinking back to its pre-aroused state.

Damp and gleaming, and still with Isaac's sex inside her, Crystal smiled lazily to herself and gazed down at her lover's gorgeous, prostrate body. Stretching her long limbs contentedly, she sighed and yawned. Then she eased herself away from him and lay down by his side, resting on one elbow and carelessly twining a few strands of his damp chest hair in her elegant fingers. 'Mmmm . . . that was wonderful.

Do you behave like that with all your fans?' she asked him with a mischievous grin, her voice soft and shy like a little girl's.

'Only if their name's Crystal Clearwater!' Suddenly Isaac sprang into action, taking Crystal by surprise and gathering her to him in a bear hug, kissing her lightly and repeatedly on the end of her nose before nuzzling her throat and her damp, fragrant hair. 'But normally I'd kick off by offering them a coffee before coming on with the full, heavy seduction number,' he said softly. 'I know this is the wrong way round, but I just couldn't help myself. Fine host I make, don't I? Wrestling my guests to the carpet and plying them with rampant nookie before I've even offered them a cuppa. Must contravene just about every rule of etiquette in the book.'

Crystal laughed, her eyes glittering with amusement. 'You could say that, but I can't pretend I'm not flattered! Anyway, now you come to mention it, I could murder a cup of something.'

Chapter Two

Mid-morning autumn sunshine streamed through the window in Isaac's kitchen, which was warm and fragrant with the aroma of sizzling bacon and freshly brewed coffee. Clad in a pair of faded, cut-off jeans and nothing else, Isaac stood over the hob, frying eggs and singing along with a track from Keith Richard's latest album which was emitting raunchily from a pair of built-in speakers in the corners of the room. In the centre of the kitchen, draped in a bath towel and reading a copy of *Rolling Stone*, Crystal sat with her feet on the scrubbed-deal table and sipped from a large tumbler of mango juice, toes curling and uncurling to the rhythm.

'Bugger it! Hope you don't mind broken egg yolks, I've managed to destroy both these two.' Isaac grimaced and slid the eggs onto two warmed plates, deftly adding several rashers of crispy bacon from the eye-level grill.

'The way I feel this morning, Isaac, I could demolish an entire hen house, birds included. I don't know about you, but all this sex is turning me into a ravening beast. I'll be asking for raw meat next. Just toss me over that leg of lamb out of the fridge, would you?' Crystal smiled at him and swung her long legs to the floor, twisting her long hair, wet from the shower, into a sleek top knot before inhaling deeply from the mouthwatering plate which Isaac had placed in front of her. 'Mmmm . . . ever thought of a career in catering? I'm sure I could find you a nice little job at High Links. What do you say?'

Isaac laughed and sat down at the table opposite her. 'I'd say cut the wisecracks and eat. Hey, I've got a great day lined up for us. We've barely stuck our noses outside the front door since you arrived. I've practically forgotten what London looks like.' Isaac took a mouthful of bacon and winked at Crystal across the table. 'It's all your fault, you randy bitch. Teaching me bad habits . . .' Just about managing not to choke on a piece of toast, Crystal took a swipe at him, grinning through a mouthful of crumbs. 'Anyway, I think it's about time we got some fresh air, so how about we take my kite onto Hampstead Heath for a quick blow, then we can do the market this afternoon and pick up a few bargains. Tonight we can tart ourselves up and eat out. Agreed?'

'Agreed!'

A strong autumnal breeze swept the Heath, its chill fingers warmed from time to time by patches of spasmodic sunshine. Isaac and Crystal dodged and laughed under the eddying clouds as they took it in turns to control the kite – a giant Chinese dragon with a long, fluttering scarlet tail – their voices lost in the vastness of their playground. When it was Crystal's turn, she ran as though the devil were after her, barely stopping to gather her long purple coat around her so that it streamed out behind like a flag, her eyes fixed heavenwards, smiling into the wind as she chased Isaac's dragon across the sky.

That afternoon, arm in arm against the cold which was

growing more apparent as the day progressed, they meandered back and forth amongst the stalls and small, bijou shops of Camden Lock Market. An inveterate hoarder by nature and keen collector of the beautiful and the exotic, Crystal was entranced and excited by what she saw. Cunning or whimsical antiques and finely wrought crafts jostled for position along the narrow walkways with rails of faded tea gowns and 1950s boleros in shot silk and fine wool; trays of delicate, diamanté jewellery and colourful, jazzy buttons in bright, primary shades and pearly pastels – refugees from bygone fashion eras. Stallholders and their friends in scarves and mittens and dangly earrings swapped anecdotes and discussed the state of the nation, nodding sagely to each other as they smoked cigarettes and sipped from large mugs of tea. Once or twice, Crystal was aware of the odd knowing glance of recognition being cast in Isaac's direction, but he was a familiar, if somewhat occasional figure in these parts, and nobody took it upon themselves to spoil their privacy by coming up and attempting to bend his ear.

Crystal was in her element. She felt like a child let loose in a sweetshop and, magpie-like, homed in on arty trinkets and various pieces of ephemera which caught her eye. She bought a Victorian fan in painted silk and a tiny beaded purse; then a Spanish mantilla in iridescent mother-of-pearl, pierced and figured with pictures of flowers and long-plumed birds and complete with a length of exquisite, cobweb-fine black lace. Isaac laughed at Crystal's obvious delight in her purchases and steered her towards a stall selling flapjacks, slabs of homemade cake and steaming beakers of coffee and chocolate, where they stood for a while in companionable silence, surveying the scene and warming their hands on their cups.

Eyes shining, Crystal turned to Isaac and smiled, blowing a strand of hair away from her face before taking a sip of hot chocolate. 'I can't remember when I last enjoyed myself so much,' she said. 'Being here, with you, right now, today – it's almost as good as sex! Well, it comes a close second, anyway.' She giggled, then looked wistful. 'I wish it could last forever and that I didn't have to end it all by going back to High Links and the daily grind tomorrow.'

Isaac stroked her cheek, tenderly tracing the fine, aristocratic contours with his fingers. 'Hey . . . why talk about things like that now? The weekend's far from over. Besides, we still have tonight . . .' Narrowing his eyes mysteriously and raising one eyebrow he gazed theatrically into the middle distance like a hammy, nineteenth-century actor in a Shakespearean tragedy. It had the desired effect, Crystal took one look at him and burst out laughing, her sombre mood evaporating into the ether.

Relieved at this welcome turn in the emotional climate, Isaac continued: 'But before we go back to the house, there's something I want to show you.' They returned their empty cups to the stall and Isaac took Crystal's arm, guiding her through the milling crowds in a purposeful manner. 'It's a little place I noticed ages ago. I've been dying to take a closer look but it sells mainly women's stuff and I figured the people running it might get the wrong idea. Anyway, you're my perfect excuse. Come on.'

Within a moment or two they were on the far side of the market and there, on the opposite corner, was a tiny boutique, painted all in black and with its name picked out in ornate silver lettering. Its single window was veritably stuffed – swathes of fabric, '20s beaded hats and velvet stoles on aged, gold-painted shop-window mannequins, vases of ostrich and peacock feathers. Excited, Crystal drew in her breath. 'Wow! What a find . . . Shall we?' Taking Isaac's arm she led him across to the shop and in through the door before he had a chance to change his mind.

The interior of the dimly lit boutique perfectly lived up to the promise of its exterior and, for Crystal, it was like stumbling upon the contents of a long-forgotten ancient Egyptian tomb. In terms of size, it had little more than the capacity of a front room in an ordinary Victorian semi, but the damson-painted walls were lined with some of the most outrageous and exquisite antique clothes that Crystal had ever seen. The ceiling was hung with feather boas and fine silk scarves in butterfly hues; long, gleaming necklaces in amber and coal-black jet; sequinned evening bags and delicate Victorian pouches in glossy satin and soft kid leather.

Reclining decorously at a tiny, lacquered card table in the corner of the shop was a creature of immense style and languorous beauty. She was dressed in cream silk harem pants and a satin smoking jacket in darkest bitter chocolate which, open to her breastbone in a plunging V and without a stitch of clothing underneath, revealed somewhat more than a glimpse of tantalisingly shadowy cleavage. The young woman's chestnut hair, marcel-waved, was short and sleek, revealing the elegant curve of her pale, swanlike throat. The whole, stunning vision was completed by her dark, heavy-lidded eyes, scarlet Clara Bow lips and long, blood-red fingernails from which drooped a slim, Turkish cheroot whose exotic aroma permeated the atmosphere of the shop, along with the unmistakable scent of gardenia blossoms.

Crystal couldn't help noticing that the creature's manifold

charms were far from being entirely lost on Isaac, but she really couldn't blame him. She was as knocked out by the woman's appearance as he clearly was.

'May I help you, or will you be happy just to browse? I'm sorry it's so cramped in here. In fact, there's barely enough room to swing a cat, as they say.' The woman's lips curved into a lazy smile as she gazed from one to the other of her prospective customers. Her voice was soft and deep and betrayed a hint of Middle Europe. By the sound of her, and on closer inspection, she was a little more mature than she'd first appeared. Mid-thirties, perhaps. At first glance, the tiny, characteristic lines around her eyes and mouth had been softened and somewhat disguised, no doubt, by the minimal lighting. 'But no matter, there's plenty here to take your mind off the close quarters, I think. Please, just go ahead. Pretend I'm not here.' Taking a long pull on her cheroot, she picked up a dog-eared copy of *The Antique Collector's Guide* from under the card table and began to leaf through its pages in the confident, methodical manner of a woman well versed and at ease in her chosen trade.

'Thanks, we'd love to have a look round.' Crystal smiled as she spoke, feeling instantly at home with this easy-going, extravagantly dressed woman and her dim, womb-like boutique with its scent of flowers, old, good-quality fabrics and expensive tobacco smoke.

Crystal and Isaac spent a good fifteen minutes examining the clothes and accessories which filled the shop, stroking the expensive, sensual materials and pressing them against their cheeks like delighted children, pausing to marvel at the milky sheen on a wide, twisted choker of tiny seed pearls or the rhinestone sparkle of a midnight-blue evening top. From time to time, the woman looked up from her reading and watched them benevolently, explaining in her smoky, charmingly fractured English about the origins of this or that item of clothing or piece of jewellery which had captured their attention.

Rifling systematically through a crowded rail at the back of the shop, Crystal's eagle eye fell on something which made her stop dead in her tracks and do a double take. 'Bloody hell,' she whispered with feeling, 'I think this is it. This is the one I should go for. Come over here and take a look, Isaac. See if you agree with me.'

Isaac returned the bottle-green velvet slouch hat he'd been examining to its stand and went over to join Crystal, curious to see what it was she'd discovered that was causing such bubbling excitement. Rounding a high rail stuffed with ball gowns, Isaac came face to face with her, eyes glittering with pleasure and mischief and a wide smile on her face as she proudly held up a lengthy, lean-lined creation in deep scarlet panne velvet which glowed sinfully in the dimly lit shop like dark, wet blood. Straight away, Isaac felt as though he'd received a powerful though oddly pleasurable blow to the solar plexus. 'Yes, I see what you mean,' he said with a note of quiet reverence and a slight break in his voice. 'Er . . . why not try it on?'

Isaac had to admit that he was impressed with Crystal's choice. Very impressed. In fact, the thought of seeing her inside the gorgeous garment, the luscious fabric stretched sensually over her hips and bottom and draped artfully across her breasts and shoulders was, quite literally, making him weak at the knees. He forced down the lump which had formed, quite inexplicably, in his throat and hoped to God that neither Crystal nor the gorgeous, Garboesque owner of the shop were aware of the rapid beating of his heart or, indeed, the light sweat which had broken out on his forehead and upper lip, not to mention some rather more intimate areas of his anatomy.

Why in heaven's name, he asked himself, was he acting like a goddamn schoolboy in a brothel? Hadn't he made a habit over the years of spending time in the company of beautiful, often scantily clad ladies in a wide variety of sensual situations such as this? It had to be said, of course, that his feelings for Crystal were a great deal stronger and more profound than any he had experienced for previous lovers, but that wasn't the full story by a long chalk, and he knew it. There was a great deal more behind Isaac's discomfiture than merely the sight of Crystal, beautiful and slightly tousled from the effects of the wind and their trek around the market, striking a theatrically provocative pose whilst eagerly pressing the sexy garment against her slim body in an attempt to coax him towards a similar level of enthusiasm to the one which she herself felt.

Indeed, the seeds of Isaac's feeling of excitement and expectation had been sown the moment he and Crystal had entered this alluring and idiosyncratic shop and his first, electrifying sight of its stunning proprietress had a great deal to do with the feeling subsequently taking root and growing to its present, somewhat fevered state.

The woman seated at the card table closed her book and placed it back on the floor, then looked up and glanced across to where Crystal and Isaac were standing. Isaac was intrigued to notice a momentary and almost imperceptible widening of her eyes as though she, too, were moved by the sight of

Crystal and the scarlet dress and only too well aware of the delicious possibilities of the situation. Overcoming her mild surprise, she addressed the subject of her appraisal: 'Yes . . . a wise choice. It's beautiful, isn't it? 1940s, or thereabouts. It was brought to me last week by an elderly lady – an ex-diva, I believe. It had been one of her performance dresses, and although she hated to part with it, she disliked even more the idea of it languishing in her wardrobe, unworn. I have to admit that I considered it for myself, but now, imagining it on you . . .' The woman's sultry, painted eyes seemed to glow as though with an inner light and she sat back slowly in her chair, reclining, as though to afford herself a more favourable view. The movement was strangely masculine, almost like that of an Edwardian gentleman of leisure, taking his ease in a somewhat morally suspect salon full of young ladies of the night. 'Come, my dear,' she continued, 'let us see if the dress is as charming on as it is off . . .' Rising gracefully from her chair she stalked slowly across to her customers, hips rolling seductively as she moved, gaze not once deviating from her goal.

The woman's last, somewhat loaded remark had been spoken with quiet deliberation and Isaac was convinced he could detect some other element in her words – an element of simmering, carefully controlled desire. His heart, which was already beating nineteen to the dozen, felt as though it were about to fail him entirely. Quietly catching his breath, he struggled to control the insidious trembling of his limbs, desperate not to give himself away but not at all sure that this were possible.

If Isaac were entirely honest with himself – and how could he possibly be anything else, faced as he was by the heady cocktail of visual and tactile delights to be found in this shop at this moment – he had to admit that the highly arousing combination of Crystal and the delectable owner, close enough to scent each other's perfume and feel the other's breath on their skin, had sent him into a flat spin. It was as though between them, by some unspoken, mutual consent known only to themselves they'd agreed to deliberately set out to bewitch him. Moreover, there was no doubt whatsoever that their plan, if that was what it was, had worked, and very successfully so. Isaac had fallen under their spell, helplessly and irrevocably. Moreover, he was unwilling, and still less able, to untangle himself from their tantalising web. As far as he was concerned they could do whatever they liked with each other and, by inference, him. And the sooner the better, too, if his mounting lust, manifesting itself with a merciless insistence deep in his groin, was anything to go by. Quite simply, he was putty in their manipulative hands, and more than happy to be so.

As though to confirm his suspicions, Crystal gazed levelly back at the woman standing opposite and answered her expression with a slow, secret smile of recognition, her shining eyes glowing with a fire of their own and tenderly exploring the other woman's beautiful, stunningly made-up face. He couldn't swear to it, but Isaac was almost entirely convinced that at that moment the two women exchanged tiny, almost imperceptible nods of silent complicity. Lowering her eyes seductively so that her long lashes cast spidery shadows across her upper cheeks, Crystal watched her own hands as they moved sensually over the soft, lush velvet, almost as though they belonged not to her but to some favoured lover. She began to stroke the scarlet fabric, pressing it against her slim, curvy frame so that her generous breasts stood out in heart-stopping relief. Then, revelling in the sensation and the feel of her own soft hands caressing her body, Crystal began to sway slightly from side to side, gently and erotically, enjoying every moment of what she was doing and exquisitely aware of the effect she was having on her rapt audience of two.

Watching Crystal, a warm flush suffused the other woman's face and her eyes narrowed and glowed darkly. A small, trembling sigh escaped from between her lush, parted lips and she made as though to reach out a hand and touch the object of her desire, but then changed her mind and spoke softly instead in her halting English, her voice heavy with desire and erotic promise. 'Come . . . Come upstairs to my flat. I'll close the shop. It's time, anyway. Bring the dress with you . . .' Seemingly in charge of her emotions once more, the woman moved gracefully across to the door and locked it with a small key, pushing home the bolts at the top and bottom to ensure their privacy, as well as the safety of the shop's contents. Then, opening a panelled door behind and to the right of her card table desk, she moved out into the dim hall beyond, pausing to beckon to Crystal and, almost as an afterthought, to Isaac, urging them to follow her.

Hopelessly aroused and yet oddly perplexed by the turn of events which, apparently out of his control, seemed to be moving forward with consummate speed, not to mention a sense of inevitability, Isaac paused for a moment as though rooted to the spot. His head swam with a mixture of lust, fear and confusion. Was this really happening, he asked himself? Only a few minutes ago he and Crystal had been happily exploring the contents of the shop, albeit, he had to admit, with a certain erotic frisson, given the dark, sensual ambience of the place and the close proximity of the beautiful owner and his own stunning partner. But now all that had changed. Any degree of levity which had existed between the three of them had evaporated like smoke from a recently extinguished candle and been replaced by a burgeoning cloud of hot, urgent sexuality which seemed to hover, demon-like, between the two women, drawing him into its siren embrace in a way which rendered him disturbingly powerless and devoid of rationality and free will.

It had to be said that the main source of Isaac's feelings of disquiet lay with Crystal and the overt wantonness of her behaviour towards the other woman who, despite possessing a sexual allure of extreme potency, evidently merciless in its effect on men and women alike, had after all been a complete stranger to them both until a very short while before. While Isaac felt himself to be in a better position than many to vouch for Crystal's profound, not to say rampant, sexuality, the current circumstances appeared to be highlighting certain shadowy elements of her erotic nature which had hitherto remained unknown to him. He had to admit that, despite being turned on to an almost obscene degree, he was more than a little surprised by Crystal's apparent willingness to collude with the sexually sophisticated older woman. Had she hinted to him before of her proclivities in that direction, he might have been better prepared for what was evidently about to follow but, as it was, he felt himself to be completely lost at sea, drowning in a whirlpool of sudden, galloping arousal, utterly at the mercy of the two women and their burning need for sexual congress.

The electrifying facts of the situation, rapidly dawning in

his seething imagination with a white-hot, burning clarity, rendered Isaac quite unable to prevent himself from being lured upstairs to the foreign seductress's private apartment. As he climbed the dark, rickety staircase – eyes fixed mesmerically on the curvy, swaying backsides of the two women in front of him – Crystal turned and treated him to a wide smile, winking conspiratorially and sealing the silent promise of her continued love and desire for him with a little, pouting kiss. Isaac felt his heart swell with relief at the knowledge that all was well, if a trifle bizarre, and that Crystal had not temporarily lost control and taken leave of her senses.

'So, here we are,' the woman announced on reaching the first floor. She was a little breathless from the climb but nevertheless there was a small hint of triumph in her voice. 'Please, make yourselves comfortable and I'll fetch us some liquid refreshment, yes? Wine, perhaps?' Fixing Crystal quite shamelessly with a glance of open, burning intensity, which was willingly returned to her by its equally horny recipient, the woman seemed to be making it quite clear that this was not so much a polite enquiry as the presentation of a firm *fait accompli*.

Crystal smiled easily, her expression of confidence hinting at an innate belief in her own sexual power, and sat down in a large, brown leather armchair. She crossed her long legs in a single, fluid movement, aware of the other woman's eyes on her face and languorous body. 'Thank you, I'd love a glass of wine. White, if you have it.'

'I'll have the same, if that's okay.' Trembling a little now, uncertain of his position in the scheme of things given that Crystal and the woman clearly had eyes only for each other, Isaac sat down on a low, damson-brocade sofa which was pushed against a wall under one of the windows. He perched on the edge of it as though to more easily make good his escape should it suddenly become necessary to do so.

The woman, obviously aware of Isaac's discomfort and keen to make him feel more at home, slinked up to him and crouched to bring herself down to his level, her deep, creamy cleavage rising and falling between the silky lapels of her bitter chocolate smoking jacket. Then, touching his arm solicitously with a manicured hand, her long, scarlet nails lightly grazing the black leather sleeve of his jacket, she gazed into his eyes. 'Darling, I'm aware that you seem a little worried about something. Am I right? Please don't be. My God, anyone would think I was planning to eat you or something!' Amused, she chuckled deep in her throat and Isaac, far from being convinced by her protestations to the contrary, was put in mind of a beautiful black widow spider, carefully and systematically seducing her prey. Her voice softened and lowered to little more than a whisper as she continued: 'On the contrary, the three of us are going to have a little fun. You might even end up enjoying yourself, who knows? Just sit back, darling, and enjoy the show. The wine will help you loosen up a little.

'Baby?' Still crouching, she turned to Crystal and began to address her in the same low, soothing tone that she'd adopted for Isaac. 'While I pour our drinks, why not slip into my bedroom and try on the dress? But be sure to show us, now, before you take it off . . .' She nodded towards a rose-pink painted door in the corner of the room. Crystal smiled mysteriously at her and rose slowly from the armchair, picking up the scrap of scarlet velvet from the low table where she'd dropped it. She made her way confidently towards the bedroom, slipping her coat from her shoulders as she went and allowing it to fall, discarded, to the floor. Her curvy backside swayed seductively as she walked and her long, silky hair tumbled like a shiny black waterfall down her sinuous back. The woman watched her go – eyes focused snake-like on Crystal's voluptuous, gently undulating bottom – and took a tiny, excited breath, biting her lower lip before running the pink tip of her tongue over its glossy surface. Then, with a little sigh and a small shrug of her shoulders, she managed to regain her composure. Rising to her feet, she made her way to a small kitchenette in the corner of the spacious first-floor apartment.

While the woman was occupied with opening a bottle of chilled Chablis and filling three long-stemmed glasses, Isaac took the opportunity to explore the room with his eyes. Apart from the separate bedroom in the corner and, presumably, a bathroom, the first floor had been made into one large room with tall sash windows on two facing sides, hung with creamy, old-fashioned lace and heavy, rust velvet. The floor, scattered here and there with good-quality though slightly faded and threadbare tasselled rugs, had been stripped bare and varnished a dark mahogany. The somewhat aged furniture was comfortably roomy and nicely lived-in, well padded and upholstered in soft animal hide and plum figured damask which glowed expensively in the subdued light from a large, emerald-beaded 1920s Tiffany lamp on a small table in the corner by the door. Old clocks, vases, figurines and teapots lined the mantelpiece above the small fireplace and covered just about every other available surface. The entire effect, eclectic in the extreme, was one of warmth and a certain eccentricity.

It was beginning to get dark outside and the woman moved silently from window to window, closing the heavy drapes and shutting out the light from the recently illuminated street lamps, casting the room in a shadowy, seductive glow which, combined with his just-acquired glass of wine, went a long way towards calming Isaac's slightly troubled spirit. Indeed, if it weren't for the fact that Crystal was still missing from the scene, changing into the scarlet dress in the woman's bedroom, he might actually believe that he were starting to enjoy himself. In fact, it had to be said that the tension in Isaac's groin, which had subsided somewhat as a result of his recent nervousness, was slowly but surely returning to full, pulsing strength, aided by his mental image of Crystal divesting herself of her clothes and pouring herself into the sexy red dress for his and the woman's imminent delectation.

The sweeping strains of Vivaldi's *Gloria* filled the room, a little fuzzily, from an ancient gramophone by one of the windows, returning Isaac's floating mind and senses to the present, just in time for him to see the bedroom door open and a vision appear, almost saintly in its powerful, commanding beauty and yet decidedly unsaintly in its pure eroticism. Closing the door behind her, Crystal turned to gaze triumphantly from the woman to Isaac and then back to the woman again, her expression altering to one of sultry moodiness as her eyes fixed on those of her desired object. Her cheeks flushed fetchingly and her pupils dilated with pleasure at the effect she was clearly having on the other woman's fevered senses.

And Crystal had every reason, Isaac thought with a fresh

rush of pulsing blood to his already stimulated sex, to be supremely confident of her sexual allure. She stood before them like a demonic, scarlet-sheathed angel, dark eyes flashing dangerously with sensual promise, voluptuous flesh as pale and smooth as lilies. Her shiny, raven-black hair was spread wantonly across her almost completely bare back, her naked shoulders and the generous, milk-white upper spheres of her scandalously exposed breasts, a tiny pulse beating above her heart as she breathed. Brief by even the most lascivious of standards, the dress's bodice was expertly boned and strapless to reveal as much of the wearer's breasts and upper torso as possible without plunging quite low enough to reveal her darker, swollen areolae to the watchers' lustful, impassioned gaze. Lower down, the glowing, scarlet velvet stretched tightly like a second skin across her hips and thighs, embracing the soft, womanly flesh before flaring out almost to the floor in a swathe of long handkerchief points. Placing one hand on her hip and the other behind her head like a 1940s pin-up, Crystal grinned like a mischievous child and raised herself onto her bare, varnished tiptoes, pirouetting prettily to reveal a long fish tail of gleaming velvet at the back of the dress, long enough to trail a little on the floor.

Isaac was completely, irreversibly spellbound. Never had Crystal appeared to him so stunningly beautiful and yet so shamelessly wanton. Eyes glittering with excitement and heart pounding nineteen to the dozen, he took a long slug of his white wine and relaxed back onto the couch, legs spread carelessly. The woman, in contrast, rose to her feet and moved, wraith-like, across to where Crystal was standing, her expression betraying a mixture of deep, boiling passion and rapt, professional interest. 'Yes, it is as I thought. A perfect fit, no?' She turned to Isaac with an enquiring look and he nodded silently in agreement, his eyes not once leaving the pulsing swell of Crystal's creamy, alabaster bosom. 'In fact,' the woman continued, slowly circling around Crystal like a fashion designer covetously surveying her favourite model, 'I wonder if I might try a little experiment. I have this crazy notion that the jacket I'm wearing will complement the dress to perfection. May I try it and see if I'm correct?' Crystal smiled lazily and nodded, tantalisingly aware of the woman's plans for her.

Isaac began to tremble with pent-up emotion, his fingers shaking nervously as he downed the remains of his wine in a single gulp. Underneath the satin smoking jacket the woman was completely, breathtakingly naked and the notion of feasting his eyes on her bare tits sent a delicious shiver through his entire body, reverberating from the roots of his hair to the tips of his fingers and causing his cock to jerk and grow stiffer still. Like a ferret watching a rabbit, he watched her as she stood in front of Crystal, as close to her as she dare so they could feel the gentle draught of each other's quickening breath against their skin. Slowly she undid the three buttons of the jacket like an expensive whore. Eyes narrowed and fixed on Crystal's, she allowed the jacket to gently fall open, revealing the full length of her cleavage and a tantalising portion of the curved undersides of her breasts. Lost for a moment in the sweet erotic pleasure of her slow striptease, the woman closed her eyes and bit her bottom lip. She then took a deep, soft breath and shook herself a little, returning once more to the reality of the moment, and eased the jacket aside, shrugging it from her and catching it in her right hand before draping it lovingly across Crystal's shoulders, at the same time gazing with sensual promise into the other woman's eyes.

Although not quite possessing the full, voluptuous proportions of Crystal's, the woman's breasts were arguably the most exquisitely formed that Isaac had ever been fortunate enough to witness. Their almost perfect spheres were plump and firm and tipped with large, Bordeaux-dark nipples, youthfully uptilted and already fully erect as a result of her increasing excitement. An excitement delightfully mirrored by that of her captivated audience. After a moment or two, the woman appeared once more to regain her original composure and stood for a while, head on one side and chin cupped reflectively in her hand, examining the effect of the chocolate satin against the scarlet velvet. In a sudden moment of inspiration she tore her gaze away from Crystal's stunningly adorned body and slinked, panther-like, across to a large ottoman covered in blush-pink shot silk and hung with fat, shiny tassels of the same hue. As she walked, her delicious breasts jiggled and shook, gleaming smoothly in the subdued light like ripe fruits, the magnificent dark nipples jutting proudly. Dropping to her haunches she lifted the lid of the ottoman and drew forth from it a veritable cornucopia of scarves and shawls and belts, coloured feathers and long, beaded necklaces of every description.

Behind her, Crystal gasped in amazement, excited by what she saw and by her dawning realisation of the woman's possible intentions. Still crouching, the woman turned to face Crystal, her beautiful face impish with mischief. Without a word Crystal grinned back, eager for whatever sexy fun and games and girlish naughtiness was on offer. Once the entire contents of the ottoman had been transferred in an exotic, tangled mass to the floor, the woman closed the lid and stood up, laughing softly as she slipped the cream silk harem pants over her curvy hips, wriggling her bottom to assist their progress so that the flesh of her backside jiggled and her perfect breasts bounced and shook with titillating abandon, allowing the shiny scrap of material to drop with a soft swish to the floor. Underneath the woman was wearing a pair of brief, pale peach-coloured lacy French knickers, petal-soft and semi-transparent so that the shadowy cleft of her bottom and the dark V-shaped cloud of her pubic hair was plainly visible. Parting her long legs a fraction and arching her back so that her tits thrust forward invitingly and her elegant head was thrown back a little, she hooked her thumbs into the top of the revealing knickers and lowered them, inch by heart-stopping inch, lazily undulating her lower body and thighs like a seasoned stripper, lavish cats eyes half-closed in ecstasy and full, scarlet lips parted in a starlet pout.

Aroused beyond belief, Crystal smiled delightedly and bit her lip as she watched the knickers drop noiselessly to the ground, fully revealing the woman's silky, chestnut-haired pubis. Then, unable to stop herself, she took a deep, trembling breath and made her way across to the shamelessly naked vision, licking her lips like the cat that got the cream – or, at least, the cat that was about to get it – her eyes dark and glittering with sexual longing and her heart beating wildly in her fevered breast as the other woman posed and preened before her like a beautiful, coquettish harlot. Her wanton, kohl-smudged gaze joined with Crystal's as she swayed her curvy bottom and stroked her big, dusky nipples. When Crystal reached the woman she quickly removed the smoking jacket, not once averting her burning gaze from the uninhibited spectacle before her, and tossed it carelessly onto the ottoman. Then, with her back to Isaac and aided by the woman amid soft giggles and whispers, the long zip at the back of the scarlet dress was lowered fully, revealing a sinuous gash of creamy back and the top inch or two of soft bottom cheeks with their invitingly shadowy cleft in between. Obviously deciding that Isaac should be a party to this highly provocative display, even if only a spectator, Crystal turned to face him with an expression of extreme mischief, her long, shiny hair wild and loose about her face and shoulders and both hands clasping the boned, blood-red bodice against her generous breasts so that they rose above it in full, milky half-moons of firm flesh, rising and falling as she breathed deeply in her state of advanced arousal. Then, with a wicked smile, a wink and a little pouting kiss she flung out her arms in a gesture of lewd abandon, allowing the dress to fall to her bare feet in a soft, bloody puddle of gleaming velvet as she stood before him, aware of her own immense feminine beauty and eroticism, preening and stretching like a sleepy, voluptuous goddess.

Never had Isaac been so turned on by a woman as he was at that moment, and his arousal was all the sweeter and more intense given the fact that the women in question was promised to another – for the time being at least. Blushing hotly, he gulped down the lump which had formed in his throat and, wincing, arranged his long legs to better facilitate the huge, throbbing erection which was threatening to burst forth from the top of his tight jeans. Struggling to control his emotions and his growing compulsion to leap from the chair, fling Crystal to the ground and fuck her as she'd never been fucked before, Isaac settled back once more, somewhat uncomfortably, onto the couch.

Meanwhile, Crystal and the woman circled each other like a pair of alley cats as the sensual strains of Vivaldi swooped and soared about them, purring softly, their naked, gleaming bodies flushed and firm, tensed with an exquisite, controlled passion. Glancing at the muddle of strewn frippery at their feet, Crystal was seized by a sudden, compelling desire to embellish her lover's sexy, naked body with some of the beautiful, tangled jumble lying there. Ducking down with the zeal of an excited child she gathered together armfuls of floaty scarves, feather boas and long rope necklaces of pearls and glass beads which glinted in the lamplight. Then, filled with rapt concentration and shivering with anticipation of the finished effect, she wound and wrapped and draped the woman's neck, breasts, arms and waist with feathers and silk and shiny beads until she looked like a diva from some exotic opera or a titillatingly rude dancer from the *Folies Bergère*. Task completed, Crystal stood back to examine her handiwork and, chuckling with delight, clapped her hands together gleefully, thrilled with what she'd managed to achieve.

Caught up in the mood of the moment, the woman became still further aroused by the sensual and unexpected feel of soft silk and feathers and cold glass against her warm, bare skin; brushing her soft belly, full of butterflies, and her dark, turgid nipples; causing her to shiver deliciously and little goose-bumps of pleasure to rise involuntarily on her body. Tiptoeing across to the large mirror above the fireplace, beads clicking and flashing and scarves floating behind her, displaying tantalising glimpses of bare, bouncing breast and jiggling bottom as she moved, she studied herself in the glass, turning this way and that in admiration of her exotically decorated, sex-flushed self. Then, laughing with delight, she returned to

Crystal and repaid the honour by decorating her in the same sensationally sexy manner, the two of them giggling and whispering together like naughty schoolgirls, soft hands and breasts and lips and varnished toes brushing and touching as they ducked and stretched and moved together in a sensual dance of mutual admiration.

At last, similarly decorated, Crystal stood back to be admired by her audience with a flirtatious smile and a theatrical flourish, thoroughly enjoying the frank exhibitionism of this highly sexual charade. Then, unable to help herself, she began to move sensually to the music, eyes closed in ecstasy. She threw back her ebony mane so that it tumbled wildly down her naked back, sinuously stretching her slender arms and fingers in the faultless rhythm of an Eastern temple dancer whilst flexing her parted knees and circling her voluptuous thighs and belly. As she moved, the silky scarves around her breasts and waist shimmered and glowed, parting from time to time to reveal heart-stopping glimpses of her gorgeous, nude body – a generous curve of swaying breast topped with an erect strawberry nipple, a shadowy belly button, a glossy tangle of black pubic hair with, underneath, more than a passing hint of the dusky pink outer lips of her flushed sex.

The woman watched her, eyes on fire, like an Indian snake charmer transfixed by a favourite serpent and, when Crystal opened her eyes with a lazy smile, filled with sexual promise, and held out her hands to her, she was powerless to resist. Fingertips touching and eyes mesmerically locked, the two women swayed and shivered together, luxuriating in the music, the sensation of the heavy beads and luxurious fabrics against their bare skin and their own powerful, joint sexuality. The close proximity of their lush, womanly bodies bathed in the room's seductive glow and the heavenly, feminine scent of each other which rose to their nostrils like expensive perfume, caused a light film of gleaming sweat to break out on their foreheads and upper lips, between their full breasts and softly parted thighs, so urgent was their desire to possess and be possessed.

Beside himself with unrequited lust, Isaac threw back his head and screwed his eyes tight shut, trembling with sexual disquiet and the discomfort of his throbbing penis which, were it not hampered by the tight jeans, felt dangerously close to the point of ejaculation. How could the bitches do this to him and not invite him to at least rest a nerveless hand on a hot, wriggling bottom or jiggling breast while he relieved himself of his agony? What he really wanted, of course, was to jump on them both and drown in their soft, scented feminine flesh before gratefully penetrating them in turn while the other watched, enthusiastically encouraging whilst begging him to do the same to her. Fumbling nervously with the front of his jeans he lowered the zip and freed his turgid cock with a moan of relief, groaning and breathing heavily as he massaged its virile length, enjoying the feel of its pulsing hardness in his hot, sweaty fist. As he masturbated, his head thrown back against the couch, a steamy mental image of the two women rose like a red mist in his fevered imagination. Attempting unsuccessfully to fight the urge to peep and urged on by a series of soft feminine giggles and squeals, he gave up the unequal struggle, gratefully opened his eyes and, with a delicious shudder of amazement, feasted them on the scene before him.

Crystal and the woman were swaying together in a pool of

soft lamplight, perspiring bodies entwined in an embrace of such urgent ferocity that anyone who'd failed to observe what had gone before might have thought they were caught in the midst of a physical dispute, like a pair of she-cats fighting over some tasty feline morsel. Eager hands reached out and clutched at long hair and quivering bottoms, pulling frantically at the tasselled shawls and scarves which partly obscured their bodies so that their swollen, heaving breasts and trembling thighs were once more fully revealed to each other's loving gaze. Naked now except for a single rope of creamy pearls and a narrow drape of gossamer-fine black silk across one bosom and an erect nipple, the woman closed her eyes, stretched out her arms and gathered Crystal to her with a deep sigh of tactile pleasure. The soft, damp flesh of their breasts squeezed together, puckered nipples grazing and touching with thrill upon electric thrill which rippled like shock waves down to the tight muscles of their vaginas, causing them to contract and shiver with erotic sensation. Moaning gently, Crystal threw back her shoulders and backed away slightly, rubbing her glorious breasts and nipples lewdly against the other woman's, arching her back a little whilst pushing out her bottom and wiggling it suggestively at the dumbstruck Isaac so that he caught a quick glimpse or two of her pouting labial lips and silky tangle of black pubic hair.

She's putting on the full, raunchy number for effect, he thought with a further rush of hot blood to the groin. Posing and play-acting like a randy-arsed porn queen from one of the Italian sex videos he and the lads had watched in their hotel suite in Amsterdam. His fingers flew to his exposed cock and he began once more to frig himself madly as he watched Crystal bend her knees slightly, flick back her long hair and lower her full lips to the woman's nipples, sniffing their heady scent. She nuzzled the firm flesh like a kitten, before taking them one at a time in her mouth and nibbling, licking and sucking until the woman could bear it no longer.

'For God's sake, you gorgeous bitch . . . you're driving me to distraction!' With a wild moan of distress she took Crystal's smooth head in both hands and forced her to stop, gazing into her eyes before covering her wicked, mobile lips with her own and insinuating her hot tongue between them in a deep, passionate French kiss. Then, lips still joined and breasts and pubic mounds pressed urgently together in a cloudy cocktail of soft ebony and chestnut, the two women backed up to the damask ottoman, their bodies moving as one, and fell back against it as though captured on slow-motion film. Underneath, Crystal wriggled free from the woman and, pulling herself up onto it sensually stretched her sexy, naked body along the ottoman. Her skin was like clotted cream against the burnished pink, her head fell back and her hair cascaded to the ground like a gleaming black waterfall. Arms outstretched and dangling over the sides in an attitude of abandon, fully revealing her pale, voluptuous breasts which rose and fell with the movement of her breathing, she deliberately placed the soles of her bare feet firmly on the ground and spread her thighs as completely and shamelessly as a seasoned whore, turning to the woman with a wanton, come-hither smile and a suggestive lick of her luscious lips. The woman flushed hotly and her eyes narrowed with lust. She stared for a moment or two at Crystal's exposed pussy, transfixed, and then knelt down between the shamelessly parted thighs, taking a firm grip on her curvy hips and lowering her face to the dusky, scented heaven of secret female folds and creases which was soon to become the centre of her sensual universe.

Breathing deeply, she savoured the warm, spicy perfume of Crystal's aroused sex and then, with tongue fully extended, licked her bare cunt with long, wet strokes, nibbling lightly on the fragrant flesh and causing Crystal to writhe and moan in ecstasy whilst attempting to spread her thighs still further apart and thrust upwards as though to cram even more of her cunt into the woman's mouth. In answer to this lewd plea, the woman clutched the soft flesh of Crystal's arse and, parting the swollen lips of her inner labia, thrust her tongue inside the tight wetness of her vagina, feeling the slick, muscular walls tighten around it in a symphony of tiny, flickering contractions.

Lost in the throes of her prolonged orgasm, Crystal's thighs tensed and the muscles of her bottom flexed as her breathing became fast and shallow. Little rivulets of sweat ran across her pulsing belly and between her heaving, naked breasts. After a while, a delicious shiver ran through Crystal's body from the roots of her hair to the tips of her elegant toes and she began to relax a little. She sighed contentedly and sank back against her damask bed, a raven's wing of hair partly obscuring one eye and her lips parting in a drowsy smile of gratitude directed at her beautiful lover. 'That was one of the nicest things I've ever had done to me by a woman. You've been practising, I can tell.' She giggled and continued, her voice low and sexy with renewed desire: 'It's a funny thing, but I suddenly feel this mad urge to return the compliment. Come here and sit on my face. Let me eat your cunt . . .'

'Darling, I can think of nothing I'd like better.' The woman's voice was thick with lust and her eyes shone with excitement as she fixed them on Crystal's. Then, with the speed and grace of a jungle cat she climbed onto the ottoman and, kneeling down with her slim thighs one each side of Crystal's face, tensed her slender, womanly body. Slowly she lowered herself until her breasts hung quivering and suspended and her warm, moist sex came into contact with Crystal's soft lips and tongue. Crystal closed her eyes and, with a shiver of ecstasy, sniffed the tangy aroma of the other woman's cunt. Then she extended her tongue and thrilled to the sensation of the tender, fleshy genital lips, glistening with musky juice and her own saliva. She stroked her wet tongue back and forth along the swollen, pouting slit, causing the recipient of her caresses to tremble and moan with pleasure, causing her to wriggle her bottom slightly to extract every ounce of tactile enjoyment from the exquisite sensation. Finally Crystal homed in on the tiny, fleshy · nub of the woman's clitoris. Concentrating at first on the narrow shaft and hood, she wiggled her naughty tongue with expert precision, flicking the already aroused flesh and causing her lover to cry out in ecstasy.

'My God!' she panted with urgent intensity. 'You're killing me, darling . . . I'm going to come!' The woman's hips and bottom shivered and bucked wildly, causing Crystal to temporarily lose contact with her intimate feast, and her flushed, swollen breasts bounced and trembled as she threw back her head and yelled with joy, tears of passion streaming from her closed, smoky-lidded eyes as spasm after orgasmic spasm wracked her hot, sweat-sheened body.

After what seemed to Crystal to be the mother of all climaxes, the woman became calm and drowsy, her movements lazy and content with released passion. Bending her gorgeous, gazelle head and kissing Crystal tenderly on the lips, she climbed from the ottoman and yawned sleepily, stretching her gorgeous naked body and long limbs before padding into her bedroom and slipping into a loose, silky kimono. Emerging once more, she removed the Vivaldi from the still-rotating gramophone turntable and replaced it with a Wagnerian opera, the rich, dark strains providing a welcome release from the 'phut, phut, phut' of the previous, spent record. She stood for a moment or two in the centre of the dimly lit, rather eccentric room, emotionally lost to the music's opening bars. Then, humming softly to herself, she glided distractedly across to her empty glass and refilled it with fresh wine before lighting a long, Turkish cheroot with a tiny gold lighter. Seeming suddenly to remember the existence of her guests, she turned and peered at them, her expression betraying a note of faint surprise at their continued presence.

By now, Crystal was dressed once more in the clothes she'd arrived in and had joined Isaac on the low couch. Still excited though slightly shaken by the experience of watching the two women make such passionately inventive love to each other, he had managed to calm himself and rearrange his clothing after reaching his own solo climax. Feigning a nonchalance he was far from feeling, he crossed his legs and draped a casual arm around Crystal's shoulders, appearing blissfully unperturbed but sneaking the occasional incredulous glance in her direction. He was maddeningly unable to challenge his inner astonishment at this previously unguessed-at facet of her personality, yet relieved by the expression of calm and utter serenity on her face.

'Another drink?' The woman addressed them almost as an afterthought.

Crystal and Isaac looked up at her, surprised and a little embarrassed by the apparent change of mood. 'Er, no thanks,' they replied together. 'We'd better be going, actually,' Isaac added, clearing his throat; 'We've a table booked at Charlie's Brasserie. We'll need to get back and shower and stuff. You know what I mean . . .' He hesitated.

The woman seemed relieved. 'Ah . . . Charlie's. An excellent choice. Do remember me to him, won't you.' Then, turning to Crystal, she continued, an unmistakeable hint of amusement in her voice as she appraised her face and body as though seeing her for the first time in spite of their recent ecstatic congress: 'Dear Charlie, of course, is a complete darling, but something of a hedonist, too. Especially where women are concerned.' Pausing, she lowered her eyes and smiled secretly, remembering some almost forgotten incident from her shadowy past. Returning to the moment she focused once more on Crystal. 'You'll need to look your best if you're to visit his restaurant. It's his pride and joy, you know. His 'wife', his 'family', his *raison d'être* . . . Darling, I want you to accept the scarlet dress with my compliments.'

Taken aback by such generosity, Crystal made as if to protest, but clearly the woman would brook no such argument. Holding up a slim, admonishing hand she continued: 'Please . . . Just a little token. When he sees you in that dress, Charlie will die for you. Think of it as a modest gift from me to you – and to Charlie, also. Now, if you'll excuse me . . .'

'Yes, of course,' Isaac and Crystal rose to their feet, shrugging into their jackets and collecting their market spoils. The woman glided towards them with arms outstretched, embracing them in turn and kissing them lightly on both cheeks, lingering a little longer over Crystal than was strictly necessary whilst pressing the revealing velvet dress into her hand and gently squeezing her bottom before ushering them both to the door. 'Goodbye, and thank you. Do visit again when you're passing.' The woman turned to her lover as she said this, her body tantalisingly close enough for Crystal to detect little flecks of gold in her dark, mysterious eyes. As she gazed into them, enthralled, the pupils dilated suddenly and she quickly looked away, flushed and surprised by her own response and by the rapid beating of her heart.

Once outside in the early evening dusk, heading across the deserted marketplace towards the street where Isaac lived, the two of them felt somewhat lost for words. Shivering a little and huddling close to Isaac for warmth, Crystal glanced back over her shoulder at the shop, in darkness now but with a faint, rosy glow emanating from the windows on the first floor. 'Well, that was interesting,' she said, turning to Isaac with a mischievous smile.

'Interesting's not the word which springs immediately to my mind,' Isaac replied, placing an arm around her shoulders. 'Bizarre comes closer to the mark. I wonder if she's like that with all her customers? We didn't even find out what her name was.'

'Tanya.'

'What?'

'Tanya. Tanya Biechonski. There was an invitation addressed to her on the mantelpiece. I had a crafty look at it when she wasn't looking. It was for a masqued ball at the Ritz. She's obviously a lady with connections in high places.'

'Connections is right,' Isaac said with a grin. 'But what sort, I ask myself?' Crystal gave him a friendly dig in the ribs. 'And what's all this stuff about Charlie? I knew he was a character but I hadn't realised he made a habit of shafting his female patrons. I'll have to keep an eye on you, won't I! Seriously, though,' he continued, 'do you think you'll visit our exotic friend again when you're next in London?' Isaac wasn't entirely sure what he wanted Crystal's answer to be. On the one hand he found the idea of her making love to another woman wildly exciting, and on the other he had to admit to feeling a little bit jealous.

After a pregnant pause, Crystal stopped walking and turned to him with an enigmatic smile. 'I don't know for sure . . . but I might do.' They were standing under a streetlamp and its light cast a golden gloss on her tousled mane and clear, glowing skin. As she looked at him, her eyes glittered with vitality and passion.

Devouring her with a smouldering gaze, Isaac hugged her to him and sighed deeply, resting his chin contemplatively on the top of her head and breathing in the scent of her hair. 'You're nothing but a gorgeous tease, Crystal. A beautiful cipher. You turn my guts to jelly. And you've turned my life upside down . . . Come on, woman,' he said, his voice husky with desire. 'Let's get back before I embarrass us both by doing something to you in public I might later regret.'

Laughing together, they hurried on towards the warmth and familiarity of Isaac's house.

Chapter Three

It was the 24th of December – Christmas Eve at High Links Hall. Crystal Clearwater was jogging briskly, at about one and a half times her normal speed, through the wintry early-morning gardens of the illustrious health spa. When she'd first set out she'd been damn glad she'd had the presence of mind to don two pairs of leggings and a couple of sweatshirts beneath her tracksuit. The exercise, though, had helped her build up a good head of steam and right now she was simmering nicely. Warm and exhilarated she skirted a small copse of trees, admiring the sight of the watery winter sun rising over the horizon to the east and marvelling at the way the delicate hoarfrost had iced the rough tree bark and the tiny, bare twigs with a skill which surpassed even that of the High Links head chef, whose somewhat unlikely passion for exotic cake decorating was legendary amongst the staff and any favoured guests who happened to be celebrating an anniversary of some kind during their stay at the Hall.

Crystal enjoyed her morning work-outs (in the summer she swam in the outdoor pool) and adhered to her daily routine with the fervour of a religious fanatic. It wasn't that she was terminally stuck in a rut, or unwilling to accept alternative ways of attacking her morning schedule, but merely that this was the one time of the day when she could be truly alone with her thoughts, free from interruptions and the day-to-day pressures of her work as High Links' PR Manager. Today, like most days, Crystal's thoughts turned to affairs of the heart, which in her case had for some months adopted the slim, lanky form of Isaac Mallory. With a warm glow she recalled the last time they'd been together, when she'd stayed with him for a long weekend during the autumn at his house in Camden Lock, stealing a precious few days of intimacy before he embarked on yet another international tour with his rock band, the Steel Dinosaurs. She remembered the fun they'd had, especially on their last night together when they'd dined at the famous Charlie's Brasserie, she in the stunning scarlet velvet sheath dress, given to her by the exotic owner of the boutique they'd visited that afternoon, and Isaac in Hungarian peasant shirt and brocade waistcoat, his dark, freshly washed hair in shiny tendrils around his face and neck.

Charlie himself had deigned to grace them with his redoubtable presence, wooing his favoured guests with finest Colchester oysters, fresh Scotch salmon and seemingly endless bottles of Krug – many of them on the house – which he'd shared with them at their table whilst taking a break from pandering to their every culinary whim. Tanya Biechonski, the boutique owner, had been correct in her prediction that Charlie would be bowled over by Crystal's erotic presence in the outrageous scarlet dress. He'd been mesmerised by her glacial, raven-haired beauty and had barely taken his eyes of her. Even whilst pouring the champagne, his fevered gaze had moved from her full, dewy lips to her slim curvy hips and bottom as she'd shifted provocatively in her chair, finally coming to rest on the scandalously exposed semi-spheres of her creamy breasts, eyes burning like hot coals and a film of sweat beading his flushed forehead.

Crystal chuckled at the memory of that evening, especially when she recalled how she'd played up to the overt adulation unmercifully, accentuating the depth and inscrutability of her gaze and sensually bending forward at every conceivable opportunity, cruelly exposing just the right amount of creamy flesh and deep, shadowy cleavage to induce a fit of the vapours in her hapless male admirer, but not quite enough to send him completely over the edge by affording him an electric glimpse of bare, rosy nipple.

Far from being jealous at Crystal's provocative behaviour, Isaac had been delighted and amused, not to mention highly turned on, by the show. Later, when they were alone once more, he'd likened it to the female mating rituals of some of the exorbitantly priced, designer-clad whores whom he'd seen in action on the arms of certain well-known captains of industry and withholders of the 'British way of life' who, far away from the prying eyes of their well-bred, county spouses, were apt to enjoy the occasional licentious night on the town at their shareholders' unwitting expense.

When they'd finally parted company, Charlie had placed a chubby, covetous arm around Crystal's smooth shoulder and, under the cover of bidding her a fond farewell, had whispered throatily in her ear, the unmistakable bulk of his erection pressing against her velvet thigh. 'I'll swing for you, darling,' he murmured. 'Trust me, you heavenly bitch, you've not seen the last of me. Charlie's not so easily satisfied. One day you'll pay for your coquetry . . . in full. One day, when it pleases me and not before, you'll dance to *my* tune . . .'

Placing a stubby, beringed hand on her curvy bottom he'd patted her like a favourite pet and then squeezed the soft flesh with the firmness and assurance of a man used to achieving his desires. At the time, Crystal had been somewhat taken aback at the menacing power of his words but later, on reflection, she'd reasoned that Charlie was unlikely to make the journey to Somerset from London just to get his end away with her when he must have countless beautiful, willing women gracing the tables of his restaurant every day of the week. Or maybe he would make the effort after all . . . With a small shrug she'd put the matter to the back of her mind. She hadn't bothered mentioning the episode to Isaac, although she'd been somewhat tempted to do so. It crouched in the far reaches of her consciousness like a small, malevolent raincloud on an otherwise cloud-free horizon.

Mildly rattled suddenly by her memory of Charlie, Crystal quickened her pace and was soon in sight of the stately, grey stone majesty of High Links Hall with its wide, sweeping gravel drive. As she approved, she was just in time to observe the slow progress of an ancient, dove-grey Daimler as it manoeuvred with the quiet grace of an elderly ballroom dancer into an empty parking space, its aged exhaust belching small clouds of carbon monoxide into the frosty, early-morning air.

Crystal slowed to a walk and, panting slightly from her run, approached the stationary car, puzzled by its early arrival. As a general rule, the High Links guests tended to arrive at slightly more civilised times, the hours between 7 and 9 a.m. being mainly reserved for the passage of laundry and delivery vans to and from the Hall.

As Crystal reached the car, the driver's door opened amid the metallic creaking of unoiled hinges and out stepped a gentleman of advancing years. Crystal immediately recognised him as the famous society photographer and distant cousin to the Queen, Claude Pettifer-Jones. In the split second it took for her to recognise him, images of Pettifer-Jones during the 1960s – a gay young blade in somewhat gentrified Carnaby Street togs as befitted his station in society, a blonde on each arm and a battery of Hasselblads and light meters slung around his neck and shoulders – fluttered across her imagination like faded newspaper cuttings from her early childhood. Looking at him now, despite the passage of time, it was easy to see why he'd achieved such popularity with the world's press, not to mention the endless procession of pretty young starlets and models whom he was reported to have squired with the almost indecent, single-minded obsession of a young man in full awareness of his manifold, masculine charms.

Crystal gulped. Despite herself, she was instantly attracted to the suave, easy-going image he presented as he stood quietly beside his car and gazed contemplatively up at the Hall. His slim frame was greyhound-lithe, albeit slightly stooped, and he was dressed somewhat eclectically in faded denims, a worn Harris tweed jacket with leather elbow patches and a pink paisley-patterned shirt circa 1965 or thereabouts. A pair of wire-rimmed spectacles attached to a leather thong, presumably a driving aid, hung suspended across his broad chest and his sleek, silver-grey hair, thinning slightly around the temples and on the crown of his aristocratic head, was worn long and clasped at the nape of his neck with a discreet rubber band.

Suddenly aware of Crystal's presence behind him, the gentleman turned swiftly on his heel with the uncanny agility of a teenager. He greeted her with a warm smile and an expression of polite enquiry, which quickly transformed itself into a look of practised, calm appraisal as he took in her smooth, vibrant beauty. When he spoke his voice was deep and well-modulated, almost mesmeric in quality. Crystal found herself blushing and becoming uncharacteristically flustered by the almost palpable charm and sensibility of the man which seemed to flow from the very core of his being like the scent of an expensive cigar box or a replete wine cellar.

'Good morning, Miss, er . . .'

'Crystal Clearwater, sir. We spoke on the telephone the other morning, if you remember. Welcome to High Links Hall. If you'd like to follow me I'll show you to your room and rouse one of the porters to fetch your luggage from the car. It's still a little early so I can't guarantee that there'll be anyone at the reception desk.' Crystal, regaining her customary air of professional unflappability, smiled at him.

'Thank you so much, my dear, but I only have a holdall and a couple of camera bags with me. I'm sure I can manage to carry them up to my room myself. But I must apologise for materialising on your doorstep at this unearthly hour. The fact is that I was forced to attend a private viewing in London last night at one of those horrendous little bijou galleries in the centre of Knightsbridge.' With an amused chuckle he added confidentially: 'And truly awful it was, too. The artist in question must either be blind or singularly lacking in talent. Anyway, I decided to cut my losses and drive down here straight after the show. I have to admit, though, that my recklessness has left me feeling a trifle frayed around the edges, so I think I'll grab an hour or two's shut-eye before I jump out at poor Sadie.' He paused and politely stifled a small yawn. 'By the way, my dear, we did agree to keep quiet about my arrival, didn't we? I'd hate to spoil the surprise.'

'Of course, sir. I haven't mentioned a word to her about your phone call. She'll be in seventh heaven when she knows you're here.' Emboldened by the easy camaraderie which had grown between them, Crystal continued: 'By the way, may I be rude and ask how you two know each other? I mean, Sadie being Sadie and you being thirtieth in line for the throne and everything . . .'

Momentarily nonplussed, Claude Pettifer-Jones threw back his head and laughed out loud, the deep melodious guffaw filling the silent drive with its joyful resonance. Embarrassed, Crystal shifted her weight from foot to foot and, blushing once more, bit her bottom lip. 'My dear girl!' he spluttered, 'you must be possessed of a quite extraordinary fund of inconsequential information. Am I *really* thirtieth in line for the throne? Heavens above, let's hope it doesn't come to that! And please call me Claude. "Sir" makes me sound like such a pompous old prig.

'Anyway, in answer to your question, Sadie and I go back a long way. She was one of my favourite photographic models, you know. Quite, quite charming in her youth – like a frightened doe, although possessed of a worldliness quite in advance of her tender years.' He paused and smiled, reminiscing. 'Anyway, I suspect that she hasn't changed one iota and I can't wait to feast my eyes on her darling form once more.' As his dark, expressive eyes met Crystal's they glittered mischievously, reducing her to a fit of impromptu giggles, delightfully caught up in the schoolboy naughtiness of this illustrious gentleman's plans for her girlish employer. But

then, unbidden, an image of Sadie floated across her mind –
pink, rather fleshy and peroxide blonde, a far cry from the
silky, milk-white goddess she'd been in her youth – and she
stopped giggling, offering instead a silent prayer to the gods
that be that neither Sadie St George nor her erstwhile,
hopelessly romantic paramour would experience the bitter
pang of disappointment.

'I'm afraid I'm going to have to hurry you, sir. I'm being
relieved in five minutes.'

Frankie de Rosa grinned at the tall receptionist whose
name, according to the plastic tag attached to her festive
scarlet uniform, was Glynis. 'Relieved of what, Glyn? Your
virginity?' He winked at Sharon and gave her a crafty dig in
the ribs with his elbow and the two of them dissolved into a
fit of helpless giggles.

'I knew we should never have had that third Madeira,
Frank,' said Sharon, almost choking with the effort of trying
to control her mirth. 'It's bloody lethal that stuff, you know.
Especially on an empty stomach. A girl like me could find
herself in all sorts of trouble.'

'Exactly, my love,' said Frankie with a leer. 'Why do you
think I suggested it?'

This produced a fresh barrage of staccato merriment from
Sharon who, wobbling dangerously on the high spiky heels
of her black PVC thigh boots, grabbed hold of Frankie's arm
for support.

Glynis, unmoved, raised her eyes to heaven, readjusted the
sprig of holly pinned to her lapel and proceeded to drum her
scarlet talons on the polished veneer counter top. Then,
catching sight of her reflection in the gilt mirror on the

opposite wall, she patted her glossy auburn curls, did a quick check on the staying power or otherwise of her lipstick and removed a stray false eyelash from the corner of one perfectly made-up eye. Turning her imperious gaze once more to the pair of morons on the other side of the counter she sighed, exasperated, and continued, a hint of steel adding a distinct edge to her clipped, carefully enunciated words: 'Well, will you be requiring breakfast in bed tomorrow morning or not?' Glynis's expression of exaggerated enquiry thinly disguised an air of distinct disapproval. 'It's one of our more popular options, sir, here at The Spotted Cow. Especially with our regular customers.' She hoped to God that these two pillocks weren't about to fall into that particular category. She'd seen enough of them already to last a lifetime. 'We charge extra for the service, though, of course.' Pity the staff themselves couldn't charge extra for the dubious privilege of dealing with the likes of these two, Glynis thought darkly. Honestly, the class of client visiting the place these days was going from bad to worse. It was all terribly depressing. She was really beginning to think she should take her boyfriend's advice and enrol for a shorthand-typing course.

Frankie scratched his head and considered his options. It had to be admitted that the prospect of an extra hour in bed on Christmas morning with the lovely Sharon, breakfast thrown in, followed by a spot of rumpy pumpy if he could still get it up after the previous night's exertions had the distinct advantage over tea and toast with polite conversation in the dining room. 'Oh, what the hell, Sharon,' he said with an expansive flourish, 'let's go for it, shall we?'

Sharon nodded eagerly, her black-rimmed eyes wide with instant complicity. 'Whatever you say, Frankie.'

'Good, that settles it, then. Toss us over the key, Glyn, and we'll get our stuff stowed away before lunch.' And if he remembered to play his cards right, Frankie thought to himself with an instant constriction to the groin area, their stuff wouldn't be all that'd get stowed away – if the telltale glint in Sharon's eye was anything to go by.

Gratefully, Glynis turned and snatched the key to room number thirteen from the wall behind her, dumping it unceremoniously on the counter top before glaring at her wristwatch and somewhat pointedly diverting her attention to the glossy magazine she'd been perusing before having been so rudely interrupted.

'Oh look, Frankie. Room number thirteen. Unlucky for some, but not for us, eh, Frank?' Sharon giggled nervously and, glancing at Glynis with an expression of girlish camaraderie, was rewarded with an icy stare. 'Oh well, can't win 'em all. Come on, Frank.' Tugging down her lime-green lycra mini she followed Frankie through the glass double doors which separated the reception area from the main body of the coaching inn, spike heels clicking obediently on the polished parquet.

With a gleam in his eye, Frankie opened the door to room thirteen with a flourish and, with a discreet bow, stood aside to allow Sharon to enter. Sharon blushed fetchingly through her pancake make-up and bit her bottom lip. 'Thank you, lover, I don't mind if I do.' Wriggling her upper torso a little in readiness for her entrance, proudly raising her chin and breasts and with eyes fixed straight ahead, Sharon wiggled her way provocatively into the hotel room and gave a little gasp of pleasure. 'Cor blimey, Frankie, come and look at this lot. It ain't half posh. *Really* tasty.'

Frankie, who'd been following hot on her heels, eyes fixed on her curvy, lime-green derrière, chuckled to himself and surreptitiously adjusted the front of his trousers. 'But not half as tasty as you, my darling . . . Come on, let's cut the preliminaries. I'm desperate for it!' Advancing on Sharon like a man possessed, Frankie pulled her into his arms and crushed her to his mohair suit before she had a chance to protest. Staggering a little on her stilettos, propelled backwards by the impact, she was prevented from falling by Frankie's bear-like grasp.

''Ere, watch it, Frank! Mind my hair, for gawd's sake. I only had it done this morning.' Extricating one nervous hand from his firm grip she reached up and carefully patted her blonde coiffure, checking the high, sexy French pleat for signs of damage.

'Bugger the hair, Sharon. There are some things which won't stand on ceremony. I'll buy you a dozen hairdos if you'll give us a kiss.'

Sharon smiled and clicked her tongue. 'Ooh, Frankie, you're terrible, you are. Honestly, what's a girl to do?' She sighed prettily and shook her head.

Interpreting her coquettish hesitance as straightforward female acquiescence, Frankie growled like a tiger and covered her pouting lips with his own in a long, sensual kiss which sent shivers of desire up both their spines and reduced their limbs to jelly. As they necked with increasing urgency, Frankie was aware that smears of Sharon's plum lipstick were transferring themselves to his face, but he couldn't have cared less. He relished the sticky, glossy feel of it against his skin and its sweet cosmetic taste in his mouth, combined with

71

the by-now familiar scent of Sharon's perfume and shampoo and clean, womanly breath.

Frankie liked women with make-up. Lots of make-up. It turned him on. Momentarily coming up for air, he gazed into Sharon's erotically crafted eyes, glittering now with excitement and her own bodily need, and devoured their sexy, carefully contrived beauty. As he looked at her, his eyes scanning her gorgeous kitten face, she pouted and peered up at him through her long, spiky lashes – an unmistakeably wanton, come-hither expression adding further piquancy to the moment. Then, extending her tongue, she licked her shiny lips provocatively and wrinkled her pretty nose in a playful grin. 'Come on then, baby,' she said in a maddeningly sexy half-whisper, 'let's play . . .'

With her eyes burning into Frankie's, Sharon took a deep breath and deftly unfastened the top of his trousers, lowering the zip in a single, fluid movement. Preferring not to allow himself to dwell too long on Sharon's evident familiarity with the task in hand – or, at least, soon to be in hand – Frankie gave himself up to a long, low groan of pure erotic pleasure. With his trousers concertinaed around his ankles and his underpants pulled down a few inches to hug his lean thighs, revealing his bare arse and his monstrous, throbbing erection, Frankie closed his eyes and shivered with sensual anticipation.

Quickly, Sharon shrugged out of her tight black-leather bum-freezer jacket and tossed it to the floor behind her. Then, adjusting the thin, lacy shoulder straps of her tiny half-cup bra and easing down the front of her low-cut skinny rib sweater still further, she pushed out her generous, exposed cleavage and swiftly gave it the once-over to check for erotic effect. Narrowing her eyes, ready for action, she once more ran her kittenish tongue over her luscious lips. Then, with a whisper of sheer, glossy nylon and the subtle creak of gleaming black PVC, she sank to her knees on the deep-pile carpet, reaching round and clasping Frankie's tensed buttocks in a firm grip before opening her mouth and placing the very tip of his penis between her soft, full lips. Gently running her tongue over the shiny purplish skin of his glans, she licked away the drop of clear semen which had gathered at the tiny opening.

Frankie moaned and tensed, trembling with desire as Sharon's tongue found the intensely sensitive point on the underside of his prick where the glans joined the foreskin. Quite unconsciously he began to slowly piston his lower body back and forth in a desperate attempt to push more of his cock into her mouth. Squeezing Frankie's bare, quivering bum in her expert hands, her long, polished fingernails digging into the warm, pale flesh and leaving flushed, red weals in their wake, Sharon relaxed her throat muscles and, with the enviable skill of an international porn queen, took the entire length of his prick into her mouth, clasping it tightly – the warm, wet pressure of her lips and enveloping tongue resembling nothing so much as the vagina of a freshly plucked virgin, penetrated for the first time.

Delighting in the sensation of Frankie's pulsing hardness in her mouth and luxuriating in the feeling of power it afforded her, Sharon closed her eyes in delight and sucked on his cock like a baby, squeezing its base between her glossy lips and sensually encircling the rigid warmth of it with her hot, wet tongue.

'Bleedin' hell, Sharon, where in God's name did you learn

to suck cock like that?' Frankie gasped. 'On second thoughts, don't tell me. Just do it . . .' With his eyes squeezed tight shut and jaw clenched in a frantic effort to prevent himself from coming too soon and spoiling the fun, Frankie felt himself on the point of swooning, his self-control stretched almost to breaking point. At his crotch, Sharon felt Frankie's prick shudder involuntarily a couple of times and, following a well-developed animal wisdom borne of years of experience, slackened her oral grip and reluctantly withdrew. Relishing the lingering taste of him in her mouth she licked her lips and sat back on her haunches, smiling up at him.

'Enjoy it, Frankie? There's plenty more where that came from . . . if you're interested, that is.'

Frankie heaved a long, shuddering sigh of contentment and opened his eyes, the beginning of a lascivious smile crinkling the corners as he spoke. 'Interested? Are you kidding? It'd take a saint to refuse one of your blow jobs, Sharon. A chance to be fellated by you should be offered free on the National Health to every male over the age of fourteen. Put the spunk back into the nation's manhood. Metaphorically speaking, of course. It'd be nothing short of a mission of mercy. Get this godforsaken country back on its feet in no time at all.' Frankie chuckled to himself and then gazed down at her with the quickening fire of a fresh bout of lust in his eyes. 'Meanwhile, my little Florence Nightingale, before you set out to cure the nation's ills, there's the little matter of unfinished business with yours truly. Get your gear off, woman, and spread 'em for me . . .'

Never one to refuse a request from the heart, especially when accompanied with such blatant admiration and erotic relish as Frankie's, Sharon rose slowly to her feet, wriggling her shoulders and leaning forward, being careful to display as much thrusting cleavage as humanly possible. 'I thought you'd never ask, Frankie,' she whispered huskily whilst gazing into his eyes and climbing out of her boots. With a sexy little shake of her upper torso which made her breasts jiggle like a pair of gleaming milk jellies inside her tight top, she pulled the skinny rib up over her head and tossed it to the floor. Then, wriggling her hips and bottom, she lowered her tight lycra skirt and sheer tights in a single movement, stepping out of the flimsy garments and carelessly kicking them aside with the pointed, varnished toes of one dainty bare foot.

Frankie gulped and took a sharp intake of breath as he feasted his fevered gaze on Sharon's palely voluptuous, skimpily clad body, drinking in the heart-stopping beauty of her spectacular breasts – the creamy skin luminous as they rose and fell with her breathing, separated and scandalously uplifted with the aid of an improbably tiny black-lace bra. Tearing his eyes away from her luscious tits, Frankie shivered, eyes on stalks, and allowed his gaze to travel downwards over her smooth, lightly curved belly to her slim, womanly hips and thighs and the little wisps of silky blonde pubic hair which peeped over the top of her minuscule, semi-transparent panties.

Delighted with the effect she was having on her lover and keen to capitalise on it fully, Sharon bent over and retrieved her shiny black thigh boots, stepping into them and smoothing the cool, gleaming PVC across her warm, naked thighs. Then, with a coy wink at Frankie and a sexy wiggle which sent her practically naked breasts and bum into delicious motion, she turned on her high, spindly heels and teetered across to the double bed. Placing her bottom decorously on its edge, she swung her long, booted legs onto the pale pink candlewick bedspread and arranged herself along its length like a Playboy centrefold, complete with narrowed eyes, pouting lips and high, gleaming blonde hair-do.

Momentarily transfixed by the prick-stimulating image she presented, Frankie swiftly stepped out of his shoes, trousers and underpants, divesting himself in seconds of his mohair suit jacket, shirt and knitted silk tie before proceeding, despite his eagerness to make love to the vision on the bed, to fold the garments carefully – though it has to be said that he lacked his usual faultless attention to detail. Completely naked now, his stiff prick throbbing with a maddening urgency and bobbing crazily against his belly with every step, Frankie hurried across to the low stool by the chintzy dressing table. He placed his clothes on it and made his way to the low divan, climbing onto it with a single-minded resolve of an automaton. Panting with his need for physical release, he straddled Sharon's prone body and whispered huskily in her ear, the inflamed tip of his turgid cock nudging against the soft, white flesh of her quivering belly. 'Jesus, Sharon, are you a sight for sore eyes or what? I'm going to screw the fucking arse off you now, woman. Take the rest of your togs off.'

'Take them off yourself, big boy,' Sharon replied in a soft whisper, her wet tongue protruding suggestively between her teeth and full, glossy lips. Frankie didn't need asking twice. Tugging at the tiny scraps of black lace like a man possessed, he quickly pulled them away from her trembling breasts and arse, while Sharon obediently lifted those portions of her anatomy from the candlewick to better facilitate their removal. Naked at last apart from her thigh boots, she gave a long sensual stretch designed, no doubt, to display her voluptuous nude body to its best advantage. Reaching her arms above her head she arched her supple back, which made her breasts bounce and judder and her big, erect nipples point impertinently ceiling-wards. Then, tensing her long legs and bending her knees amid a squeaky symphony of PVC, spike heels impaling the soft, pink bedspread like flick-knives, she spread her thighs wide to reveal the dusky gash of her glistening pussy. Adjusting her position a little, she ran a slow, wet tongue over her lips once more and, with lazy, narrowed eyes, gazed down the length of her gorgeous, naked body at Frankie, her expression of mild interest betraying an innate confidence in her own sexual beauty.

And Sharon had every reason to be confident. Once more, Frankie was charmed and amazed at the sight of her naked cunt, marvelling yet again at the woman's desire for erotic credibility which had prompted her to bleach her pubic hair a pale baby blonde, a perfect match for her glossy beehive. Artificial it may have been, but the electric effect of it on Frankie's already bursting genitals couldn't be denied. In fact, he'd be happy to challenge any red-blooded heterosexual male, even one who got his rocks off over more natural-looking bints, to gaze on the fleshy lips of Sharon's gorgeous peroxide pussy without creaming his jeans in an instant. Frankie, luckily, had managed to cultivate a little more self-control. But not much.

Trembling with lust, his dark eyes devouring her luscious body and beads of sweat gleaming on his sex-flushed forehead, accentuating a single throbbing vein across his right temple, Frankie was tensed and ready for action. With a swift, easy athleticism which mirrored the urgency of his advanced sexual need, he positioned his slim body above Sharon's with her shapely legs, bent at the knees, one each side of his thighs. After only the briefest of pauses while he ran his eyes once more over the beautiful, willing body he was about to plunder, he took his erect penis in his right hand and positioned it, tantalisingly, at the pouting outer lips of Sharon's swollen peroxide pussy.

Sharon sighed and gave a tiny shudder, spreading her thighs still further apart, confident that she was about to be penetrated by him. But Frankie had other plans. With a low, excited chuckle, his body wracked with the excruciating tension of holding back his fast-approaching climax, he stroked the turgid, inflamed tip of his penis along the slick gash between Sharon's pubic mound and tiny, puckered anus. Sharon yelped with surprise and pleasure, her genital muscles fluttering delightedly in an involuntary series of minute, preliminary contractions as she wriggled her bare bottom against the soft candlewick, tensing her slim thighs, her shiny spike heels stabbing the pink fabric with increased ferocity.

'You're a bastard, Frankie,' she gasped, panting now with desire, her naked breasts rising and falling as she breathed and trembled with the rapid beating of her heart. 'Don't tease me, Frank. Can't you see I'm dying for it? For Christ's sake, *do* something!' As she pleaded with her lover to put an end to her erotic agony, Sharon's voice grew shrill and tight with emotion. At last, unable to bear the sensation of Frankie's stiff cock nudging at the entrance to her pussy a moment longer – so near and yet so far – she let out a scream of frustration and, arching her back, grinding her bare arse against the bed and thrusting her swollen cunt at him, she yelled in something close to rage bordering on sexual delirium:

'Fuck my frigging cunt, you sodding bastard, before I ram my fist up your bleedin' arse!'

With a brief stab of embarrassment, fearful in case Sharon's less than tender words had been overheard by the occupants of the rooms on either side of them – indeed, of the rooms on the other side of the building – Frankie was unwilling and still less able to hold out any longer. 'Okay, bitch, you asked for it!' Grabbing hold of her hips and repositioning his prick at the entrance to Sharon's dripping cunt with the deadly accuracy of a crack marksman, he tensed his buttocks and stabbed forward, gritting his teeth in concentration as he impaled her fully and completely, before withdrawing as far as he dare without losing his purchase on her pussy, then stabbing forward once more.

In less than no time Frankie had established a swift, dynamic and powerful rhythm which, his position being such that with every thrust of his prick he managed to massage her inflamed clitoris, was as satisfying for Sharon as it was for him. In fact, so mind-blowingly stimulating was the sensation of Frankie's prick pistoning in and out of her cunt that she squeezed her eyes tight shut, opened her mouth and screamed, long and loud with the pure, undiluted pleasure of it before finally yelping with joy as her orgasm was upon her, each heavenly wave eliciting fresh bursts of vocal ecstasy.

Lost in the final throes of passion, Frankie was past caring. Limbs tingling and trembling with the intense exertion of his powerful fucking, Frankie rode the waves of Sharon's orgasm and, as they gradually dwindled and he felt her body become loose and fluid with lazy satisfaction, he allowed himself at last to give full rein to his own climax. 'I'm coming, woman!' he panted hoarsely. 'Wait for it . . .!' With a final, triumphant thrust he quickly withdrew his prick, glistening with musky juice from Sharon's sated cunt and, straddling her belly and holding it proudly in both hands like a small boy with his first imitation firearm, whooped with joy as he shot a veritable stream of spunk across her large, flushed breasts. Then, sighing deeply with spent passion he fell, exhausted and face down, beside her.

Bleedin' hell, Frankie thought to himself as he lay there, drunk with sex and on the threshold of sleep, if this was a taste of things to come over the next couple of days, he'd be good for nothing when he finally returned to work. He hadn't even minded much about the racket Sharon had made while he'd been fucking her. With the enviable accuracy of an inveterate cocksman, Frankie had correctly categorised the lovely Sharon Neavis as a prime 'screamer' from the moment he'd first set eyes on her. It was perfectly obvious, he'd told his colleague, Nick Knack, over a cup of tea in the tiny office-cum-cubbyhole they shared at High Links. You could tell just by looking at her. Nick had remained unconvinced, preferring to maintain an air of brooding scepticism along with his usual surly menace, but then Nick's track record as far as women were concerned was less than encouraging. In fact, it could be said that it fairly reeked of failure and disappointment. Frankie remained unswayed, and rightly so, as it later transpired that Sharon was a shouter *par excellence*. So much so that Frankie had frequently had to clap a silencing hand across her mouth in an attempt to save both their blushes.

Sharon stretched her body and cooed softly, placing an arm behind her head which further disrupted her already somewhat dishevelled blonde mane. Turning to smile contentedly at the exhausted Frankie, she considered her recent performance. Not bad, she thought. Not bad at all. Unless she was very much mistaken, and if she was any kind of a judge of men (which she was, she added smugly) Frankie de Rosa was hers for the taking – for the time being at least. She had him right there in the palm of her hand, whether he was aware of it or not. Sharon prided herself on her understanding of the male sex. They were all little boys in grown-up bodies really. And, if she was lucky, they had a clutch of credit cards burning holes in their pockets in place of smouldering cap guns.

A gob of semen had landed on Sharon's left cheek and she scooped it up with one finger, transferring the sticky fluid to her tongue as though it were finest caviar. She smiled contemplatively, savouring its musky saltiness in her mouth and, pushing out her chest, glanced down at her full breasts which were still slightly flushed from their lovemaking and liberally spattered with Frankie's spunk. With an erotic thrill spreading like quicksilver from her breasts to her vagina, she noticed that a particularly large dollop had ended up on her left nipple, which instantly flushed and hardened as she looked. Now for the good bit, she thought with a shiver. Head thrown back and eyes closed, she smeared the sticky spunk over her breasts and belly with both hands until they were slick and gleaming. Then she began to flick and tickle her big, shiny nipples with the tips of her long, polished nails, pinching them between her fingers and whimpering incoherently with renewed lust before losing herself to the rapid, intense orgasm which raced through her like an Australian bush fire.

After a minute or two, sticky and somewhat sleepy, she

opened her eyes and yawned, then raised her head and glanced at Frankie who was lying on his front beside her. His head was turned towards her and his eyes were closed. As she watched him, his back rose and fell rhythmically as he breathed and an almost imperceptible snore escaped his open lips. He looked so innocent and tranquil when he was asleep, she thought. Hard to relate the image he presented now with the wise-cracking, sharp-suited Mafioso lookalike she knew and loved. Just a little boy, really, deep down. She smiled tenderly at him and stroked his dark hair. Sharon's little boy . . .

Pulling herself together she glanced at her watch and gasped. 2.00 p.m.! Her tummy rumbled, as though on cue. She was famished, she realised. She could murder a steak and chips if the restaurant was still open for lunch, and she hoped to God it was. No point in rousing Prince Charming from his slumbers. He probably wouldn't thank her for it. But she, on the other hand, had every intention of enjoying her stay at The Spotted Cow to the full, which included partaking of breakfast, lunch and dinner with gin and tonics thrown in and the odd packet of fags added to the bill if she thought she could get away with it. After all, who knew when a man like Frankie would treat her again to a buckshee break?

Quickly climbing off the bed, careful not to disturb Frankie, she climbed back into her bra, panties and the discarded lycra. Forsaking the sheer tights in her haste, she quickly unclipped her small handbag and removed a long, menthol cigarette from a mock-croc case. Lighting it with an airport disposable she inhaled deeply, gratefully expelling a blue, smoky plume before poring over her near-ruined hairdo in the dressing table mirror and minimising her smudged eye-liner with a tissue from the box thoughtfully provided by the management. She'd do, she decided happily, mentally attacking the juicy fillet, medium-grilled with a hint of pink in the centre, just the way she liked it. Eyes gleaming with anticipation she grabbed her bag and set off in search of the dining room.

'What did you say your name was, dear? I don't believe we've had the pleasure before, have we?'

'Sidney, madam. No. I don't believe we have.' Without losing his rhythm, the young masseur glanced at the curly blonde head and pink, fleshy back on the treatment table, shiny with an oily, aromatic cocktail of almond, lavender and rose absolut, and raised his eyes to heaven. Could she really have forgotten his name so soon? For crying out loud, he'd only told her what it was a minute ago. Manageress of High Links Hall she may be, and let's not forget about the hiring and firing and the paying of wages, but Sadie St George reminded him of a character from one of those 1960s *Carry On* films his parents had been so potty about – all fluff and knickers and not much else. Right now she was addressing him as though he was tripping the light fantastic with her at the Palais Ballroom, rather than administering her daily massage – face down on the couch, beached and sleek like a seal and naked save for a bath towel over the soft curves of her bare bottom – in her private office at High Links. He had to admit, though, that she was a tasty bit of woman-flesh, despite her daffiness. A bit long in the tooth for him, maybe, and a little on the voluptuous side, but he could see how his mate, Casper, had fallen for it. Casper, though, had met with a sticky end, courtesy of the ominous Nick Knack and his size twelves, and had since joined the dole office queue, armed with P45 and a complete set of bruised ribs.

Served Casper right, really. He should have remembered which side his bread was buttered – and who buttered it – and kept his sticky paws off all those young bits of stuff he'd insisted on playing around with on the side. Hell hath no fury like a woman scorned, Sidney thought, and Sadie was no exception. Beneath the bouncy, kittenish exterior there lurked a vengeful she-cat. He recalled the way Casper had been when he'd come to him for help after being given a seeing to by the resident thug, broken and sobbing, wet with tears and blood. Sidney shivered and continued massaging the smooth, womanly shoulders and neck with extra solicitude.

'Mmmm . . . my dear boy . . .' Sadie half whispered, her voice husky with emotion, relishing the sensation of Sidney's firm, masculine young hands on some of her countless erogenous zones. 'You have the touch of an angel, I swear it. Just like darling Casper. You know, you remind me a little of Casper, my dear. Silly boy . . .' Sadie's voice trailed away.

Blissfully unaware of Sidney's brief, panic-stricken start which caused him to pause for a split second in his work, she allowed her erotic imagination to drift, fuelled by the blatant sensuality of Sidney's strong, male hands caressing her nude body. Like a billowing cloud of soft, scarlet feathers Sadie's libidinous consciousness floated on the current of her bodily sensations and finally came to rest on the tall, ebony-black image of the 'late' Casper Jones, the bitter-sweet memory of whom continued to tug on her heartstrings with an insistence borne of a mixture of remembered lust and sentimental longing. She thought of his soft, Bournville eyes boring into hers as they made love, his hot, urgent breath on her cheek, the firmness of his young buttocks and the absurdly generous dimensions of his penis which, when fully erect, gleamed like polished mahogany, the sensitive, silky skin stretched tight like a drum across the burnished glans as he stroked it with exquisite tenderness across the entrance to her eager, blushing pussy . . .

Suddenly, there was a knock at the door. Disgruntled by the unexpected interruption to her racy reverie, Sadie gave a deep, shuddering sigh and, without opening her eyes, addressed Sidney in a small, disappointed voice. 'Bother! Who on earth can that be? Run along and see who it is, Sidney, there's a dear.'

Obediently, Sidney wiped the oil from his hands and hurried to the door, opening it with an expression of enquiry, which turned at once to surprise and puzzlement when he saw who was standing on the threshold. The figure silently responded to Sidney's obvious discomfiture with a warm smile, raising a placatory hand by way of reassurance and waving a crisp twenty pound note with the other by way of persuasion.

'Who is it, dear?' asked Sadie from her prone position on the treatment couch.

Unsure of how to reply but eager to earn his twenty pounds, Sidney glanced at the figure for a moment, grappling for inspiration. With a mischievous grin, the mystery guest licked an imaginary envelope and hoisted a phantom postbag. 'Oh . . . it's only someone from the mailroom with the afternoon post.' The silent visitor smiled warmly at Sidney, pleased with the explanation, and handed over the money, indicating to the young masseur with a rapid series of graphic gestures that they should surreptitiously swap roles whilst being careful to avoid alerting Sadie to what was taking place.

'Oh, goodie! I wonder if there's anything from that dishy accountant in Bristol. Put the letters on my desk, sweetie, and come back over here. Auntie Sadie's been missing you badly . . .' She'd taken quite a fancy to young Sidney. With a little bit of imagination and with the lights turned down low, or maybe turned off completely, he was a dead ringer for darling Casper. But let's hope he wasn't as foolish as that particular young man.

'Okay, madam, I'll be right over,' Saved by the bell! Inwardly sighing with relief, Sidney shook his head, amazed yet highly amused at the fortunate turn of events, before smartly swapping places with the visitor, closing the door firmly behind him and setting off down the corridor away from Sadie's office with a lilt in his step and a song in his heart.

Alone with her at last, the visitor walked quietly over to the blonde, recumbent form and smiled down at her with an expression of tender remembrance. Yes, it was the same old Sadie all right. Despite her maturity, she was as beautiful and alluring as ever. So what if she'd gained a pound or two in weight and the blonde, carefully styled curls were achieved courtesy of salon perms and tints rather than being naturally sun-kissed and sexily wind-tossed as in previous incarnations? The passing of the years since they'd last met appeared to have done little to dim her fire and the woman inside was still very much the same, her warmth and female allure continuing to radiate that particularly potent brand of sexuality which had made her name as one of the most sought-after photographic models this country had ever known.

After first squeezing them together to maximise their warmth, the visitor placed tender, exploring hands on Sadie's shoulders and back and began to gently caress her smooth flesh in a series of long, sweeping strokes. 'Now then, my dear, what's all this I hear about dangerous liaisons with young boys? I feel quite sure that none of it can be true. After all, you always managed to maintain such an excellent taste in men. I mean, look at me, for example . . .' As he continued to stroke Sadie's silky, voluptuous back he heard, though could not see, her take a sharp intake of breath and felt her muscles tighten and become rigid with shock.

'Yes, it's me, my pretty little Sadie. Come back to haunt you after all these years. Now, what do you think about that?' With a low, amused chuckle, Claude Pettifer-Jones bent over and kissed Sadie tenderly on one bare shoulder, then helped her turn over onto her back and sit up rather shakily. He graciously averted his eyes (for the time being, at least) while she quickly covered her breasts with the towel which had covered her bottom.

Sadie sat and stared at him, her blonde hair sensually tousled, her eyes round and wide with amazement, baby blue and unblinking. Her pretty cupid's bow mouth dropped open in disbelief. 'Claude . . .?' she whispered hesitantly. 'Is that you? It's been so long . . .'

'Too long, my precious.' Claude smiled, delighted at Sadie's evident pleasure in seeing him again. As he watched she gulped prettily and shrugged her shoulders, finally accepting with a warm rush of pleasure that the man standing before her really was her former lover and favourite photographer. Blushing like a girl, she bit her lower lip and continued in a small, shaky voice, high with shock and excitement: 'Well, I think this calls for a celebration, don't you? The champagne's in the fridge . . .'

Chapter Four

11.15 p.m. High Links Hall stood silent and shadowy on that crisp, frosty Christmas Eve, its many occupants safe and warm inside, preparing in their various ways for the following day's festivities. Outside, all was still until a sudden, chill wind disturbed the frozen, silvered branches of the trees which lined the sweeping gravel drive and the distant purr of an approaching car, growing louder by the second, broke the enveloping calm of the wintry, night-time scene. A moment or two later, twin searchlight beams swept off the road onto the drive, closely followed by the vehicle itself – a midnight-blue Citroën Light 19. The car progressed with stately deliberation, like an eerie phantom from a Maigret novel, crunching across the gravel to a parking space between two trees, several yards away from the other stationary cars.

The engine stopped and the scene was once more plunged into silence, save for the distant hooting of an owl and the faint ticking of the car's machinery as it cooled and came to rest. A minute passed. Then two. Then three. With a metallic creak the driver's door swung open, startling a young vixen who, disturbed in her nightly perusal of the rubbish bins which tonight provided particularly rich pickings, streaked off through the trees as though the devil himself were after her.

The figure which finally emerged from the car's interior was small, dapper, rather plump and somewhat pasty in appearance. He was dressed in an immaculate dark suit, an expensive camel-hair coat thrown casually over his shoulders, and a slate-grey Fedora which successfully hid his greying, rather sparse hair. With all the time in the world at his disposal, he placed a small leather holdall on the ground at his feet and took a final pull on his Havana before crushing it with the toe of a black, polished shoe. Then he turned to gaze contemplatively up at the Hall, leaning against the car for support. Allowing himself a modest smile of self-congratulation at having come this far, he pushed away from the gleaming metal, retrieved the holdall and began to walk towards the main entrance of High Links, slowly, deliberately and with a slight, almost imperceptible swagger.

'Come on, love. It may never happen, you know. You look like someone who lost a tenner and found a sixpence. What's up?'

Despite herself, Crystal looked across at the small Scottish chef sitting opposite her in the High Links dining room and laughed out loud. He looked so comical with his chef's hat crammed down over his swarthy, Italianate forehead and his dark, liquid eyes, soulful at the best of times, full of mock-melancholy. 'Christ, Fernando, you don't give up, do you?' she remonstrated through her laughter. 'Can't a girl mourn the absence of her lover on Christmas Eve without being set upon by madmen brandishing desserts?' Chuckling to herself in a resigned sort of way she reached out and pulled the little dish of *crème brûlée* towards her, sinfully creamy and topped with a brittle shell of golden, caramelised sugar. 'But on the other hand, I'm rather glad she can't. Yummy! This is just what the doctor ordered. Thanks, pal.'

The reception area was practically in darkness, save for the minimal glow from one or two wall lights and a desk lamp. Allowing the heavy, double doors of the main entrance to swing silently shut behind him, the man looked around in a somewhat distracted way at the aged oils lining the panelled walls – wreathed with holly, sprigs of mistletoe and shiny streamers – and the expensive Persian floor-coverings, but his attention was focused elsewhere so that were he to be invited at some later date to describe the scene, he would find himself unable to do so. Not that this would worry him unduly. Right now he had far more important things on his mind.

Through a partly open door to the right of the wide staircase came the sound of voices, punctuated by muted laughter – a man's and a woman's. The stranger cocked his head in the direction of the sound and listened, then smiled, recognising one of the voices. Shrugging off his camel-hair coat he tossed it, together with his hat, over the plump arm of a low sofa and sat down, biding his time, the small leather holdall at his feet.

Fernando smiled indulgently at his favourite lady and watched, head on one side, anxious to ascertain her approval or otherwise of his gloriously wicked confection. Aware of Fernando's eagle-eyed scrutiny Crystal slowly raised a delicious, heaped spoonful to her parted lips like somebody from a TV advertisement, tilted back her head, closed her eyes in voluptuous ecstasy and took her first taste amid a plethora of extravagantly gooey Oohs and Aahs and Mmms. Well pleased, Fernando's round face broke into a broad, beaming smile and he sat back in his chair, arms folded across his chest, and watched her demolish the remains of his offering with a little more decorum than before but no less relish.

'Fernando, if there's a chef in this world who claims to make a better pud than you, he's a filthy liar. Must be something to do with your Italian lineage, I reckon. Anyway, thanks a lot. I needed cheering up.'

Fernando shrugged happily and stood up, good deed completed, and removed the empty dish. 'Don't mention it, sweetheart. It was nothing. What's a *crème brûlée* between friends? But listen, seriously, don't be too sad about spending Christmas at High Links with the rest of us waifs and strays with no homes to go to. We'll have fun, Crystal, you'll see. Tomorrow night, when the last of the guests have buggered off to bed, we'll have a blow-out in the kitchen with the seasonal leftovers and a bottle or two of vintage claret. How's that sound?'

'Sounds like a great idea, Fernando,' said Crystal, smiling. 'Give me a nod and a wink when the party's about to start and I'll be there like a shot. Might even be able to winkle a bottle of champers out of petty cash for good measure, who knows?'

'Good girl! Right, I'm off to my pit. Busy day tomorrow. Sweet dreams, my love.' Yawning, Fernando glanced at his watch and disappeared back into the kitchen with the empty dessert dish. Crystal watched him go, guilty about feeling miserable when she recalled that her own emotional woes were a veritable picnic compared to his. Before Fernando had joined the senior kitchen staff at High Links, he and his Italian wife and four children had lived in Edinburgh. He'd been head chef at a fashionable city centre restaurant and was earning a healthy living there, fast building an enviable reputation as one of Scotland's finest. So much so that when the restaurant came on the market he was all set to buy it and turn it into his own. But then, disaster struck. His wife left him and she and the kids went back to live with a former lover of hers in Rome. Fernando, devastated, had fled to England in his grief, desperate to be as far away as possible from the land of his marital break-up and shattered dreams.

But despite all he'd been through, Fernando invariably managed to hide his hurt and disappointment beneath a sunny and amiable exterior. He was a real darling. One of Crystal's favourites. She sighed and looked at her watch. 11.45. Almost Christmas Day. In a few hours' time the place would be jumping like a kangaroo on speed. And if Sheba, the world-famous rock star and notorious ruffler of Establishment feathers arrived with her retinue in time for Christmas lunch, as promised, Crystal would well and truly have her work cut out. She smiled when she remembered how she'd taunted poor Frankie a few days before with lurid hints of Sheba's proposed Yuletide descent on High Links, and how she'd tantalised him by refusing to divulge the 'mystery' guest's identity. Crystal giggled, recalling Frankie's consternation, then yawned, suddenly overwhelmed with fatigue. Better get some shut-eye before the fray. Wearily she began to rise from her seat.

'Good evening, my dear. Surely you can't be thinking of turning in so soon? Not with the night still so young.'

Crystal froze and her heart skipped a beat. She immediately recognised the man's voice, though she'd only heard it once before. How could she forget it? Hadn't she been over that particular scene a hundred times in her mind's eye? Slowly straightening her body she turned to face him with a feeling of unease. 'Charlie,' she whispered. 'So, you meant what you said, then. I didn't think . . .'

'My friends know me to be a man of my word, Crystal, and do you know what? I think you're about to become one of them. A friend, that is – a rather special one, unless I'm greatly mistaken . . .' His voice was silky smooth, but his breathing was fast and audible – disturbingly so. A light sweat had broken out on his forehead and his eyes were dark and bright as they moved from her lips to her breasts and back to her lips again, scrutinising her, assessing the power of her beauty. Gaze unwavering, Charlie held the edge of the table as he lowered himself slowly into the seat opposite her. She noticed that her hands were trembling. Surprised at herself and of her weakness in the presence of this man, insidious and somewhat threatening though it was, Crystal sat down also.

Charlie took a deep breath and smiled at her, revealing a glint of gold filling, his beringed hands forming a chubby pyramid beneath his chin. 'Now then. This is cosy, isn't it? How about a drop of cognac for old time's sake? And to welcome the season in, too. What do you say? Come, you wouldn't refuse a friend, would you? Not when we have so much to talk about.'

Crystal's mouth was dry and her heart was hammering in her chest. What the bloody hell was all this about? Why was she so scared of this little ponce with his inflated ego and his empty threats? Her mind raced back to his words that evening last autumn in the restaurant. He'd tried to seduce her then. He'd undressed her slowly with his eyes, then he'd called her a bitch, assuring her that he'd be back for more . . . For crying out loud, Crystal thought angrily to herself, I've eaten more intimidating men than Charlie for breakfast. Besides, the place was stuffed with potential saviours. All she had to do was raise the alarm. But something – some buried instinct – stopped her. Slowly, silently, she rose to her feet and walked shakily across to the bar, now in shadows, and poured two large measures of brandy into balloon glasses before returning to the table and sitting down once more. 'What do you want with me, Charlie?' she said, her voice and demeanour remarkably composed despite her inner disquiet.

Charlie began to laugh, the sound rising from his chest in a way which made Crystal squirm. 'Want from you? Come, come, baby. Surely it's more a case of what you're going to give me. Freely and willingly. And you will give it to me, Crystal, I have no doubt about that.' He paused and his eyes dropped once more to her breasts, the smile leaving his face as he lingered there, gazing salaciously as though by some strange magic he were able to clearly see their full, pulsing voluptuousness beneath her blouse.

The way Charlie was looking at her, Crystal might just as well have been naked. Like a hostess in a topless bar, she thought suddenly. Bare-breasted and wanton, willingly at the mercy of all those who chose to feast their eyes on her nudity. A lump formed in her throat and she gulped, alive with a mixture of emotional discomfort together with a strange, unidentifiable sensation which spread through her body from the tips of her toes and fingers and the crown of her smooth head, making the surface of her skin tingle and the fine, downy hairs rise on her arms and at the base of her neck. Like warm honey, the sensation flooded inexorably to her genitals and, with a sense of horror, she felt her nipples harden and press with exquisite tension against the fabric of her top – an event which was far from lost on Charlie, whose eyes shone with lust as he gazed at them, his lips curling in a satisfied smile.

Crystal felt her heartbeat quicken. Raising her brandy glass to her lips with trembling fingers she took a large swig of the dark liquid and closed her eyes as its fiery passage burned her throat. Immediately, it seemed, her trembling ceased and her muscles grew loose and drowsy. Thanks to the alcohol, she was beginning to feel in control of the situation once more. Replacing the glass on the table in front of her with careful deliberation, she fixed Charlie with a steady, unsmiling gaze, willing him to remove his eyes from her breasts and meet her eye contact with his own. 'And what if I refuse to play?' she asked quietly.

Charlie was unswayed. 'A good question, sweetheart. Allow me to answer it with one of my own. Tell me, do you value your position here at High Links?'

Crystal sighed and nodded, exasperated by his impertinence and by his apparent evasion of her straightforward query. 'Of course I do. Why do you ask?'

Charlie continued: 'So you'd be somewhat inconvenienced, to put it mildly, if it became known about your little dalliance with a particular friend of mine – someone with whom it was more than a tiny bit reckless to have an affair, however transitory.'

Crystal's disquiet turned to anger. Her eyes blazed. 'What

the hell are you talking about, Charlie? If you're referring to Isaac, then it's common knowledge around here that we've—'

Charlie cut her short. 'No, not Isaac, my dear, impetuous lady. Someone far more dangerous. The person I refer to is Tanya Biechonski.'

Crystal blanched and she stared at Charlie for several seconds, her mouth open, lost for words, and her brow furrowed with incomprehension. 'Tanya . . . But why?' she finally managed to whisper. An image of the beautiful, voluptuously eclectic Eastern European with whom she'd made such passionate, creative love a few months before swam into her consciousness. Tanya Biechonski was one on her own, certainly. Mysterious and somewhat vague, yet highly sophisticated in the erotic art of sexual seduction, she'd swept Crystal off her feet with all the innate charm and poise of a royal courtesan, not to mention the power of her stunning, vibrant body. But dangerous? Surely not.

'Dear Tanya. Such a shame.' Charlie agitated his brandy glass, releasing the warm, intoxicating aroma, and took a generous swig before gazing into its glowing depths and shaking his head sadly. 'Right now she's in Holloway, you know. A guest of Her Majesty, pending trial. And over Christmas, too.' He clicked his tongue with distaste at the thought. 'I wonder if they serve brandy butter with the pudding in prison . . .'

Despite the lingering warmth of the dining room, icy fingers stroked Crystal's spine and she began to shiver. 'Prison . . .' she whispered, 'Tanya . . . What in God's name has she done to deserve that?'

Charlie paused before answering, enhancing, whether

inadvertently or otherwise, the dramatic impact of his reply. Crystal couldn't be sure at the time but when, on subsequent occasions, she relived the scene in her mind's eye, she'd have been prepared to swear on a stack of bibles that Charlie was smiling. But for now, the shock of his unfolding revelation and the dawning realisation of the reasons behind it succeeded in blunting her perceptions. 'Drugs,' he said, his dark eyes studying her. 'Heroin to be exact. Tanya Biechonski is – or was, should I say – one of the most notorious drugs traffickers in Europe. She supplied them all. All the big boys. She was a junkie herself once, but she kicked the habit several years ago when she became more interested in the business side. She was clever enough to know that one should never mix business with pleasure.' Charlie paused, downing his cognac in a single gulp before continuing: 'The drugs squad have been chasing her for years and now they have her just where they want her . . . Poor baby. She doesn't stand a chance. And I don't suppose she's having much fun at the moment. The stories one hears about the way they treat people like her in prison . . .'

Tears of shock and fear stung Crystal's eyes. She screwed them tight shut and buried her head in her hands, a shiny curtain of raven hair obscuring her temporarily from Charlie's unwavering gaze. In the space of a few short minutes, faced with this man who, after all, was little more than a stranger to her, Crystal had moved through the full gamut of emotions, powerless to halt their relentless progress – surprise, anger, burgeoning lust, disbelief, disgust, and now terror. Finally, dangerously close to breaking point, she managed to find her voice once more. 'But the shop . . .?'

'Merely a front for her other, rather more profitable

activities. Anyway, my dear, let's move on to the purpose of my visit.'

Falteringly, Crystal removed her hands from her face, placing them on the table in front of her and, with a little sniff of defiance, looked Charlie straight in the eye. Charlie stared right back at her and his expression did little to assuage her discomfiture. Despite her obvious charms and powerful attractiveness to men, of which she was fully aware and constantly reminded, Crystal had never been faced by such a look of bare, naked lust. So much so that after a couple of seconds she was forced to avert her eyes and gaze instead at her hands on the table, which were pale and trembling. Quickly, she moved them to her lap.

When Charlie spoke it was in a tense, dangerous whisper, low with suppressed passion. His face was flushed and damp with sweat and his eyes, dark and glowing with desire, hinted at something which Crystal was loath to acknowledge – something hot, pulsing, venomous, perverse. 'I want you, Crystal Clearwater. From the first moment I saw you in my restaurant. You aren't like the others. Those bitches – they're just a bunch of high-class whores, the lot of them. All hair and arse. Always ready to screw. Open their legs at the drop of a hat or the wave of a credit card. But you're class . . . real cool. You have to really want a man before you'll let him fuck you, am I right?'

Glancing at Charlie momentarily, Crystal nodded, amazed at herself for her own complicity, for being so prepared to go along with his game – thus far at least – without calling his bluff by raising an alarm. All she had to do, she told herself, was get up and walk away. The police would be here within minutes. As for the blackmail attempt, if he tried to spill the beans about her affair with Tanya Biechonski, it'd be his word against hers, and she had a pretty shrewd idea about who'd be more believable out of the two of them. But to her utter dismay, Crystal found herself unable and, worse still, unwilling, to take decisive action. Something about Charlie stopped her. It was some subtle element in his voice, his stance, his whole demeanour. It was almost as though he were willing her to take control of the situation. To dominate it, in fact. Crystal had seen this sort of reaction in men before. It excited her, made her feel powerful, horny . . . So, she thought to herself, if that's the way he wants to play it, maybe I'll condescend to go along with the pathetic little bastard. After all, that's all he was. Naked and vulnerable, he'd be nothing but a heap of shit . . .

Under the table, Crystal curled her toes and pressed her thighs together, feeling the sweat rise where flesh touched flesh. The throbbing in her sex was warm and insistent. She wriggled her bottom on the chair and felt her breasts jiggle inside her blouse, the erect nipples rubbing with exquisite friction against the soft fabric, sending darts of white fire to her belly and below. Opposite her she could hear Charlie's breathing grow fast and ragged. He, too, had sensed a sea-change. And he was glad.

Leaning forward a little to allow him a tantalising glimpse of her cleavage, Crystal tossed back her long, ebony hair in an imperious gesture and gazed, unsmiling, into Charlie's eyes, her expression betraying nothing of her earlier discomfort. Charlie quickly averted his eyes from her cool, level gaze and gulped, beads of sweat standing out on his forehead. 'My suite's on the ground floor at the back of the building, overlooking the rose garden,' Crystal said to him, her voice an icy, authoritive monotone. 'Be there in ten minutes. I'll leave the door ajar.'

Slowly she rose to leave, relishing the almost tactile sensation of Charlie's greedy, panic-stricken eyes on her sinuous body. His eyes focused on her breasts, he opened his mouth as though to say something but then thought better of it, fixing her instead with a pleading gaze.

'Yes, what is it?' she snapped at him.

Charlie recoiled, startled and contrite at the harshness of her voice, then bent and hesitantly pushed the leather case along the floor towards her. 'Please . . .' he whispered, his voice trembling, 'if it would increase your pleasure . . . A small gift. Take . . .'

Crystal stood for a moment, considering his offer, prolonging his agony. Then she appeared to reach a decision. With a small sigh of impatience, as though annoyed with herself for pandering to the fickle whim of a small child, she picked up the case and, without a word, turned on her heel. As she headed out of the dining room and towards her suite, her silky, waist-length hair and curvy backside swaying hypnotically with every assured step, a small smile began to play about her lips. 'Better and better,' she thought to herself.

Charlie sidled, crablike, along the wide corridor towards Crystal's suite. It was midnight and most of the wall lights had been extinguished leaving the moon to cast a warm glow over the soft blue carpet and the walls lined with paintings, and making the gash of light escaping from the partially open door to the room in question clearly visible. Charlie's mouth was dry and his armpits and forehead damp and clammy. Try as he might, he was unable to stop himself from trembling, a condition made all the more acute when he dared to allow his mind to dwell on his unexpected good fortune. He could hardly believe his luck. Everything was happening exactly as he'd imagined it in the countless, feverish fantasies with which he'd entertained himself since he'd first met Crystal. Something deep within him had responded to her, almost as though he recognised in her some quality which mirrored his own. A fondness, perhaps, for a particular brand of sexual expression which many would find distasteful, indeed perverse, but which, presented with the opportunity, he and Crystal would be only too delighted to embrace with gleeful relish. It would appear now that he had been right to form such an assumption. With the minium of hesitation Crystal had taken the bait. Charlie congratulated himself on being a superior judge of character.

The light from the semi-open door to Crystal's suite glowed like a guiding beacon, entrancing him, exciting him with notions of what lay on the other side, across the threshold. All was silent. Charlie braced himself and took a deep, trembling breath, flexing his fingers and slowly circling his neck in an effort to loosen the tense, knotted muscles beneath the surface. Then he walked slowly and deliberately towards the door and nudged it open with the toe of his shoes, closing his eyes as it swung slowly open in delicious anticipation of the sight which he fervently hoped would greet him.

And Charlie was far from disappointed. When he first saw the woman (she was barely recognisable as the Crystal he'd parted company with in the dining room), the strength drained from his legs and it was as much as he could do to stop himself from falling. She sat facing the door in a high-backed rattan chair, several feet away from him towards the back of the room in front of a pair of tall, velvet-draped windows. The room itself was stylishly decorated and subtly lit by several small table lamps and one large ceramic one which had been artfully placed on the floor beside the king-size, clothes-strewn bed. Only a blind man would fail to have been moved by her appearance as she reclined there in the warm glow. Her face was pale and still, accentuating the dark, brooding eyes which were heavily rimmed with smoky liner. Her full, slightly parted lips had been uncharacteristically painted a lush scarlet and her long dark hair fanned across her shoulders and bare arms, dropping to below waist level like smooth, shiny molasses.

Charlie dampened his dry lips with the tip of his tongue, willing his racing heart to slow down for long enough to allow him to fully grasp the awesome beauty of the vision before him. His eyes moved from her face and hair to the voluptuous semi-spheres of her alabaster breasts, generous portions of which pulsed and strained above the skintight, laced bodice of a minuscule corset. Fashioned from shiny, blood-red leather, it was as smooth and supple as the naked skin of the woman inside it, clasping her narrow waist in its erotic embrace and ending just above the dark cloud of her pubis, which was quite naked, the soft skin as pale and flawless as her breasts. The woman's thighs were spread slightly apart, allowing Charlie a tantalising glimpse of her bare genitals, the shadowy slit already swollen, damp and dusky with lust. Despite the distance between them, Charlie fancied he could detect the scent of her cunt – the dark, female spoor hanging on the air between them like a steamy, siren cloud. The smell of her maddened him. He gulped convulsively and allowed his eyes to continue their downward scrutiny of her body. Stretched tight around her bare hips, aligned with the bottom of the brief corset, she wore a suspender belt crafted from the same soft scarlet leather. Its strappy fastenings dripped along her creamy, naked thighs like fresh blood, fingers of soft animal skin pressing into the voluptuous white flesh, firmly tensing the sleek, super-sheer black nylon seamed stockings in which her long, elegant legs were encased. On her feet she wore a pair of high, spindly heeled scarlet satin mules.

The outfit could have been made for Crystal alone. Feasting his eyes on her, a horny sex goddess in skimpy garments the exact shade of wet blood, Charlie congratulated himself once more – this time on his choice of female underwear and for correctly assessing the woman's physical dimensions. He made a mental note to pay particular tribute to the designer with which he'd placed his commission for them. Charlie was well pleased. His aroused penis throbbed inside his trousers. It was then that he noticed the narrow, black riding crop, held lightly in the fingers of her right hand, Surely he hadn't . . .

'How dare you . . .' Crystal's voice was low and deadly. Charlie started, alarmed at the sudden intrusion, and his heart leapt. Nervously he wet his lips with the tip of his tongue. 'How dare you enter this room fully clothed. Undress immediately and leave your clothes outside the door. I've no wish to see them in here.' If anything, the menace in Crystal's voice had intensified, her delivery quiet yet perfectly audible, staccato and slow.

Charlie began to tremble uncontrollably now and fresh beads of sweat broke out on his forehead and upper lip. Clumsily, he began to fumble with his clothes, loosening his

tie, unbuttoning his shirt and stepping out of his shoes and
trousers as quickly as he could manage without losing his
balance. He didn't want to upset the woman by seeming to
take his time. He could feel her eyes on his emerging body –
cold and critical, with a hint of distaste – and he blushed with
embarrassment, instantly self-conscious and ashamed of his
flabby midriff and veiny legs. Stripped down to his vest,
socks and boxer shorts he stopped and glanced fearfully at
Crystal, silently pleading with her to allow him to keep them
on. But he was wasting his time. Crystal was beginning to
enjoy herself. She appraised him coolly, biding her time
while stroking the riding crop along her sleek, stockinged
thigh. Her expression registered her displeasure. 'So? What
about the rest of your things? Surely you can't imagine that
I'll get turned on by the sight of your pathetic little limp dick?
Christ! Give me credit for some taste.'

Charlie was crestfallen. He bit his lip and twisted his
hands together, glancing nervously at Crystal with an
expression of hang-dog supplication. Her harshness thrilled
him. Inside his pants his penis began to expand and stiffen
against his groin, its rubicund tip threatening to appear at any
moment from the leg of his shorts. Summoning his courage,
he pulled his vest off over his head, mussing his carefully
combed hair and revealing his upper torso with its pelt of
grizzled, grey-brown hair. Then he unbuttoned his pants,
pulling them down to his feet and stepping out of them in his
stockinged feet. When he'd finished he stood, terrified in his
naked vulnerability, unable to meet her gaze as his erect
penis protruded at right angles from the base of his belly,
dark and throbbing with anticipation, a visible tribute to the
effect the woman was having on his erotic sensibilities.

Crystal sighed with impatience and addressed him with measured over-emphasis as though he were a backward child. 'I might have guessed you'd be the type who fucked with your socks on. It seems I wasn't to be disappointed. But leave them on, anyway. It amuses me.' A small, satisfied smile played about Crystal's glossy, scarlet lips as she scrutinised the naked, albeit be-socked, figure of the man standing before her, but her eyes told a different story. Beautiful and heavy with cosmetics, they shone with a kind of brooding contempt mixed with excitement, like those of a cat contemplating the next cruel move in her one-sided game with a captive rodent. Transferring her attention to the pile of discarded garments on the floor, she clicked her tongue and nodded her head sharply in the direction of the door leading on to the corridor outside.

Quickly, hoping to avoid her further displeasure, Charlie hunkered down and gathered the clothes together, screwing them up into an untidy ball, mindless of the superior quality of the fabric in his haste to do as he was told, before putting them down outside the door and daring to close it quietly behind him. Too late, he wondered if this were expected or, indeed, desired. After all, Crystal hadn't actually asked him to close the door. Maybe she'd . . .

'Good. Out of sight, out of mind.' Crystal appeared not to have noticed his imagined *faux pas* regarding the door, or at least she was choosing not to respond to it. Inwardly, Charlie melted with relief. 'Now, there's a couple of things I want to get straight before we go any further,' she said briskly. 'Number one, you call me Madam. Number two, you do exactly as I say at all times, no matter what I ask you to do. And number three, you keep your mouth *shut*!' Charlie jumped at the last word, which was delivered with such strength and brevity that he was left in no doubt whatsoever that she meant it and that failure to comply with her wishes would signal a demonstration of severe displeasure.

Her next words were softer but no less authoritative. 'Now, lick my cunt.' Leaning back into the chair and draping her languid arms over its sides, Crystal spread her legs and placed her bare bottom as far forward as she could so that the dusky folds of her pussy were fully revealed to Charlie, the inner labia slightly open and gleaming with her increasing arousal. Her lip was curled slightly as she watched him stare, wide-eyed, at her exposed sex, and her dark eyes narrowed with interest and pleasure. Charlie's heart missed a beat and the blood drained from his perspiring face. Bereft suddenly of energy, his muscles sagged and became limp with shock. He staggered a little and the trembling in his limbs became acute and uncontrollable. Finally managing to get a grip on himself, he began to move towards the reclining female, slowly and with single-minded deliberation as though on automatic pilot. Part of him wished the floor would open and devour his poor, quivering body and another part was terrified in case the woman changed her mind, snapping her legs shut and denying him the unspeakable treat on offer between her open thighs.

'Not so fast!' Crystal snapped, making Charlie's heart leap so that he thought it would burst from his chest. 'What do you mean by coming at me like that? You're nothing but scum, are you . . .? Well, *are you*?'

Charlie gulped and struggled to find his voice, which seemed for a brief, terrifying moment to have deserted him entirely. 'Yes, Madam . . .' he whispered, his eyes fixed on the ground. 'I mean, no, Madam,' he added quickly before she had a chance to pounce on his mistake.

'Louder,' Crystal ordered tersely.

'No, Madam.'

'Good. That's better. Now, get down on your hands and knees and grovel like the scum that you are.' She watched, fascinated, as Charlie did as he was told, intrigued and excited by the sight of his erect penis which bobbed crazily from side to side as he moved. Hot with the desire to feel Charlie's lips against her throbbing cunt, Crystal hardly dared to dwell on the effect this little charade was having on her mind and her body. It all felt so right. Disturbingly so. Her power over this man seemed to have enveloped her. It was as though she were addicted to it, wanting it never to end. She closed her eyes briefly and placed her smooth head against the back of the chair, breathing rhythmically through her nose in an attempt to still her galloping emotions, which were threatening to race out of control at any moment. After a second or two, relieved beyond belief, she found herself becoming mistress of the situation once more. No sense, she thought, in spoiling it all at this stage of the proceedings by falling to the ground in a quivering heap of exposed sexuality and begging Charlie to fuck her to within an inch of her life. That wasn't what the game was all about at all, and it certainly wasn't what Charlie wanted. This way was far more fun. 'Well,' she breathed, 'What are you waiting for? Surely you know how to eat pussy . . .'

Crystal stared at Charlie's pale, trembling body as he shuffled clumsily towards her on all fours, his eyes bright and glowing with excitement and his breathing heavy and uneven. She watched as his large penis, dark with lust, bounced against his belly and his heavy testicles wobbled between his legs. Gone was the smooth, dapper manipulator of less than an hour before. This creature was like an animal, stripped of all pride and higher emotions along with his clothes, plumbing the depths of base, physical sensation, desperate only to fuck and be fucked, to penetrate and to be cruelly manipulated whilst doing so. A tremor of lust flickered through Crystal's corseted body, setting her on fire and raising the fine hairs on her arms and at the back of her neck, despite the enveloping warmth of her private suite. She closed her eyes once more, luxuriating in the heady eroticism of the moment, and waited . . .

At last, Charlie was within centimetres of Crystal's pouting cunt. He stopped and sniffed, reeling at the smell of her, suddenly drunk with the intense femininity of her musky scent. Slowly he extended his tongue and dared to allow himself a taste, running the warm, wet tip along the length of her outer lips between her anus and the tiny pink nub of her clitoris. The skin of her pussy was soft and warm, blush-pink and swollen with arousal. The dark pubic hairs tickled his lips and tongue. He loved their wiry springiness against the sensitive skin tissue inside his mouth. Sometimes, with other women, the sensation had made him want to gag, but not this time. Above him the woman began to moan, easing her bottom further along the seat of the chair towards his face, her cunt wet and gleaming with a mixture of her own lubrication and Charlie's saliva. 'Poke me with your tongue,' she whispered huskily. 'Stick it right into me. Fuck me with it . . .'

With intense sensual relish, Charlie found the dark opening to her vagina and nudged the tip of his tongue against it, pushing between the soft dusky folds of flesh and up into the narrow channel beyond. He wiggled his tongue against the firm, muscular walls of her pussy, feeling them pulse and contract around it, and rubbed his lips against her quivering vulva. Right now Charlie was feeling hot – hot with blind lust and single-minded concentration. Without thinking, he grasped his cock in his right hand and began to masturbate wildly, frigging the warm flesh like a man possessed, causing the loose skin to slick back and forth along its length and the shiny purple glans at its tip to burst forth again and again. In his mounting excitement, aroused almost beyond endurance, he removed his lips and tongue from Crystal's cunt and gasped, panting like a racehorse, desperate to reach his climax.

'Stop!' Shaken back to full consciousness, Charlie stopped what he was doing and glanced up at Crystal, his body shaking still with desire. 'I don't believe you could have understood my instruction earlier. Tell me, are you deaf, stupid or both? I suspect the latter.'

Though spoken quietly, Crystal's words were loaded with simmering menace. 'How dare you . . .' she hissed. 'How dare you go against my wishes. Are you incapable of leaving your prick alone for five minutes? You're pathetic, do you know that? A pathetic little wanker. And I'm going to punish you for what you've just done. Bend over . . .'

A white hot flare of anger erupted in Crystal's belly. As she spoke, she rose majestically to her feet, intensely beautiful and statuesque in the high satin mules. She stood looking down at the object of her ire with her legs apart, breathing evenly with nostrils flared and creamy breasts rising and falling above the brief leather corset, the lips of her naked pussy plainly visible now through the cloud of dark pubic hair. 'Well . . . what are you waiting for?' she whispered.

Petrified, Charlie glanced, wide-eyed, at the narrow black whip with which Crystal had begun sensually to caress her bare thigh, moving its cruel length closer and closer to her already aroused sex, then stroking it along her tender labial lips and shuddering with pleasure, head thrown back and eyes momentarily closed.

A thousand images flashed through Charlie's fevered mind. Visions of previous sexual encounters with innumerable women – wives of wealthy clients, attractive female staff, countless prostitutes. As different as each experience had been, they all had one thing in common – Charlie's perverse desire to be sexually manipulated and cruelly controlled. He made a point of choosing his lovers carefully, seducing only those women whom he felt would be able and willing to satisfy his need. As a result he'd developed a kind of sixth sense and could tell at a glance whether a potential sexual partner had the qualities necessary to assume the role of dominatrix, often before they knew it themselves. And Charlie had seldom been disappointed, surprising himself again and again with the accuracy of his hunches, marvelling constantly at the seemingly endless capacity for physical cruelty present in the average woman. Or maybe it was he who brought it out in them.

Charlie rose unsteadily to his feet, eyes fixed on the ground, and scurried over to the brass bedstead like a chastened hound. Whimpering slightly and muttering unintelligibly, he positioned himself with his back to Crystal, legs apart, leaning over the high brass rail whilst grabbing hold of it with both hands. His erect penis throbbed with excitement, the hot, turgid flesh bobbing against the cold metal and sending tiny, delicious shivers through his tensed body. Now, having assumed the position, he waited impatiently for the degradation to begin, trembling with erotic anticipation, painfully aware of Crystal's cool scrutiny of his body. He was glad she'd made him keep his socks on, exquisitely aware of the extra ridicule they afforded him.

Crystal began to laugh, but the sound was cold, joyless. Charlie felt the laughter scorch through his body like a heated knife, bringing tears of humiliation to his eyes and fresh gouts of pulsing blood to his already bursting member. Then the laughter stopped and he was aware of her walking towards him on her spindly satin heels across the soft carpet. She stopped just behind him and he jumped with fright as he felt her stroke what he assumed to be the narrow thong of the whip with extreme care down the entire length of his back, stopping when it reached the point where his buttocks separated. Charlie cowered at its uncharacteristically tender touch, every sensitive nerve-ending in its path alive and tingling with a mixture of terror and delight.

After what seemed like a lifetime the woman spoke, her voice dark and forbidding, heavy with barely suppressed rage. 'So, you've been a very, very naughty boy indeed, Charlie. You leave me with no choice but to punish you, and punish you severely. It's for your own good, Charlie. I don't doubt you'll thank me for it in the long run . . .'

The woman's voice had lowered to a whisper. She was standing as close to him as she could without actually touching him. He could smell her subtle scent – a mixture of Shalimar and her own natural secretions – and feel her soft breath against his ear. He shuddered with pleasure. Then, incredibly, she closed the gap between them entirely, pressing the full length of her voluptuous body against his back so that he could feel the beating of her heart, the heavy fullness of her semi-naked breasts and, lower, the silky mass of her pubic mound as it rubbed hypnotically against his buttocks, almost as though she were trying to penetrate him. Mesmerised, Charlie tensed his anus in delighted anticipation. Momentarily unafraid yet exquisitely aware of the undoubted transience of the situation, Charlie held his breath and waited, every muscle in his body tensed and ready for the onslaught which he felt certain would follow as surely as night follows day. As he waited, sweat breaking out from every pore of his body, he felt the woman's movements against him become wilder, more frantic, her heartbeat growing faster and stronger against his back and her breathing in his ear becoming ever more ragged and uneven.

'Now!' she hissed at him through clenched teeth, '*Now!*' Pulling away, she positioned herself behind him, full-square with legs parted. Then, closing her eyes and taking a deep, energising breath, she slowly drew the full length of the whip through her long fingers before raising it above her head and bringing it down with full, stinging force across the bare back of the man in front of her. The sound reverberated through the quiet room. Charlie cried out, squirming with surprise and fright, a single, red weal immediately appearing on the pale skin. Crystal gazed at the wound, shocked and amazed at the reality of what she'd done, yet strangely exhilarated, lit from within by a mysterious, deadly fire of passion which seemed to devour her very soul, threatening to overtake her with its erotic intensity.

At that point, or shortly after, Crystal seemed almost to lose all reason. Yet something, some innate, previously unacknowledged wisdom of the strict rules of the game furnished her with sufficient self-restraint to prevent her from losing control entirely. With a whoop of satisfaction, eyes blazing, she brought the whip down again and again across Charlie's quivering back, scorching the surface of his skin and turning it a dark, angry red, criss-crossed and sore. Throughout Crystal's cruel ministrations, Charlie maintained a firm grip on the brass bedstead, writhing against it, twisting and turning this way and that like a steak on a spit, attempting in his own hopeless way to escape the stinging lash, knowing full well that his efforts would prove fruitless.

He cried out in pain and anguish, agonisingly alive to the sharp, ugly sensations in his back yet aroused beyond belief, weeping with boiling passion, intent on the rapidly approaching tide of his own, pulsing release. Through his agony and his tears, Charlie felt the cutting blows move ever lower, stinging his buttocks, the narrow, pointed tip catching the tender, wrinkled skin of his scrotum and causing him to shriek with fresh pain.

'Oh my God! Stop . . . stop it *now*!' Charlie's testicles convulsed, shrinking upwards into his groin, and from the tip of his inflamed penis came the first thick gob of his emission, its warm translucence landing on his clenched fist, a second and then a third dollop appearing on the bedspread and then on the floor at his feet. By the time his ejaculation had dwindled away to nothing, the whipping had ceased and all was quiet. Gone were the grunts, moans and cries – both male and female – of a few moments earlier.

A warm, satisfied glow spread from the toes of Charlie's feet to his thinning crown. His muscles stopped twitching, relaxing and becoming still. Knowing his face was obscured from the eyes of his 'tormentor' he allowed himself a small grimace of discomfort, followed by a little smile of pleasure and release. Conscious only of his own intense relief, he failed to be moved by the sound of weeping coming from behind him. Crystal's.

Crouched on the floor in a foetal position, the whip several feet away where she'd cast it from her in disgust, Crystal's body was wracked with quiet, rhythmic sobs of disbelief and despair at what, just a few minutes before, she'd found herself compelled to do. She simply couldn't believe that she'd allowed herself to become so embroiled in a scene of such ugly, mindless violence against another human being, however loathsome he may have been in her eyes. She wished to God she'd had the strength to ignore the lure of his nasty little plan and walked away, head held high. Screwing her eyes tight shut she allowed the tears to flow unchecked to the carpet, hugging her knees to her breasts, praying silently for comfort.

Wiping the semen from his hand and foot with a corner of the bedspread, Charlie turned and glanced down at Crystal, his expression arch and cool once more, contemptuous of the woman whom he'd so recently referred to fearfully as 'Madam'. He clicked his tongue disapprovingly. 'Now, now, my dear. Don't feel badly. You have every reason to be proud. You're good. Very good, in fact. A natural.'

Despite his nudity, he walked with a slight swagger across to the door, opened it, retrieved his clothes and studied them carefully for signs of creasing before stepping back into them. Stooping down he checked his reflection in the dressing table mirror, smoothing his ruffled hair before replacing his hat. After a brief scan of the room he noticed the leather case which had contained the skimpy outfit lying open on the floor. He paused for a moment before closing the lid, struck by an idea as he crouched down next to it. 'You may keep the clothes,' he told her matter of factly. 'They suit you. Besides, you may find them useful if you ever find yourself contemplating a change of career.' He smiled at her and made for the open door.

Slowly Crystal looked up, her face streaked with make-up, an expression of pure hatred in her eyes as she stared at him. Suddenly, frantic with rage, she leaped to her feet and tore the scarlet leather and sheer black nylon from her tense body. Then, grabbing the velvet dress – her gift from Tanya Biechonski – from the wardrobe, she flung the whole lot down the corridor after Charlie's departing form. 'You can keep them!' she yelled. 'The whole bloody lot of them! And don't ever, ever let me set eyes on you or your filthy little schemes again!' Slamming the door of her suite behind her, Crystal staggered across to the bed and crawled under the covers, praying for the healing cloak of sleep to descend on her.

Outside in the corridor, Charlie heard the door slam shut and turned round, retracing his steps and retrieving the strewn garments, stuffing them in the leather case before setting forth once more.

At last, eyes glassy with distress and fatigue, her sobs controlled now to the occasional faint hiccough, Crystal was sure she heard the sound of a car as its engine pulsed into life before disappearing down the drive, away from High Links Hall, and her life, forever.

Christmas Day lunch at High Links Hall was, as ever, a thoughtfully conceived and brilliantly executed affair. Its magic and visual beauty were matched only by the thick white feathers of snow which were falling outside, drifting down from an iron-grey sky and covering the undulating Somerset landscape with a soft, perfect blanket of pure white. In stunning contrast, the dining room at High Links provided a brilliant medley of vibrant colour, a veritable symphony of evergreen, berry red, royal blue and purple, brought brilliantly to life with touches of glimmering gold and silver.

Crystal moved with quiet assurance amongst the dining guests, who were celebrating the season with every appearance of complete enjoyment and bonhomie, talking happily amongst themselves as well as calling across to fellow diners, sharing jokes and amusing anecdotes amid the merry tinkle of clinking glasses and tipsy laughter. From time to time she sat down with a group of revellers to catch the tail end of a joke or distribute a few more paper hats and party novelties. Her customary serene demeanour and good-natured banter did nothing to reveal the way she was actually feeling inside on this Christmas day, a day tailor-made for bubbling spirits – both actual and metaphysical – and an effervescent lightness of being.

Crystal felt anything but light. After a brief, dream-laden sleep she'd awoken at 4 a.m. and spent the next few hours reliving again and again the torrid events of the night before. The dark eroticism of her behaviour towards Charlie, and his towards her, had left its emotional mark. God knows, she was as broad-minded as the next person – probably more so in fact, when one considered the numerous kinky sex games in which she'd liked to indulge with various lovers, of both sexes, from time to time over the years – but never before had she actually inflicted harm on another person. Like some

117

kind of hypnotic, reassuring mantra she repeated over and over to herself how Charlie had wanted her to do what she'd done to him; had begged for it, in fact, and then later had demonstrated his appreciation of her performance in the customary manner. She had the stain on her bedspread to prove it and the image of it in her mind's eye made her shudder with revulsion.

There was no denying that Charlie was a nasty piece of work, cold and utterly calculating, his treachery knowing no bounds. Charlie would stop at nothing to achieve his grubby ends – not even blackmail. She hoped to God that she never set eyes on the evil little runt again. She simply had to relegate the seedy episode of the night before to the back of her mind and put it down to experience, or whatever, so that she could carry on with her life in the best and most positive way she knew how. If only something would happen to take her mind off it . . .

Suddenly there was an urgent tap on her shoulder and Crystal turned round to see that it was Bella, the relief receptionist, who appeared to be seeking her immediate attention. Bella's customary pallor and expression of pained, long-suffering weariness seemed to be at an all-time high. She'd obviously allowed herself to become severely rattled for some reason. Crystal deduced, rightly as it turned out, that something was definitely up. 'What is it, Bella? You look as though you've eaten something which hasn't agreed with you. Too many mince pies in the staff kitchen, maybe?'

'In a manner of speaking, Crystal, you're right. But not about the mince pies,' said Bella, tight-lipped with suppressed anger. 'For "eaten" substitute "been confronted with". Would you mind stepping this way and helping me to sort out a little problem in reception? Christ, did I say little? More like a bloody great problem and clad from head to foot in an endangered species to boot!' Crystal had rarely seen Bella as fed up as she appeared to be now. By Bella's standards that was saying something, notorious as she was for her somewhat neurotic behaviour and frequent bouts of emotional heebie-jeebies. Intrigued to find out what all the fuss was about, Crystal excused herself from the table of guests with whom she'd been exchanging the usual seasonal chit-chat and followed the distraught receptionist out of the dining room and into the lobby.

Immediately recognising the cause of Bella's upset, Crystal's heart did a nose-dive. Fancy her forgetting a thing like that? The events of last night must have effected her more than even she'd realised. Leaning against the reception desk as though she owned the place, her whole demeanour suggesting a pronounced air of languorous authority, ebony-black six-foot frame expensively wrapped from head to foot in arctic fox and drumming the polished desk top with her matching pure white-varnished talons, stood Trouble with a capital T. Sheba, world-famous rock star and stunningly outrageous sex symbol had descended on High Links Hall for her Christmas break and she aimed to make sure that as many people in as short a time as possible registered her arrival.

'Are you in charge here?' came the terse non-greeting which was barked – as befitted the canine source of her floor-length coat and huge cossack hat – in an accent which combined the seductive lilt of the speaker's native France with a rather less appealing Texan twang.

Shaken but not stirred, Crystal stood her ground. 'Hello,

Sheba – hope you don't mind me calling you that? I don't believe we've—'

'Cut the crap, honey,' interrupted Sheba with a note of exasperation, glancing at the unfortunate Bella with murder in her eyes. 'Are you or are you not in a position to overrule this little . . . this little . . . this person here?'

Crystal winked reassuringly at Bella, who seemed close to tears, and met Sheba's icy stare with an equally frigid one of her own. 'In a manner of speaking, yes. What seems to be the problem?'

At this, the woman in white fairly exploded, eyes flashing with rage, fashionably pale lips parted in a grimace of pure, unalloyed malice. 'What seems to be the problem . . .?' she mimicked Crystal, spitting out the words like so many tin tacks before proceeding to itemise the sources of her discontentment at a hundred decibels, counting them off on her fingers with precise, systematic fury. 'Where would you like me to start, for Christ's sake? I know, let's start at the beginning. First, the pathetic bunch of losers I call my friends called off at the last fucking moment, forsaking me for some goddamn houseparty in Buckinghamshire or some other bloody commuterland paradise, forcing me to spend my Christmas alone in this piss-poor, godforsaken outback of a place, masquerading as the English countryside. Second, my chauffeur's wife, poor bitch, chose Christmas Eve to drop her first kid, so he's buggered off on paternity leave, which meant I had to take a bloody cab down here, all the way from Kensington, which has just about relieved me of the entire proceeds of my last European tour. Third, even as we speak, if it hasn't already been nicked, my Vuitton luggage is standing on the top step outside my house, lonely and forlorn, ignored by the stupid fucking cabbie despite the fact I told him a hundred times to put it in the boot. And fourth, just to cap it all, I discover that the Queen's Suite, which I was under the impression my stupid cow of a secretary had booked well in advance, is occupied by some senile old dowager with a dicky heart, while I've been fobbed off with the Duchess Suite with en suite shower but no sodding bath. So, to neatly summarise, I'm friendless, driverless, penniless and in possession of zilch by way of clothes and cosmetics, apart from the ones I'm standing up in, and I can't even end it all by drowning in a sea of bubbles having first sunk an anaesthetising bottle of hooch! Wouldn't you be upset?' She turned to Crystal, her face a tragi-comic mask of rage and frustration.

Crystal, lost for words, glanced at Bella for inspiration, but the girl's expression of open-mouthed astonishment was more than she could bear. With a sense of appalling inevitability, she recognised the sensation bubbling up within her as helpless, hopeless laughter, occasioned not just by the bizarre circumstances she currently found herself in, but also by her immediate and intense sense of release from the tensions of the previous night. Watched by the two other women, both displaying profound if contrasting attitudes of surprise, Crystal sank slowly to the carpet in a nerveless heap of hysterical shrieks and giggles.

Chapter Five

'Now then, you naughty girl, stop teasing me immediately or I shall be forced to take you across my knee.' Claude Pettifer-Jones tried hard to look stern but was failing miserably. 'Exactly when was I foolish enough to squander a whole month's hard-won earnings on that darling coat of yours?' he continued.

With a secret little smile which made her blue eyes twinkle and lent a sensual curve to her expressive lips, Sadie St George snuggled further into the oversized wild mink, wrapping it tightly around herself and pulling the generous, furry lapels up to her ears. The lavishly showy gems at her throat, wrists, ears and on several fingers flashed expensively with every movement, caught in the warm glow of several candles which were fixed variously in old champagne bottles as well as more conventional candleholders. Reaching over, she brushed a mote of dust from the sleeve of Claude's old tweed jacket, which she'd spied a second or two earlier en route from the vaulted ceiling of the summerhouse within which they were spending a lazy, thoroughly decadent Christmas Day afternoon.

'1965, I believe,' she answered with a little sigh of remembrance, brushing a stray, platinum blonde curl from her smooth forehead. 'Don't you remember, darling? We'd just finished a photo session at a studio in Finsbury Park belonging to that rather seedy friend of yours – it was a series of shots for *Playboy*, I seem to remember – when all of a sudden, without so much as a by your leave, you ordered me to get dressed, then whisked me downstairs to a passing cab which took us all the way to Harrods in Knightsbridge. You were absolutely hell-bent on buying me a present, you reckless man, and the only thing I really wanted more than anything else in the whole world was a fur coat. So, you bought me this.' She glanced across at Claude with a mischievous smile, wrinkling her nose playfully at him.

'It was like being in heaven,' she continued, a faraway look in her eyes. 'All those sniffy sales ladies bowing and scraping, each one desperate to be the lucky recipient of the commission on the sale . . . I remember thinking, if they only knew what I do for a living they wouldn't even give me the time of day, let alone their undivided attention!' Sadie laughed out loud and bit her lip, recalling the sense of wicked glee she'd felt at the time. 'The low lights, the hushed reverence of the place. The warm scent of expensive fur and perfume, the agonising choice to be made as I tried each one on, imagining how I'd look if, underneath, I was completely naked . . . Mmm . . .' Sadie closed her eyes and shivered deliciously. 'And then we took the same cab back to the penthouse flat you were renting in Pimlico from that Duke of something-or-other – you'd told the cabbie to wait for us outside the store, remember? – and I was able to see for myself how I looked . . .'

While she reminisced, Claude had been watching Sadie with covetous interest – aware of her closeness, her bubbling excitement at being there alone with him, the subtle perfume rising from her soft, freshly bathed skin – and he was entirely, uncompromisingly delighted with her. To him she was a girl again, wide-eyed and nineteen, just the way she'd been all that time ago in London. With a little lump in his throat and a catch in his voice he spoke, the years melting magically away like snow in summer as he too recalled the scene which Sadie had so successfully recaptured for him: 'You were so utterly beautiful, my dear. Like a young goddess with your white skin and pale gold hair. Your innocence bewitched me. You were so different from the other models I'd encountered – so calculating, so mercenary . . . You were like a breath of spring in a hot, busy city which, for me, was rapidly losing its charm, and I wanted you for my own – to love and protect and cherish. Tell me what went wrong, Sadie?'

Sadie gazed, unseeing, at a pile of wrought-iron garden furniture, brought indoors for the winter months and stacked in the corner of the summerhouse. Shifting her bottom somewhat distractedly in her deckchair she stretched out her stockinged toes with unself-conscious pleasure towards the large paraffin heater which was placed a few feet away from where they were sitting, forgetting entirely about the thick snow falling outside as she luxuriated in the warmth emanating from its ancient bulk. Then, picking up her brandy glass from an upturned box beside her, she took a long, delicious sip of Armagnac before turning to face Claude with an inquisitive look. 'Do you know, darling, I had no idea you'd cared so much. And besides, even if I had known, it wouldn't have been any good. I was too young then. Inexperienced and idealistic. The stars in my eyes hadn't yet dimmed. I was just a hopeless romantic, expecting at any moment to be swept off my feet by a knight in shining armour on his snow-white charger. Maybe he was there all along and I didn't even recognise him . . .' She treated Claude to a sidelong glance from beneath lowered lashes and gave him a suggestive wink.

'Sadie,' Claude breathed huskily, aware of a sudden constriction at the front of his jeans, 'you're an incorrigible flirt – and I love you for it. Come, let's do those pictures we promised ourselves. Just for old time's sake, eh?' He smiled mysteriously and rose with an easy grace to his feet, taking Sadie's hand and helping her to rise, too. They stood facing each other, silent and grinning from ear to ear like a pair of kids. 'Well, what are we waiting for?' Claude murmured conspiratorially. 'Everything's ready. All it needs now is you and me . . .'

Sadie turned and picked her way through the stacked garden furniture to the centre of the summerhouse, where a generous space had been cleared and a number of photographer's arc lights set up. On the floor were several soft rugs, haphazardly though tastefully draped across the bare wooden boards, and scattered here and there were large, opulent-looking satin and velvet cushions. Claude watched as Sadie slipped the fur coat from her shoulders and allowed it to fall carelessly to the ground. Then she dropped slowly to her knees and arranged herself in the kind of languid, sensual pose familiar to readers of the more upmarket men's magazines. She lay on her side, facing Claude, resting on one elbow with her long legs stretched out beside her and one knee slightly bent.

With a contented smile, aware of Sadie watching him with rapt interest, Claude selected the appropriate cameras and

126

other photographic ephemera, loading film and checking light meters with the innate skill of a true, lifelong professional.

Despite having witnessed this and similar scenes any number of times before during her career as a photographic glamour model, Sadie had never failed to be both fascinated and impressed by the beauty and ceremony of it all. If only, she thought with a grin, the magazine punters knew the amount of palava which went into taking a few saucy snaps of all those naked young floozies who featured in their favourite 'adult' periodicals, they'd be happy to part with twice the cash for the pleasure of a quiet few minutes sexual titillation, ogling and wanking by turns, safely away from the prying eyes of wives, secretaries and girlfriends.

At last, preparations complete, Claude stooped to peer ruminatively at Sadie's reclining form through the viewfinder of his Hasselblad – a method of appraising beautiful women with which he was entirely familiar. As he gazed at her, assessing the pose she'd chosen to adopt, it occurred to him how utterly confident she still was in her ability to arouse, and how incredibly beautiful. Looking at her now it might have been yesterday that he'd captured her on film for that 1965 issue of *Playboy* magazine. It was true that her blonde curls may be enhanced a little with the appropriate chemicals and her smooth body was a little fuller and more curvaceous than it had been in her teens and twenties, but Sadie had always been a generous woman and the soft, ample bloom she'd discovered now in her middle years did nothing but lend substance to this fact.

First and foremost, Sadie was a woman who took the upmost pleasure in pleasing men, which was evident in the way she looked, talked, carried herself and adorned her voluptuous body. Filled with admiration and sexual longing, Claude allowed his gaze to linger on the creamy half-moons of the upper portions of her breasts, which rose and fell as she breathed, above the tight, oyster-satin basque with its deep flounces of soft, coffee-coloured lace. From the bottom of the garment – which ended at upper hip level and succeeded with firm efficiency in holding the soft, womanly flesh in delicious captivity – long, ruched satin suspenders held the tops of her sheer seamed stockings. Her modesty was preserved – though only just – with the aid of a pair of tiny satin panties, trimmed with lace, in the same subtle hue as the rest of the outfit.

Sadie, basking in the warmth of Claude's evident appreciation of her manifold charms, smiled back at him with assured confidence and a certain professional chic. As she gracefully arranged her voluptuous, corseted body in ever bolder and more alluring poses, Claude pressed the camera shutter again and again, frowning slightly in concentration and moving this way and that in his quest for the ever more imaginative erotic image. As Sadie moved her body, arranging and rearranging herself on the soft rugs, placing plump cushions and satin bolsters behind her blonde head and under the soft cheeks of her bottom which, scandalously, was all but completely revealed in the minute satin and lace panties, her breasts bounced and jiggled and her velvet-soft skin began to glow with a kind of inner fire. After a few minutes, she sensed with the unerring accuracy of a seasoned photographic model that Claude was nearing the end of his roll of film. Taking a deep, satisfied breath, she closed her eyes and slowly lay back until she was reclining against a soft pile of cushions, arms flung out in an attitude of complete abandon, one shapely leg stretched out, foot elegantly arched, and the other bent at the knee. Her face was turned towards Claude and on it was an expression of such pure sexual potency that the poor man's heart skipped a beat and he began to tremble with growing anticipation.

'Sadie, my love,' he whispered, 'have mercy on a poor, weak man who finds you unspeakably beautiful. My God, how you tempt me . . .' Claude's mouth was suddenly very dry indeed and he ran his tongue over his lips to dampen them a little, eyes dark and glittering with excitement as they explored the undulating hills and deep, shadowy valleys of Sadie's skimpily clad body. Temporarily lost for words, he marvelled silently at the stunningly alluring though subtle contrast between the shiny, almost opalescent satin lingerie, lavishly trimmed with darker lace, and her youthfully pale and translucent skin which provided a perfect foil for the heavy, glittering gemstones at her throat, ears, wrists and fingers, sparkling and flashing in the candlelight with a million tiny fires of their own.

Aware of Claude's fevered scrutiny, Sadie's cheeks flushed prettily and, beneath the sweeping curve of her mascaraed lashes, the expression in her blue eyes – already shining with a mixture of bold self-confidence and sexual desire – grew heavy and blatantly seductive. She pouted like a sex kitten and her full, glossy lower lip quivered slightly with erotic promise.

When she spoke her voice was low and hypnotic. 'Well, Claude darling, how do you like your little Sadie now? Am I as sexy as you remember me?' Sadie altered her position, pointing her pretty toes like a ballerina and sucking in her breath, which had the effect of flattening her corseted tummy and pushing out her semi-exposed breasts. She gazed down at herself with the contemplative smile of a woman who already knew the answer to her question.

'Surely you know how I feel about you, Sadie,' breathed Claude huskily as he started to move towards her. 'If anything, darling, you're even more gorgeous than you were then – so sensuous, wise, knowing . . .' Gazing down at her he bent his knees and began to lower himself to her level, stretching his body slowly and deliberately across the strewn rugs, whereupon he reached out a hand and stroked her soft cheek with trembling fingers whilst gazing into her eyes.

Sadie played up to his rather chaste, nervous caress, lowering her eyelids and breathing deeply, nudging against his hand like a playful cat, a stray blonde curl breaking free from her sexy coiffure to fall in a shiny, white-gold ringlet across her forehead and left cheek. 'Mmmm . . .' she breathed, opening her eyes a fraction and treating him to a wide, sensual smile. 'What a perfect gentleman you are, Claude. A lesser man would have ravished me by now without so much as a second thought. The thing I've always adored about you is that you allow a woman time. Time to fully respond to the situation she finds herself in. And this afternoon, darling, we have all the time in the world. So, before we go any further, I'm going to give you a nice surprise. One of my little personal services from years back which I reserve only for my very special friends.'

With these seductive words she gave a little shimmy with her shoulders and upper torso which set her breasts atrembling, then rose gracefully to her knees and began without further explanation to remove Claude's shoes and socks. Taking his bare right foot in both hands she gave it a little squeeze followed by a gentle massage before lowering her blonde head, extending her pretty tongue and lightly running its wet tip across his long, elegant toes, exploring and encircling them with slow, sensual relish.

Claude sighed deeply and closed his eyes, relaxing against the cushions. Every cell in his body was alive with a mixture of deep contentment and warm, simmering desire which seemed to pulse with ever-increasing urgency at every flick of Sadie's expert tongue. When, after what seemed like hours of pure, unalloyed pleasure but was, in reality, only a few short minutes, Sadie took Claude's big toe fully into her soft mouth and began to suck on it like a baby at her mother's breast, he thought he'd die from sheer delight. Lost in his own little world of silent reminiscence, he allowed his mind to wander back to similar situations and sensations, many of them shared with Sadie, in his earlier years as a young, virile photographer. How they'd fallen at his feet, all those sleek young starlets and models with their slim, sexy bodies and prematurely worldly faces. For most, their careers spanned before them, and glitteringly successful they were, too. But for others, the bright lights, fawning adulation and the insidious, dark temptations – thrills beyond their wildest dreams which lurked in the shadows at every fashionable event and glossy showbiz party – proved too much. Hooked on booze, drugs, predatory men or, in some cases, all three, these girls were tragically cut off in their prime, victims of the very culture which had previously exalted them.

Sadie had been one of the lucky ones. Her appealing innocence and pronounced lack of showy affectation masked a steely ambition to succeed and a well-developed talent for self-preservation. Just look at her now, Claude thought. She was as beautiful and sexy in her forties as she'd been in her late teens, a lucrative modelling career behind her and now a senior and highly desirable position within one of the world's most exclusive health resorts. The darling girl had most certainly landed on her feet, just as he'd always convinced himself she would.

Oblivious to all but the slowly mounting sexual desire within her supple body and the all-embracing desire to please and be pleased, the subject of Claude's heady ruminations turned her attention to his left foot, which she treated with equal warmth and oral sensitivity, licking and sucking with every evidence of complete dedication to her highly arousing task.

Returning once more to the moment and exquisitely aware of the delicious silky wetness around the area of his toes, Claude moaned a little and shifted his body on the rugs to better facilitate the swelling bulge between his legs. Sadie was alive to his slight discomfort and, removing his big toe from the enveloping warmth of her mouth, she licked her full lips in satisfaction at a job well done and allowed herself a tiny smile of self-congratulation. You're getting there, Sadie my girl, she told herself. Just like the old days. Any more of that and we'll be hitting the jackpot too soon. Time to change tactics.

With gleeful anticipation, her blue eyes glittering with a similar brightness and intensity to the many jewels with which she'd chosen to adorn her voluptuous body, she brushed the blonde curls from her flushed forehead and rubbed her pretty, beringed hands together in readiness for what was to follow. 'Now then, my angel, I have a notion that there's another portion of your darling body which could use a little attention, am I right?' Sadie spoke in a deep, husky whisper, a tone she'd developed and perfected as a result of her many erotic encounters with members of the opposite sex. It had never failed to elicit the desired effect, and this particular occasion was no exception. Claude nodded mutely, speechless with lust and a growing realisation of what was surely coming next.

'Good,' Sadie breathed. 'Then just lie back, relax and enjoy the show . . .' With the agility and grace of a woman half her age, Sadie quickly straddled Claude's trembling body, deliciously aware of his steamy gaze on the soft, jiggling flesh of her large breasts. Deftly unzipping the front of his straining jeans and pulling them down a little, together with his pants, she gasped with delight as the generous dimensions of his stiff manhood burst free with what seemed to be a life of its own, throbbing with heat and vitality as it finally came to rest across his naked, rapidly rising and falling belly. Seemingly mesmerised by the pure masculine beauty and power of Claude's naked member, Sadie began slowly and with fast-beating heart to lower the brief bodice of her satin corset until her big, milk-white breasts hung as naked and unfettered as nature intended, as ripe and heavy as exotic fruits, topped with full, rose-pink nipples of such girth and succulence that it was as much as Claude could do to stop himself from rearing up from his prone position and taking them both in his mouth simultaneously. Now it was his turn to gasp with surprise and pleasure, and he lost no time in expressing his joy at the magnificent sight of them.

'Touch them for me,' he whispered, unable to disguise the pronounced tremor in his voice. 'Squeeze them, play with your nipples . . .' Claude's eyes were dark and shiny with pleasure as he feasted them on Sadie's glorious breasts and his cock gave an involuntary jolt in its eagerness to become embedded in the soft, fleshy objects of his sultry desire.

Smiling sweetly, aware of the tremendous sexual power she had over him, Sadie stroked her big breasts with the tips of her fingers, closing her eyes and shuddering with delight as her own, feather-light touch sent sparks of erotic energy to the very core of her womanhood, causing her already generous nipples to become larger still and heart-stoppingly pronounced so that they stood out like a pair of luscious, ripe strawberries, the exquisitely sensitive skin a dark, dusky pink, swollen and glossy in the flickering candlelight.

Arching her back and pushing out her breasts towards her lover, she gazed at each erect nipple in turn, openly admiring them with a complete lack of self-conscious embarrassment. Then, as though in a kind of trance, she caressed them gently with the open palms of her hands before squeezing their plump fullness between her fingers, squealing with delight at the intense pleasure this afforded her. Excited beyond measure, Sadie felt herself to be rapidly losing control and she didn't care in the least. She was nineteen and in love again, thrillingly aware of the hot, handsome male eyes upon her, filled to the brim with unquestioning approval and burning passion. Panting with mounting lust, her breathing fast and shallow, she wriggled her bottom in delight and clasped her big, milky breasts in both bejewelled hands, throwing back her head and moaning with complete abandon as she kneaded and massaged the engorged flesh. Soon the pleasure became so intense that she felt the first tiny tremors of a massive climax begin to overtake her. As the first rhythmic waves flooded through her, she gave a loud cry of joy and swooped down, smothering Claude's rigid, pulsing prick in the hot, cushiony flesh of her quivering breasts until it disappeared completely, buried in the sultry warmth of her generous cleavage, squeezed and pressed and profoundly stimulated until Claude could bear it no longer.

'Stop!' he gasped from between clenched teeth. 'Enough . . . I can't stand it. Any more and I'll come immediately, and I don't want to, not yet . . .' He squeezed his eyes tight shut, panting loudly and sweating profusely with the effort of preventing himself from ejaculating whilst trapped in the powerful, fleshy grip of Sadie's breasts. 'I want to make love to you properly, Sadie my darling, the way you deserve. Come on, let's do it how we used to. The way we always liked it best, eh? Remember?' With extreme concentration, Claude had succeeded in calming his racing emotions which, for a few worrying moments had threatened to spiral out of control. Right now, safely away from the brink of orgasm, although not for long, he allowed his voice to become low and soothing, cajoling. His eyes burned with desire and his strong, tender hands stroked the soft, naked flesh of the gorgeous creature who sat astride him.

Instantly aware of Claude's plans for her, and thrilled to bits by them, Sadie's wide blue eyes shone with anticipation and she bit her lip coquettishly. 'Ooh, you naughty man!' she giggled. 'You know I love it like that!' In the blink of an eye she sprang into action, climbing off her lover and, still on her hands and knees, turned her back to him. Her full, creamy breasts hung down, erect nipples within millimetres of brushing the rug on which she knelt, and her voluptuous derrière was thrust lewdly towards him. With her legs slightly apart, Claude was treated to a glimpse of her swollen, pink-flushed labial lips through the tiny satin panties and, between them, the duskier, oyster folds of her inner sex. He licked his lips appreciatively, excited beyond measure by the scent of her distinctive musk.

'That's right, my sweetheart, I see you haven't forgotten.'

Sadie wriggled her bottom suggestively and laughed like a young girl, glancing seductively over her shoulder at him, cheeks flushed and eyes twinkling. Claude feasted his eyes on her sensational, semi-naked form for a second or two more, prolonging the sweet agony of the moment for as long as he dare. Then he reached out as though on the point of selecting the largest slice of a particularly wicked chocolate cake and, with trembling fingers, lowered the tiny, shimmering satin panties over the glowing cheeks of her glorious, curvy arse until they came to rest several inches below, stretched tight between her parted thighs. The effect was spellbinding, erotic beyond belief. Claude drew in his breath and stared, entranced at the full, alabaster spheres of Sadie's bare bum and the luscious, shadowy folds of her exposed sex, tantalisingly framed by the panties. Then, with a dramatic sigh, he advanced on her with his lips and tongue, clasping her hips while licking and sucking and gently breathing on the soft, fragrant skin of her naked bottom. Tenderly he rubbed the dark, sensitive flesh of her cunt, thrilling to the taste of her musky, aromatic love-juice in his mouth which, by now, was flowing freely and unchecked.

Extending his tongue further still and breathing through his nose, he nudged its pointed tip insistently at the entrance to her vagina until it was fully inside her, then wriggled it against the warm, muscular walls until she cried out in passionate release, lost yet again to the intense joy of a deep, shuddering orgasm.

Well satisfied with what he'd managed to achieve with his lips and tongue alone, Claude felt the time was right to try for a hat trick with the help of another part of his anatomy which was already rock-hard and filled to bursting with hot, pulsing seed, desperate for physical release. He backed away from the ripe, blonde goddess before him who, by now, was panting audibly and sighing with advanced sexual abandon, undulating her backside and wriggling her smooth shoulders so that her large, naked breasts shook wildly and swung back and forth as though with lives of their own. Then, in less than a blink of an eye, he'd climbed out of his trousers and pants and grasped his stiff prick in his right hand, rubbing it swiftly up and down a few times before advancing on Sadie once more and positioning its glossy, single-eyed tip against the entrance to her pussy. Still clasping it in his hand, he stroked it slowly and with exquisite sensitivity against her pouting sex, gasping out loud in his passion, his body hot and damp, shaking like a leaf with anticipation. Suddenly, with a shout of relief, he plunged deep inside her until his cock was buried to the hilt and his crisp pubic hair brushed against her bare bottom, tickling the tender flesh. Slowly withdrawing from her until just the sensitive glans was hidden from view, Claude plunged forward once more, commencing a highly vociferous bout of abandoned, rear-entry fucking. As his urgent groin slapped against Sadie's generous bottom, both lovers moaned and sighed and cried out loud by turns, whilst breathing steamy endearments and lewd imaginings to each other.

At last, Sadie began to shudder with the tumultuous onset of her third and final orgasm. As her gorgeous body melted in

137

her ecstasy and the muscles of her vagina tensed and released in a rapid series of fluttering contractions, Claude felt his testicles tighten against his groin. Tensing every muscle in his athletic body, he became quite still – buried deep inside the hot, pulsing woman-flesh – and with a powerful rush he ejaculated inside her, the warm, rhythmic gouts of sperm filling her to capacity.

Sated at last, Sadie and Claude remained silently locked together for some time, Claude reaching round and lazily stroking Sadie's full breasts, tickling her nipples and nuzzling the pale blonde curls at the nape of her soft neck, which made her giggle softly and wriggle against him. After a while, Sadie felt Claude's penis slowly but surely shrink inside her and the first warm trickles of semen dampen the outer lips of her sex and the inside of her thighs, drawn from her by the inexorable force of gravity. When, with a contended sigh and a winning smile, Claude finally withdrew from her and sprawled out on the rugs, resting on one elbow, Sadie rolled over onto her back next to him like a playful kitten, peering up at him through her long lashes and blowing him a little, pouting kiss. 'I think this calls for another glass of Armagnac, don't you?' she whispered softly.

Claude gazed lovingly at her smooth, stockinged legs and gently rounded satin belly. To his utter delight, he found himself becoming aroused all over again by the beauty of her large, still-naked breasts which, in repose, rose and fell as she breathed, blush-pink and luscious in the candlelight. Tearing himself away, he reached out and grabbed the bottle and two glasses, pouring generous measures and handing one of them to Sadie. Clinking glasses, they each took a sip, smiling silently into each other's eyes as they reclined there, warmed by the paraffin heater as well as by the alcohol and their recent lovemaking, naked and semi-naked on the untidy, colourful tangle of rugs and cushions, surrounded by garden furniture and the subtle scent of old paint and seasoned wood.

'I think I'd like this moment to last forever,' Claude said at last.

'No, not forever . . .' Sadie replied thoughtfully, 'though maybe until tea-time!' Amused at her own joke, the merry sound of her laughter filling the summerhouse, Sadie got up onto her knees and wriggled her body suggestively, running her tongue over her full lips, cupping her bare breasts in her hands and giving Claude a big, saucy wink as he reached out for her once more with a happy cry of renewed passion.

Perplexed for the umpteenth time that day, Crystal stood outside the door to her office and considered the options. Should she put her mug of tea down on the carpet, thus freeing her right hand to open the door, yet running the risk of leaving an ugly brown tea stain on the top-quality Wilton? Or should she hang on to the tea and put the parcel down instead? She frowned at the steaming Smarties mug and then at the sizable, festively wrapped box, sufficiently large to be barely contained under her left arm, and sighed audibly. Then she giggled at the absurdity of the situation, put both the mug and the box down on the carpet, unlocked her office door and nudged it open with her foot. Retrieving the two items from the floor, she went inside, kicking the door shut behind her. Bloody hell, she thought to herself as she kicked off her shoes and collapsed exhausted into the welcoming leather embrace of her executive swivel chair, things are coming to a pretty pass if I'm bothered by senseless minutiae like that. The events of the last twenty-four hours must be sending me well and truly ga-ga.

Crystal glanced at her watch. It was 5.30 p.m. She swept aside the pile of brochures, memos and other correspondence and plonked her feet up on the desk, then took several reviving swigs of Earl Grey before leaning back gratefully against the back of the chair and closing her eyes. It was good to be alone again at last. It gave her a much-needed opportunity to refresh herself and gather her thoughts before the next onslaught. Not that she minded hob-nobbing with the guests – they were a good-natured bunch on the whole, hell-bent on enjoying themselves and reluctant to find fault with the generally immaculate service provided at High Links – but she was still slightly rattled by the previous night's episode with Charlie.

There was precious little chance, she told herself, that he'd dare to return for a repeat performance, but would she mind too much if he did? This was the million-dollar question which had been driving her half mad. Thank goodness she now seemed to be getting closer than ever to answering it. The conclusion she'd reached during the course of the day was that she probably wouldn't mind. In fact, she thought with a certain chill dread, she'd almost certainly relish every last dirty, seedy little moment of it. Only next time she'd give Charlie more than he bargained for. Show him who was really boss by already owning all the right togs and 'equipment'. A little tremor of desire shimmied like quicksilver from her nipples to deep in her belly at the thought, and she made a mental note to check out that 'leisure and play-wear' catalogue she'd caught Frankie ogling over a few days before. Oh well, she thought with a resigned little smile, it's never too late to learn a few new tricks. It was difficult now to understand why she'd allowed herself to get so steamed up about the whole thing. After all, they were both adults and nobody had really been hurt, at least not against their will. Just think, if Charlie hadn't turned up last night she might never have known about the slightly murkier side of her sexual nature. She had that to thank him for, at least. Or maybe 'thank' wasn't quite the right word.

With a slow, melting sensation between her legs and a definite swelling and hardening around the nipple area she wondered, not for the first time, whether Isaac might also be persuaded to share one or two of her new-found proclivities. Isaac currently being several thousand miles away in Australia, the notion was almost more than she could bear. She shook herself back into reality and sat upright once more in her chair, but she was unable to banish the thought entirely from her mind and a small, sexy smile continued to lend a definite curve to her already sensual lips.

Finishing her tea and dipping into an open desk drawer for her secret stash of plain-chocolate digestives, Crystal turned her attention back to the parcel in front of her. Munching with the kind of slow, indulgent deliberation she reserved expressly for the consumption of the deliciously wicked, she turned the box this way and that, observing it from all angles, smoothing her hand across the expensive, metallic scarlet wrapping paper and beginning to untie the huge gold ribbon bow. It was definitely for her, even though it appeared to be unlabelled. Bella had told her as much when she'd handed it over half an hour before. It has arrived by messenger, it seemed. Some poor cabbie, cursing and swearing about the weather and the condition of the roads, not to mention the fact that he was having to work at all, especially on a day when most Christian folk were tucked up in front of their tellies with a box or two of Terry's Assortments and a few cans of brown ale. It was for economic reasons, apparently. He was charging double for the privilege.

Crystal couldn't imagine who'd be sending her large, lavishly wrapped and exorbitantly delivered gifts at this hour on Christmas Day. She'd already received her Body Shop gift basket from Sadie, the gorgeous bunch of white crysanths from Frankie, wrapped in crinkly cellophane and tied with a white satin bow, and the customary year's supply of American Tan tights from her parents. Crystal made a mental note to remember to drop a few unambiguous hints to her Mum when her parents arrived back from Spain – she still had last year's supply, instantly discarded on receipt and mouldering steadily at the bottom of her wardrobe amongst the down-at-heel shoes and piles of carrier bags, their contents long-forgotten.

Filled with a sudden rush of burning curiosity, mixed with a hint of trepidation, Crystal threw caution to the wind and tore at the scarlet foil, her desperation to see what was inside the parcel winning hands down over her usual reserved self-control. With a puzzled frown, she stuffed the discarded wrapping into her wastepaper basket and peered at the small furry creatures, many of them dressed in festive party clothes and carrying balloons and other childhood ephemera, which scampered across the second layer of festive paper. What the hell was going on here? Was this somebody's idea of a joke?

Amused despite herself, she giggled and bit her bottom lip, then set to work to remove this second and surely final layer. The sheet of old newspaper which greeted her was received with a howl of frustration.

Making fists of her hands and screwing her eyes tight shut, Crystal counted slowly from one to ten and then, opening her eyes, she took a deep breath and tried again. Carefully turning the parcel over, almost as though it contained a live animal, or even an unexploded bomb which had been set to detonate at the first careless move, she tore away a small strip of the newspaper and peeped underneath it. The plain, whitish paper beneath was of the sort in which fish and chips are generally wrapped and, judging by the faint whiff of saveloy and vinegar, this had been its former, somewhat noisome function.

Thoughtfully, Crystal sat back in her chair once more and pondered the situation, long and hard, scanning her mind and imagination for possible clues as to the identity of the mystery sender. Or senders. There may conceivably have been more than one of them. Had she knowingly upset anyone recently? A guest or a particularly sensitive member of staff perhaps? The more she thought the more she continued to draw a complete blank. There was one name, however, which kept cropping up in her mind with boring regularity and, when it was pushed back down again, rose once more with the tedious insistence of a tenacious terrier reunited with a particularly juicy marrowbone. No, it couldn't be him, surely . . . Or could it?

There was only one way to find out. Going at it once more with renewed vigour, Crystal tore at the chip wrapper like a woman possessed, followed by all the other odds and sods of paper, or what passed for paper, its various unsavoury origins too numerous or too dubious to dwell upon. At long last, her office resembling nothing so much as a salvage collection point or the end result of a particularly frenetic paper chase, Crystal was composed once more and holding a medium-sized, black leather pouch with a silver-coloured clasp, the size and shape of a modest Havana cigar box. Curiouser and curiouser . . .

With fluttering heart and trembling fingers, Crystal raised the pouch to her nose and sniffed at the deliciously warm, leathery scent. Then she unfastened the ornate clasp and gingerly withdrew the pouch's contents, holding the object in both hands as though it were a small, frightened bird or a priceless curio. Crystal couldn't remember when she'd last seen anything so beautiful and as finely wrought as this pure silver bracelet, fashioned in the shape of a coiled snake. The metal itself had been hammered and polished until it shone with a brilliant, mirror-like clarity and along the creature's length and on its serpent head had been set a variety of semi-precious gems – turquoise and amber, lapis lazuli and tourmaline – all of them polished and glowing with vibrant colour. The snake's eyes were two tiny coral beads and they seemed to smile up at her, the effect of its sinuous grin intensified by the fact that its many-fanged jaws were set slightly apart.

On closer inspection, Crystal noticed a tiny scrap of tissue-thin paper which had been carefully folded, origami-style, into the shape of a bird and attached between the snake's jaws with a small blob of something sticky. Holding her breath she carefully removed the tiny paper bird, gingerly unfolded it and proceeded to read the message inside, which had been painstakingly written in sloping print so spidery and minute as to be almost illegible.

> *To whom it may concern:*
> *Good fortune awaits she who wears me!*
> *Embrace me with love, warm me against your skin*
> *and tonight,*
> *all will be revealed . . .*

A tiny tremor of excitement shimmered through Crystal's body, infusing her limbs with warm treacle and quickening her breath. With eyes shining, she turned the serpent over and over in her trembling hands, slowly examining it for further clues, but she could find none. She didn't care, though. There was little doubt now in her mind about the identity of the mystery sender. She'd simply do as she was asked, follow the instructions, and maybe later . . . Her heart leapt and she shook herself in an attempt to still her racing pulse, determinedly denying herself the luxury of speculating on what might conceivably happen later. She couldn't bear the disappointment if it transpired that she was wrong. Placing the snake lovingly around her slim right forearm, she smiled into its tiny coral eyes and stroked its smooth serpent head with the tip of her finger. Time alone would tell. All she could do now was wait.

Suddenly, with an almighty crash, the heavy mahogany door to Crystal's office burst open, instantly dissipating her mood of quiet, reflective anticipation, and in stalked the slim, statuesque figure of Sheba. Dressed entirely from head to foot in glossy scarlet latex, obscenely tight and as supple as a sexy second skin, she stood four-square on her monstrously high, spiky blood-red heels in front of Crystal's desk, legs slightly apart, and hands on hips, snow-white talons drumming an impatient tattoo against the shiny, tight-stretched fabric. Her coal-black eyes flashed dangerously and a hot facial flush of mounting rage was clearly evident despite the ebony blackness of her smooth skin. Crystal noticed – somewhat inconsequentially given the simmering tension of this new, entirely unexpected, not to mention unwelcome drama which had so rudely assailed her private space – that the woman had clearly bathed and reapplied her make-up. Sheba's inky, close-cropped hair gleamed damply as it hugged her proud, elegant head. Her narrow cat's eyes were sharply and dramatically defined with shiny black liner and her sensually pronounced, voluptuously full negroid lips had been freshly painted a high-gloss, extravagantly pearlised white to match her unnaturally long, club-cut fingernails. On her breath, which came in deep, angry gasps, was the unmistakable scent of whisky.

'What the fuck kind of place is that that I can't even get a decent meal when I want one? Food, it would seem, is strictly out of bounds before dinner this evening, and right now it's five-thirty in the afternoon and I could eat a small zoo. I've had nothing but a measly Mars Bar, for Christ's sake, since this time yesterday. Do me a favour, sweetie. Would somebody, preferably you, tell the poncey dago in that stinking, so-called kitchen of yours that I'm a paying guest at this godforsaken hellhole, and as such I demand to be fed! Right now!'

A lump formed in Crystal's throat and she felt the bile rise as a deep, angry flush rose from her throat to the roots of her hair. How dare Sheba talk about Fernando like that? The way she was describing him was cruelly out of character and not at all in keeping with the comfily rotund, highly amiable head chef whom everybody at High Links, from Sadie St George down to the most junior chambermaid, knew and loved. She could only assume that the reason he'd refused to ply her with food was because she'd adopted her customary arch, disgustingly spiteful attitude towards him and, quite honestly, she didn't blame him in the least. Crystal would have reacted the same way herself, whilst delivering a swift left hook to the queen bitch's latex-clad, overly pampered solar plexus for good measure.

Crystal felt doubly miffed given that immediately after the woman's stormy arrival, taking pity on her in the face of her numerous, largely self-inflicted misfortunes and despite the ripeness of the expletives with which Crystal had been addressed, she'd taken it upon herself to ease the situation by relocating Sheba to a suite with private bathroom and walk-in dressing room. Crystal had then proceeded to raid the treatment rooms and beauty salon for armfuls of expensive toiletries and cosmetics which she'd presented to the complainant buckshee and with the compliments of the establishment. Right now it made her blood boil to see the spoiled cow standing there in front of her like goddamn royalty, bathed and perfumed on the house and reeking of free booze, looking down at her, lip imperiously curled, as though Crystal had just slithered out from beneath a pile of rotting vegetables. And, adding insult to injury, to have to listen to the bitch ranting and raving like a sozzled fishwife about poor, lovable Fernando was really more than Crystal could stomach.

Rising majestically to her feet like Venus on the half-shell from the waves, Crystal tossed back her waist-length hair and crossed her arms on her chest as though she really meant business. Narrowing her eyes and looking down her nose at the woman on the other side of her desk, she fixed her with a look of such blatant, simmering contempt that even the thick-skinned Sheba, reputedly oblivious to criticism of any kind, even from the highest quarters, was compelled to flinch slightly at the fearsomely chilly image she presented. She'd given Sheba more than enough rope to hang herself with, Crystal thought resignedly, a hard knot of anger smouldering in her gut, and now the obnoxious bitch had it coming to her – with bells on.

'When I first heard you were coming here, Sheba,' Crystal began with slow, quiet deliberation as though struggling to contain her fury, 'I was warned by one or two friends – people, incidentally, whose opinions I've learned to trust – that I may be in line for a spot of bother. It seems they weren't kidding. I thought at first they might be laying it on a bit thick, but that was before . . . Right now I reckon they were underestimating the problem.

'Tell me, Sheba, are you like this with everyone?' Crystal asked, her expression changing to one of exaggerated, sarcastic enquiry. 'Because if so, I really can't find it in my heart to blame your "so-called friends" for opting out of spending Christmas with you. I'd even go so far as to call it an extremely wise move on their part. From where I'm standing, a protracted period spent with you would seem to constitute a fate worse than death. In fact, knowing what I know now, I wouldn't wish it on my worst enemy.' Crystal paused in her damning monologue for just long enough to register the other woman's expression of shocked surprise combined with pained discomfort. Shifting distractedly from foot to foot like some grotesque albeit beautiful athlete about to attempt a world record, the worse for drink and wobbling slightly on her monstrous scarlet heels, Sheba's eyes shone with resentment as she stared back at Crystal, her stunning, chiselled features blushing a deep, burning crimson through the almost blue-black of her complexion.

'I'd just like to say, Sheba,' Crystal continued, her voice rising with emotion, 'that I don't think I've met a ruder or more pompous bitch in my entire life. And what's more, once Christmas is over and you bugger off back to your ivory tower in Knightsbridge or wherever the hell you hang out, I hope to God I never have to set eyes on you again!' By now Crystal was shouting, her limbs trembling with pent-up tension. She stopped talking and put her arms down by her sides, tensing her hands into fists, her eyes brimming with unshed tears and chin wobbling dangerously. Taking a deep, calming breath she nervously flicked her long hair back over her shoulders once more and forced herself to meet Sheba's thunderous, unblinking gaze, struggling without success to regain her formed poise and attempting vainly to assume an attitude of superior, self-righteous grace.

As though in slow motion, Sheba placed her hands on her hips and stared back at Crystal, head thrust forward menacingly, eyes like glittering black saucers and slightly hazy with drink, lips and chin set in a rigid grimace of outrage and injured pride. In the brief silence which followed, punctuated only by their rapid, angry breathing, the atmosphere between the two women was almost palpable – a dense fog of intense, brooding dislike and misunderstanding which seemed to join them as though by a live seam of exposed current, its lethal fingers of raw energy reaching out to fill all four corners of the room.

After several heart-stopping seconds during which the sanity of adult reason seemed temporarily to have vacated the minds and hearts of the two women, Sheba pulled herself up to her full height, tensed like a jungle cat and spat a large and voluble gob of spittle with unerring accuracy directly onto the left breast pocket of Crystal's pale blue silk Armani shirt. As though in a dream Crystal stared, unblinking in her disbelief, at the damp, glistening stain.

'How dare you . . .' Sheba growled in a low, dangerous monotone. 'Nobody speaks to me like that. Not one goddamn person. Least of all a jumped-up fucking typist with delusions of grandeur. You! You're nothing more than a goddamn servant. I could have you fired for this, *bitch*. In fact, that's exactly what the hell I'll do. Right now! Nothing would give me greater pleasure.' Sheba took a few steps back from the desk and stood in an insolent, drunken slouch, swaying slightly on her heels, arms folded across her shiny latex breasts, close-cropped ebony head on one side and lip curled nastily as she regarded the object of her ire through narrowed cat's eyes. Then, with an obscene gesture and an ugly grimace she turned to go, slinking insolently towards the door, voluptuous shiny arse swaying below her waspish waist with impudent exaggeration, dagger heels leaving dark, spiteful weals and scuffs on the plush office carpet. When she reached the door, her back to Crystal, she stuck out her bum and waggled it lewdly, turning briefly to leer over her shoulder and let loose a loud, resonating raspberry. 'Bye-bye sweetheart,' she cried coquettishly, 'if I pass you in the dole queue I'll toss you a coin.'

'Not if I see you first, you won't, you evil cow!' Without pausing even to walk round it, Crystal scaled her wide desk in a single bound – a physical feat which was ambitious even by her usual athletic standards, especially from a standing start – and landed silently on her feet on the other side with a look of murder in her dark eyes. In less than the blink of an eye she was level with Sheba's departing form, grabbing her roughly by the shoulder and yanking her round before delivering a hefty slap across her right cheek. '*That's* for calling me a jumped-up typist,' she hissed menacingly before raising her hand once more and slapping the left one, 'and *that's* for being the biggest fucking arsehole in the northern hemisphere! Now, bugger off out of my office before I raise the alarm and have you dragged out by the scruff of your neck!'

'Like hell I'll go! Take this, you cruel slag . . .' Despite the effects of the booze, Sheba sprung immediately into the offensive, her cheeks smarting from the blows. Clutching her opponent by both shoulders and trapping them in a painful, vice-like grip, she shook her with naked, violent energy like a dog with a rat, pulling her back and forth like a rag doll before flinging her to the carpet with as much solicitous concern as if she were a sack of vegetable peelings destined for the scrap heap. Then, with a satisfied smirk, she proceeded to jab painfully at Crystal's ribs and thighs and calves with the pointed toes of her shoes, muttering incoherently to herself, her breathing fast and ragged with almost hypnotic determination as her unfortunate victim rolled and contorted her body, yelling like a startled banshee. So absorbed was Sheba in her nasty little task that she failed to notice the arm snake out and grab her calf, tugging sharply and bringing her crashing to the floor beside Crystal in a spitting, writhing heap of teeth and nails and blood-red latex.

Managing to assume mastery of the situation, albeit a short-lived one, Crystal kneed the fallen enemy in the solar plexus before balling her hands into fists and, with a shout of triumph, pummelling her stomach and thighs and as much of her body as could be reached. Then, teeth clenched in concentration, she scratched and clawed with furious intent at the scarlet latex catsuit. However, maddeningly slippery and moulded to Sheba's body like a glossy second skin, it refused to tear or budge even an inch, despite Crystal's most frenzied efforts. Wild with frustration, Crystal cursed out loud and flung herself on top of the prone, spitting Sheba who, with a tremendous lunge and a fearful gasping groan, rolled over until she was once more in control, straddled above the panting Crystal's who, by now, was scarlet and sweating with fatigue and thwarted fury.

For the next ten minutes, the normally peaceful luxury of Crystal's plush executive office rang to the sounds of writhing bodies, locked in mortal combat and slapping angrily together, accompanied by unmentionably foul oaths and the tearing and ripping of the assorted giftwrap which lay like so much untidy refuse where Crystal had thoughtlessly tossed it, discarded and forgotten in the heat of the moment yet eerily adding its own papery symphony to the angry female cacophony raging above.

At last, exhausted and bruised, covered in scratches and weeping helplessly, Sheba gave up the hopeless struggle and rolled slowly away, rising wearily to her haunches whilst sobbing uncontrollably and wiping her eyes and nose with the back of her hand. Emotionally beaten, she looked down at

Crystal who lay on her side on the floor, curled in a foetal position, her body racked by great, gasping breaths of spent passion and her right thigh draped rather incongruously with a torn scrap of the childish rabbit giftwrap. This pitiful sight upset Sheba still further and she sobbed afresh, pressing her bunched fists into her poor, swollen eyes and sinking once more to the floor in a graceless heap.

After a while, the room silent and mercifully calm once more, Sheba glanced again at Crystal's recumbent body before crawling across to her and gently removing the party paper from her motionless thigh, sniffing pitiably as she did so. Then, shuffling painfully around on her haunches so that she could look directly into the other woman's silent, tear-stained face, she wiped her eyes once more and spoke in a quiet, low voice, filled with pain and regret. 'I'm sorry . . .' Then, wiping her hand with concerned solicitude across her glossy leg, she reached out, trembling slightly, and stroked Crystal's cheek as though it were a tiny, day-old kitten, before treating her to a wan, wobbly smile of silent contrition.

To Sheba's absolute delight, Crystal smiled right back at her, then winced a little with discomfort as she rose up onto one elbow and pushed the tangled hair from her eyes. 'Well,' she breathed quietly, 'Any more scenes like that and we'll be old hags before our time . . . Truce?'

'Truce!' agreed Sheba with a wide smile of relief, gathering her new friend into her arms as though she were a long-lost teddy bear. 'I think we're going to have fun together, you and I . . .'

Chapter Six

'Aw, go on, Frankie love, swap me a bit of your breast for a bit of my thigh!' Sharon pressed her own breast suggestively against Frankie's shoulder and shouted in his ear, voice raised against the loud, festive racket in the cram-packed dining room of The Spotted Cow. 'You got more than me, you greedy pig, and I fancy a bit of tit.' She collapsed against him, giggling tipsily at her own joke.

'You're not the only one, darling . . .' Frankie leered salaciously back at her and rubbed his dark-suited shoulder against his girlfriend's ample bosom, before transferring a succulent slice of white turkey flesh onto her plate from his own. 'There you are, my little pouter pigeon, get your laughing gear round that, but leave enough room for your afters, eh?'

Sharon attacked the pale meat with relish, licking her lips and turning to smile saucily up at Frankie from beneath a pair of huge, fluttering false eyelashes. 'I bet I know what "afters" you're referring to, you wicked bugger, and I don't s'pose it's the Christmas pud!' She turned back to her meal, smiling happily to herself in a slightly drunken, lopsided sort of way, delighted at the way things were turning out for her this Christmas. It beat the previous year's festivities, that was for sure. Four miserable days spent in her previous boorish boyfriend's flat, alternating between being gracelessly pawed and supporting him by the shoulders above the porcelain pan while he paid in the customary, unsavoury manner for his gross overindulgences. It had been the worst Christmas she'd ever had. Worse even than being left at the tender age of twelve by her boozy mum to suffer the unambiguous advances and petty indignities of Christmas with her stepfather, a sharp-suited bookie with little or no time for children generally, despite a peculiar fondness for little girls in particular. It was only Sharon's childish stealth and speedy wit which had saved her then from a fate worse than death, but she'd been forced to stare it full in the face a couple of times before her mother had finally seen fit to return home and reclaim her unfortunate offspring.

Sharon winked good-naturedly at Frankie and took a mouthful of roast potato and sage and onion stuffing, liberally smeared with cranberry sauce, and munched determinedly, surveying the room and her many fellow diners with mounting excitement and interest. The joint was certainly jumping, that was for sure. Hot and steamy from the heat of the open inglenook at the far end of the low-ceilinged dining room – which was hung with fancy brasses and shiny, flameproof Christmas decorations – the whole effect was extravagantly enhanced with the help of the liberally intoxicated, well-fed bodies of the happy revellers in their best suits and posh party gear. In fact, if one were asked to provide a near-as-dammit analogy of the scene in question, it was uncannily redolent of a spicy, Bacchanalian feast or one of those opulent and chintzy greetings cards, so beloved by accountants and retired bank managers, depicting the Victorian family Christmas, with jolly *pater familias* chomping on the post-prandial pipe and buxom matrons languishing rumbustiously amid a rosy, firelit glow in the delightful company of happy, apple-cheeked children and well-fed domestic pets.

All in all, the whole thing was completely and utterly lovely, Sharon thought to herself with a smile as she lit a mid-course ciggie and took a long, satisfied drag on it before thoughtfully blowing the smoke over her shoulder, away from the remains of Frankie's dinner. It was bloody marvellous, in fact.

On a small raised dais at the far end of the room, opposite the fireplace and lit by two or three strategically placed spotlights, set ingeniously into the wall so as not to detract from the room's olde-worlde charm, stood a three-piece band. A little long in the tooth, maybe, for younger, more up-to-date tastes, but proficient nevertheless, the three musicians – pianist, saxophonist and drummer – had been busily engaged for an hour or more in treating the assembled diners to a cosy selection of popular Christmas hits, gleaned from any number of previous musical decades.

As the strains of *Santa Claus is Coming to Town* battled it out with the rather more raucous sounds of clattering cutlery and boisterous guffaws, Sharon took a swig of Piesporter, cupped her chin in her hand and tapped her foot appreciatively. She liked all the oldies, she had to admit. They seemed more romantic, somehow. Ironic, really, when one considered her previous incarnation as a heavy metal chick, following obediently in the wake of the Steel Dinosaurs with which Kev, her erstwhile boyfriend, had been percussionist. She sighed and looked lovingly across at Frankie, whose attention seemed to have been captured by someone or something on the other side of the room. She was well out of that particular scene, she thought gratefully. She'd never been one for all those drugs, not to mention being reduced to passing the time of day with sullen groupies who, for the most part, looked in dire need of a damn good wash and a square meal. With a shudder, she recalled late nights spent chewing the fat, ankle-deep in spilled lager, in the fluorescent-lit dressing rooms of seedy dives and music venues. Better by far, she considered, to be wined and dined in a place like this by a suave man about town who really knew how to treat a woman, all needs catered for and the odd little pressie or two thrown in for good measure.

Sharon's attention turned to the gorgeous 'sapphire', surrounded by tiny twinkling 'diamonds', on the finger of her right hand which Frankie had presented her with that morning in bed as they polished off their toast and coffee. It wasn't real, of course, but who cared? It must have cost a packet and it certainly looked the business – just like Princess Di's engagement ring. A fine fix she'd got herself in, Sharon thought disgustedly. It was a wonder the daft cow hadn't worked out which side her bread was buttered before having hysterics and screwing up her inheritance. Not much fear of Sharon behaving like that in the circumstances. Anyway, chance'd be a fine thing . . . She giggled at the ridiculousness of the notion. Oh well, it takes all sorts, she added with a sigh. Frankie had said the sapphire matched Sharon's eyes. She put her head on one side and held the sparkling geegaw up to the light, admiring the way the glow from the little table lamp reflected against the shiny facets, making the polished glass stones glitter like genuine gems.

'Psst!'

Surprised out of her reverie, Sharon turned and gazed in

the direction indicated by Frankie's surreptitiously pointed finger.

'Isn't that the stuck-up cow from reception? Gorgeous Glynis from Glyndebourne, ball-freezer to the nobility? Christ, Sharon, she's changed her tune a bit, hasn't she? I almost didn't recognise her.'

Slightly taken aback at first, Sharon peered somewhat dazedly at Frankie's expression of undisguised, open-mouthed approval, and then back at the object of his excitement. Taking a sharp intake of breath, she blushed and bit her lip, stung with momentary surprise and embarrassment. Then she covered her mouth with her hand and dissolved in a fit of giggles. It was Glynis the receptionist all right, but what a change! Barely recognisable as the titian-haired ice maiden of the previous day, Glynis posed coquettishly at a small table to one side of the large dining room. She was perched precariously on its edge, shoeless and unrepentant, sleek legs crossed provocatively at the thigh and swinging girlishly from side to side, her milky curves scandalously revealed to the utter delight of the room's collective gaze.

Glynis's curvy body, bereft of its smart but severe uniform of white blouse, scarlet jacket and straight, knee-length navy skirt, had been squeezed to enormous effect into a skintight, strapless, backless and virtually frontless shocking-pink shot-silk sheath dress. Slit to the thigh, its hem gathered brazenly around her hips for ease of movement, thereby revealing a good inch or two of smoke-grey stocking top and glossy ruched magenta satin suspender. Her slim arms were elegantly encased in super-long, silky charcoal evening gloves and her glossy auburn curls hung loose to her smooth shoulders, contrasting with striking simplicity against her pale freckled skin and her shiny puce lips which were an almost perfect match for her dress. Beneath generous swathes of sooty false lashes, her eyes shone with a mixture of booze and rampant exhibitionism, mischievous and glittering wickedly with excitement and daring.

Gathered around this exotic figure like hornets around a frangipane bush, sat five or six off-duty waiters, clad casually in their best washed and pressed civvies, pints and cigarettes clasped in enthusiastic hands as they leaned back in their chairs, intoxicated with lustful anticipation, whistling and catcalling at the vision of voluptuous female beauty in their midst.

'Come on then, Glyn!' one of them shouted above the din, 'what're you waiting for? Get out there, girl, and strut your stuff. Show the lads what you're made of!' This last remark, spoken in a lecherous growl, prompted a series of loud, lewd whoops and calls from the other men and a barrage of lustful laughter. So much so that quite a few of the remaining occupants of the room dropped their own conversations and turned with interest towards the source of the racket to see what all the fuss was about. As might be expected, casual curiosity quickly turned to a combination of faint embarrassment mixed with dread, tinged with a *soupçon* of envy, not to mention bug-eyed, open-mouthed approval. More than one of the women shuddered inwardly, remembering the message inherent in that pithy, age-old adage, 'There but for the grace of God go I', grateful for once for their own relative anonymity.

Oblivious to all of this and frisky as hell, Glynis pouted seductively and put her hand behind her head in a starlet pose, winked saucily and then slowly began to uncross her shapely legs, thus titillating the waiters still further and eliciting fresh cries of appreciation and the start of a slow, rhythmic hand-clap. One of the waiters, clearly the worse for drink, took a swig from his pint glass and wiped his mouth on his sleeve before reaching out and attempting to grab a fleshy handful of the cause of the increasing tightness at the front of his already tight jeans. But Glynis was having none of it. Not yet, anyway. 'Everything comes to he who waits . . .' she murmured sexily, grabbing his wrist and pushing it away from her in a manner which belied the soft curve of her lips and the warm glow in her eyes as she looked at him. Chastened, the offending waiter shrugged good-naturedly and, leaning back once more in his chair, joined in the hand-clapping with enthusiastic vigour and a shrill, high-pitched wolf whistle.

By now, the rest of the diners had fallen silent, holding their collective breath in anticipation of what was to follow. At various points around the room, elderly couples and families with young children rose hurriedly to their feet and prepared to leave, thinking better than to stick around and be embarrassed by this brazen hussy in skintight silk who, only the day before had seemed such an efficient, well-brought-up young lady. It just went to show that you couldn't trust first impressions. Honestly, what was the world coming to?

The last to leave was a stout, grey-haired woman of advancing years, dressed rather sombrely in a chocolate-brown two-piece and pushing her unfortunate spouse ahead of her out of the room, her granite features wearing an expression of marked distaste. The poor man was clearly leaving against his will and the couple appeared to be in the midst of some sort of dispute. 'But I haven't finished my dessert yet, dear,' he whimpered with hopeless resignation, casting the odd surreptitious glance in Glynis's direction.

'Dessert be damned!' the woman hissed through clenched teeth as she propelled him towards the door, 'I'm not staying here to be insulted. And I shall make absolutely sure the management get to hear about this disgusting little charade!'

On the other side of the room, halfway through their second bottle, the hotel manager and his wife exchanged amused glances. Glynis – busy catching the henpecked husband's eye and blowing him tiny, wet little kisses in recompense for what he was about to miss – slithered off the edge of the table and rose confidently to her silky feet. Tugging her dress down a little to cover her stocking tops, she called out cajolingly to the woman in an attempt to get her to change her mind. 'Aw, come on, madam. Don't be a spoilsport. Let the dog see the rabbit, eh? It'll do the poor old bugger the world of good. Give him a new lease of life. You may even end up thanking me for it!'

With one voice, the whole room dissolved into laughter at the cheekiness of Glynis's remarks to the woman, who stood four-square in the doorway like a galleon at anchor and fixed the receptionist with an acidic glare. The room fell silent, the diners leaning forward in open-mouthed anticipation. 'If you have the temerity to be addressing me, young lady, then you deserve horse-whipping!' At this, the laughter recommenced with joyful gusto, increasing in pitch and volume and enhanced with further whistles and shrieks of approval. 'No, I take that back,' she shouted above the fray. 'Horse-whipping's too good for you! You precocious, impertinent little floozy . . . My God, I'd like to take you across my knee and give you the biggest hiding you've ever had in your life!'

With this, highly titillated by the idea, the room fairly

roared at her remark and exploded with fresh mirth. Allowing himself a sly, private little smile, away from his wife's laser-beam gaze, the husband too looked far from averse to the notion. Surreptitiously he licked his lips and coughed discreetly into his pocket handkerchief, hiding uncomfortably behind his shirt cuff. Glynis grinned and winked at him conspiratorially.

One man, rising unsteadily to his feet and egged on by his companions, joined in the argument. 'Go back to your knitting, you sour old battle-axe, and leave the rest of us to have some fun!'

Speechless with rage, the woman's face turned a dark, angry red as though, alarmingly, its owner was on the point of spontaneous combustion. She roughly grabbed the collar of her husband's jacket, yanking him practically off his feet, turned on her heel and frogmarched him from the room amid whistles and jeers of delight.

Amazed and intrigued at this wholly unexpected turn of events, Sharon and Frankie glanced at each other, lost for words, and then looked back at Glynis. Without once taking her eyes off the other woman, Sharon wriggled in her seat to find a more comfortable position and lit a cigarette from the smouldering butt of the previous one, before settling back once more to enjoy the show – whatever the show may be – and absently draped a covetous arm around her boyfriend's shoulders.

Glynis, emboldened by the wholesale adulation aimed at her by the remaining dinner guests, stepped gingerly back into her shocking-pink satin stilettos, pulled her dress down to its correct length, wriggling her bottom delightfully as she did so, and sashayed gracefully across to the small, spotlit stage amid a rousing round of applause. The three musicians, assuming correctly that their brief respite was nearing its end, slowly rose from where they'd been slumped wearily over their instruments and, watching Glynis with growing affection, they stubbed out their fags on the parquet platform and downed the remains of their pints. Wiping away the foam from their mouths on their sleeves and preparing to resume their musical labours, it occurred to all three of them, quite independently, that this was no ordinary broad who fancied herself as a popular *chanteuse*. Most of the amateur bints they'd come across in their careers, though sassy enough, bold and brassy as chicken in a basket, lacked the necessary poise and charm to make the big time. Added to that, precious few had voices which would successfully pass muster when placed in front of an expectant audience – especially a drunken one eager for instant thrills and their full money's worth.

Glynis, however, seemed to have this particular bunch of good-time goons in the palm of her soft little hand. There they were, men and women alike, hanging on her every gesture – every toss of her hair, wriggle of her hips, pout of her glossy lips – devouring her hungrily with their eyes, desperate as sea lions for anything she cared to throw in their direction by way of entertainment. The amusing little episode with the disapproving matron had helped, of course, by winning the audience over to her side. Right now she had them exactly where she wanted them, and she knew it. With a shy little smile she tossed back her hair once more and placed a solicitous hand around the microphone at centre-stage front. 'Good evening, ladies and gentlemen,' she said softly in a low, breathy half-whisper. The room erupted with a fresh round of applause and Glynis smiled sweetly with simple, heartfelt gratitude. Raising her hand for silence before continuing, her words were marked with an appealing, girlish hesitance which only served to increase the bond between herself and her audience: 'Regulars at The Spotted Cow will know that, between shifts at the reception desk, I can sometimes be persuaded to entertain them with a little number or two from my modest repertoire of popular hits. Well, tonight being Christmas night, I've been asked by the management to do just that . . .' Pausing briefly for effect and smiling mysteriously, she added, almost as an afterthought, '. . . and there may, just may, be a teensy little surprise thrown in for all those kind enough to stay and watch the show . . .' At this, the room went wild, rising to its collective feet, clapping and stamping appreciatively, rocking the very foundations with its enthusiasm.

Sharon, intoxicated by wine and by the excitement of it all, was far from immune to Glynis's charms. Leaning forward, perched on the edge of her chair, she absent-mindedly grabbed Frankie's knee as though her life depended on it, her pretty face a veritable picture of rapt admiration.

The hotel manager was well pleased with the extremely favourable response to his imaginative little plan which, despite only having occurred to him that morning, seemed to be excelling even his fondest estimates. He rubbed his hands with glee, hearing already the merry tinkle of cash registers as guests rushed to the bar for still more costly liquid sustenance. Pushing his way quickly towards the stage he scaled the steps and, gently taking Glynis's elbows and moving her solicitously to one side as though she were a piece of rare Dresden china rather than a flesh-and-blood female, he gazed benevolently out at the audience and raised both his hands for silence.

Whatever power and charisma this man possessed, it seemed to work. The room fell silent once more and prepared to listen with interest to whatever their esteemed host had to say to them. 'My dear guests,' he began, 'as you know, we're all here to have a good time and enjoy ourselves, but in order to gain fully from this delightful little bit of impromptu entertainment, I ask only one thing – that you try and stay as calm and appreciative as possible while this lovely lady here gives us the unparalleled benefit of her terrific voice, not to mention one or two other . . .' At this point the manager paused, apparently tongue-tied and flushed with embarrassment, while the room buzzed with excited speculation as to the precise meaning behind his words. Regaining his former cool the manager continued: 'But that, my dear ladies and gentleman, is for later. All will be revealed in the fullness of time, have no fear on that score.' With a somewhat glassy leer he placed a covetous hand on Glynis's curvy bottom and gave it a salacious squeeze, planting a big wet kiss on her soft cheek before turning once more to the audience and completing his statement: 'But now, ladies and gentlemen, I give you our own, our very own, gorgeous Glynis Gabriel!' With a crafty wink and an expansive gesture towards the lady in question, he left the stage and headed back to his table while the applause died down and those present prepared to be entertained.

With a serene, self-assured smile, seemingly unrattled by her employer's uncalled-for familiarity, Glynis waited patiently for a modicum of quiet to descend before daintily clearing her throat and addressing the gathering in the low, silky-smooth tones of a young woman in full knowledge of her personal magnetism. At this moment, even the magical Monroe herself would have been hard-pressed to match this woman's practised calm and belief in her ability to please. 'Well, after an introduction like that, what more is there to say?' she said softly. A gentle titter of approval circumnavigated the room as she continued: 'Except, perhaps, to ask if anyone has a request . . . ?' With a look of enquiry and chin raised expectantly, Glynis's sensual, feline gaze caressed her audience.

A young, rather portly gentleman, seated at a table near the stage with his wife and two other couples, rose nervously to his feet and coughed apologetically. 'Er, what about *White Christmas*? I think we all know that one, don't we?' Smoothing his hair with his right hand in a distracted sort of way, he quickly sat down once more, almost missing the padded Dralon completely in his haste and blushing furiously at his own ineptitude. No one, it would seem, was oblivious to or untouched by the brilliant spark of electric current which hung suspended above the room, threatening to break free at any moment in a lightning flash of pure, undiluted sensual excitement.

'Excellent choice, cobber!' came an enthusiastic voice from towards the back of the room, belonging it would seem to one of the off-duty waiters. 'Couldn't have chosen better myself. Come on, Glyn, let's have it!' After a momentary silent consultation between Glynis and the three musicians who, by now, would have been prepared to play *The Death March* if requested to do so, the opening bars of *White Christmas* filled the room. After a moment or two, the soothing strains of the popular Christmas hit were skilfully embellished by the addition of Glynis's seductively husky, engagingly vibrato voice which succeeded in weaving its potent, highly charged magic in the minds and groins of all those fortunate enough to be within earshot.

At last, reluctantly, the song drew to its close and after a second's hesitation the room erupted into a warm barrage of applause, punctuated with the odd cry of 'Bravo!' and 'More!' and, from the table of increasingly vociferous waiters, 'Get 'em off!'

Glynis smiled engagingly and stuck her tongue out at the deliverer of the last remark, before consulting briefly with the musicians once more and breaking into her next number, a delightfully slow, romantic rendition of *We're Almost There*. Completely spellbound, the audience attached itself like treacle to every soft, emotionally loaded word and when, at the song's completion, Glynis gave a little shimmy of apparent sensual pleasure and blew them all a lingering kiss, they fairly erupted with unbridled delight, tense with excitement and anticipation.

From the far side of the room Glynis caught the manager's eye and responded with a sensual smile and a tiny nod of complicity, waiting patiently for the applause to die down before continuing: 'And now,' she breathed huskily when calm had descended once more, 'the bit we've all been waiting for . . .' This latest remark was too much for some of the male members of the audience who rose instantly to their feet, calling out and whistling at the outrageously sexy and brazenly provocative image before them, eyes bright with pent-up desire. Drunk with her own power, Glynis carried on regardless, stepping out of her high satin shoes as she did so. 'You've been such a wonderful audience,' she breathed, 'that I think you all deserve a little treat . . . Gosh,' she said with feeling, wiping her brow and gazing distractedly at the air conditioning, 'is it me or is it hot in here?'

Frantic yells and whoops of delight filled the increasingly steamy confines of the crowded room followed by the beginnings of a slow hand-clap. This was swiftly taken up by everyone present until its urgent, hypnotic beat awakened the deepest, most basic instincts of all concerned, like the siren call of African tribal drums. As though in a trance, head held high and arms held out towards her adoring audience, Glynis began to slowly undulate her hips to the rhythm like a milk-white, flame-haired goddess, attracting further and even more adoring vocal responses with every move of her body.

Biding his time, the hotel manager watched from the sidelines, pleased as Punch with himself for having dreamed up such a lucrative little scheme at such short notice. Takings, he thought ruefully, were woefully down on the same time the previous year, undoubtedly a direct result of the recession and the general feeling of uneasiness amongst the general public at the prospect of spending money unnecessarily. But he was no slouch when it came to gauging public taste, and there was one particular commodity upon which one could almost invariably rely to make an extra bob or two when times were lean. Sex. Rubbing his hands together, he rose from his seat with an attitude of practised authority and made his way towards the small stage with the air of a man who meant business. Which was exactly what he was.

'Right here in my hands,' he shouted above the noise, 'I hold the key to the realisation of all your wildest dreams and fantasies. Indeed, ladies and gentlemen, one of these tickets,' he said, 'will be the passport to a veritable garden of delights for the lucky winner. In short, whoever wins the prize in this highly unusual raffle will be offered the rare chance to escort our gorgeous receptionist, every stunning inch of her, to their very own private room and feast their eyes on her manifold charms away from the prying eyes of the rest of you lecherous buggers. In fact, to be perfectly blunt, Glynis has agreed to do a private striptease for the owner of the winning ticket!' At this mind-boggling news, the room erupted once more before pulling itself together and transforming itself into a hive of fevered activity while pockets and wallets were emptied of cash and anxious men of all shapes, sizes and descriptions descended on the scheming manager, fists held aloft and filled with coins and notes of the realm, desperate to take their chance and secure a generous slice of voyeuristic bliss with the delectable Glynis Gabriel.

Never one to let the grass grow under his feet, Frankie de Rosa was first in the queue of flushed and sweating men, palpitating with the best of them and offering a silent prayer to Bacchus, mythical master of sinful orgies and cornucopias of lush goodies, as he held out a crisp fifty pound note and was rewarded with a clutch of ten raffle tickets. If that little lot doesn't earn me a bite of the cherry, Frankie thought, even if only as a just reward for the capital outlay, than I'm a Dutchman. Gloating confidently, he treated the hotel manager to a sly wink and was rewarded with a somewhat sickly grin which, though promising, did nothing whatsoever to assure him of his ultimate success regarding the raffle.

Undismayed, Frankie returned to his seat, eyes shining with excitement, and was surprised and mildly concerned to discover that Sharon had seen fit to disappear during his brief absence. Surely, he thought, the daft cow hadn't got the hump because of his eagerness to take part in the little bit of harmless fun thoughtfully offered up by the management?

She must have got the message by now that, at the end of the day, when all was said and done, it was Sharon he was really interested in. It was just that, well, the notion of feasting his eyes on the gorgeous Glynis Gabriel in the raw had somehow got under his skin, and he was frankly unable to pass up the golden opportunity of watching her reveal those gorgeous boobs and that voluptuous bum just for him and him alone. If he asked nicely, maybe she'd keep her stockings and suspenders on for him while she posed, bare-arsed and brazen as a bitch on heat. His prick gave a jolt and, under cover of his trousers, began its slow ascent of his belly. He wondered idly if her pubes were the same colour as her hairdo, in the same way that Sharon's were. But then, his Sharon was a perfectionist amongst women, he thought with a modest swell of pride. With Sharon, everything matched – lingerie, finger and toenails, even body hair. Yes, there was no doubt about it, Frankie de Rosa was a lucky man where Sharon was concerned – he knew a great many men who would give their eye teeth to have a crack at her. And if lady luck had the grace to smile on him tonight and grant him a legitimate eyeful of the lovely Glynis, he was shortly to become more fortunate still.

Lost in thought for a moment, Frankie was barely aware of Sharon's silent return to the table. Easing her bottom into the seat next to his, mindless of the fact that her micro-mini, stretched tight around her curvy hips and revealing several tantalising inches of silky upper thigh, was in grave danger of resembling nothing so much as a wide belt, she wriggled a little with sheer pleasure and ran her tongue unself-consciously over her freshly lipsticked lips whilst curling her toes with delight inside her high-heeled shoes. Leaning forward a little, poised and ready and eyes fixed wantonly on the delectable, shoeless redhead onstage, Sharon glowed inwardly with a warm, erotic fire, simmering wickedly with a delicious, slow-mounting excitement. She wondered idly whether, in the rugby scrum panic to buy tickets, Glynis Gabriel's brief absence from the manager's side had been noted. Pouting sexily she blew a tiny kiss towards the stage, a gesture which, though subtle in its execution, was duly noted by the recipient and mirrored back to her.

Frankie, aware at last of Sharon's presence next to him, noticed with a small start of alarm the undeniably salacious gleam in his girlfriend's eye and the confident tilt of her pretty chin as she gazed stagewards. He could almost feel the heat rising from her skin. Talk about the cat that got the cream, he thought to himself. Unless he was greatly mistaken, the lovely Sharon Neavis was up to something. He'd seen that look before and it generally meant trouble. Trouble with a capital T. In fact, the last time he'd seen her look like that was on a day trip to Boulogne. On board the ferry coming back, intoxicated with the romance of *la belle France*, tipsy with cut-price brandy and laden with duty-frees, she'd insisted they make love in the staff toilets, an event which, though highly memorable in terms of the knee-trembling frisson it evoked within them both, almost succeeded in bringing an untimely end to the *entente cordiale* between our two illustrious nations. But that was history whereas this, most definitely, was right now.

Frankie gave a small, nervous cough and shuffled awkwardly in his seat. 'Er, you okay, doll? Don't mind me asking only I was wondering where you'd buggered off to just then. Thought maybe you'd got the hump or something . . .' He shrugged apologetically and looked at Sharon expectantly, ready for an explanation as to her obvious, rapt interest in the post-prandial proceedings, though not at all sure he was going to get one. At least, not one which would satisfy his growing concern.

As predicted, Sharon was unforthcoming. She turned to him with the face of an angel, eyes wide with surprise at his apparent nervousness, the very picture of purity and divine innocence. 'I'm fine, thank you, sweetie. Golly, what ever made you think I'd got the hump? I'm having a lovely time, Frankie, and all thanks to you.' She smiled sweetly, wrinkling her nose appealingly at him and reaching out a soft hand to tickle the underside of his chin. 'I only went to powder my nose, darling. That's all . . .' she concluded in her maddeningly titillating little girl voice.

Quite sure now that his worst fears were about to be confirmed, though painfully in the dark as to their precise nature, Frankie smiled back at Sharon and gave her knee a brief, unconvincing squeeze before settling back awkwardly into his chair and gazing fixedly and with mounting disquiet at the stage, raffle tickets clutched with a vice-like grip in his anxious fist. Oh well, he thought with weary resignation, if the evil bitch really was up to something, there was sod all he or anybody else could do about it. He'd learned that from bitter experience. Better just to relax, sit back and take it on the chin. He only hoped they didn't wind up getting kicked out as a result of whatever Sharon had in mind, forced to roam the countryside in search of alternative accommodation. Not a particularly heart-warming prospect at the best of times but, on Christmas night, damn near suicidal.

'Right now, ladies and gentlemen,' shouted the manager

from the stage, struggling to compete with the noisy hubbub, 'if everyone has their tickets, we'll begin the raffle! The fourth prize is this here litre bottle of excellent French brandy,' he expounded, holding it aloft amid 'Oohs' and 'Aahs' of approval from the audience, 'and the winning ticket number is . . .' Turning to Glynis, he watched her draw one of the tiny folded scraps from the cut-glass bowl she was holding and, taking it from her, called out the number. A small, rotund lady with a too-tight dress and an ash-blonde perm descended on the stage to claim her prize with a little skip and a whoop of excitement, encouraged on all sides with rapturous applause and loud wolf whistles. The third and second prizes, a two-pound box of chocolates and a set of wineglasses, were collected in similar manner. Then, gesturing for a bit of hush, the manager paused dramatically before announcing the winner of the first and final prize . . .

Breathing heavily and wiping the sweat from his brow with his pocket handkerchief, he nodded towards the percussionist, who commenced a slow drum roll, growing faster as the tension mounted. Gazing theatrically out into the now-silent audience for a second or two, chest rising and falling with exertion, he allowed his fevered mind to dwell for the briefest moment on an image of himself sitting at his desk, systematically counting the profits of his seedy scheme. Then, turning suddenly to Glynis with a surreptitious wink and an unmistakeable gleam in his bloodshot eye, he was duly handed the lucky ticket, news of whose number was eagerly awaited by the entire assembly. 'And the winning number is . . .' As one, each member of the audience drew in their breath and held it. '. . . number sixty-nine! Who'd have believed it!'

With an audible sigh of relief mixed with disappointment at the realisation that he didn't in fact own the winning ticket, rapidly turning to a mounting fit of pique at his own foolhardiness in parting with a precious fifty quid on the strength of nothing more than a whim, albeit a seductive one, Frankie tore up his tickets in disgust and stuffed them in his breast pocket. Then, rather reluctantly, he began to cheer and clap with the rest, peering around him in an attempt to ascertain the identity of the mystery winner.

Oh gawd, not again! Frankie thought with a sudden jolt and a twist of anger. Where the hell was she off to now? Sharon, who had risen to her feet along with several others when the winning number had been called out, was moving away from him, establishing a slow though steady passage through the yelling throng. Surely she couldn't need to take another leak. Not so soon after the last one. Maybe he'd got the wrong end of the stick and she wasn't hatching a plan after all. Perhaps she'd just had enough and decided on the spur of the moment to call it a day and turn in. She might have alerted him to the fact, though. And anyway, he thought petulantly, the very least she could have done was stick around to assuage his disappointment at not having won the raffle.

Not even a measly box of chocs to show for all that lost loot! A glass or two of French brandy would have gone down a treat, too. Frankie sighed. Forfeiting his eyeful of Glynis Gabriel he could cope with – if anything, it was something of a relief not to have to turn on the charm at this hour of the night. In any case, it went without saying that it would have been beholden on him to suggest the two of them round off the evening by putting on a performance of the beast with two backs – no point in insulting the girl by not doing so – and the thought of Sharon's reaction to that inevitable little scenario made him cringe. But having said that, to be refused the opportunity of at the very least putting the final touches to the evening by getting his end away with Sharon was more than he could stomach. No bloody gratitude, that was the trouble. Feeling sorry for himself Frankie stopped clapping and folded his arms resignedly across his chest, slumping balefully back into his chair and turning his downhearted gaze back towards the stage.

The sight which greeted him made him sit bolt upright once more. Simultaneously his mouth went dry and he began to sweat. His heart skipped several beats and it was a good job that he was sitting down because, had he not been, his nerveless legs would have landed him on the deck. The hotel manager, flushed with success and grinning from ear to ear like Luciano Pavarotti taking his umpteenth curtain call, stood at centre-stage, one arm thrown casually around the bare shoulders of the gorgeous Glynis Gabriel and the other – horror of horrors! – linked solicitously with Sharon's, for all the world as though he were a favourite uncle or beneficent godfather. As Frankie watched, wide-eyed with shock, the three of them descended from the stage amid wild applause and, courtesy of the three-piece combo, the opening strains of *The Stripper*. Kissing the manager on each cheek and giving his bottom little squeezes of gratitude which sent him all ashiver, the two women gently circled each others waists and slowly allowed their lips to meet in a tender welcoming kiss. Then, sashaying elegantly through the crowd of onlookers, as bold as brass and not in the least embarrassed, the two women made for the door, heads held high and soft, probing hands resting on curvy bottoms as they allowed it to be opened for them by a rapturous waiter and then closed smoothly behind them.

Several minutes later, the other guests having retired to their rooms, many of them set on satisfying the insistent gnawings occasioned by the recent events in the dining room, Frankie was still sitting in his chair facing the stage, motionless with disbelief and fatigue. Images of his Sharon and that receptionist bint floated unbidden into his mind, paused a while, and then gently floated out again. How could she do it to him? Stitch him up like that. And tonight of all nights. The whole event had obviously been fixed, he thought grimly. His stomach knotted as he recalled Sharon's apparently innocent little trip to the powder room. The randy bitch must have set it all up then – bought a ticket and slipped it to her lady love to produce, as if by magic, at the optimum moment. Crazy as he was he hadn't even realised the horny pair of tarts fancied each other. In fact, if his and Sharon's arrival in reception the previous lunchtime had been anything to go by, he'd have sworn they hated each other's guts. But then, he'd never understand women. Like creatures from another planet, the whole bloody lot of them. Daft as brushes and twice as prickly.

Not much point going to bed. Not tonight. Sharon and Glynis were doubtless up there now, stripped to the buff and going at it hammer and tongs like a pair of demented she-cats. Downing the remains of his wine and grimacing theatrically as the bitter dregs slipped painfully past the lump which had formed in his throat, Frankie slumped further down in his chair and prepared to call it a day. He sighed and closed his eyes.

'You look like a man who could do with a top-up. Fancy a drop of the hard stuff? On the house, of course.' Frankie blinked and looked up. The manager, clutching a bottle of Irish whisky and a couple of glasses, sat down next to him and poured two generous measures. 'All the bloody same, these women,' he opined heavily. 'All cast in the same mould when it comes down to it. No rhyme or reason to their behaviour, really. The wife's gone off with a headache – one of her phantom ones, I shouldn't wonder – so I'm not exactly overjoyed with the fair sex myself at the moment.'

Instantly on the ball despite being a little fuzzy around the edges, Frankie sat up and took his glass, nodding conspiratorially and trying as hard as he could to look sympathetic. As far as he could see, there was little point in refusing the manager's generous offer of a buckshee tipple. Any port in a storm, as they say, and besides, he might as well salvage something from the evening, even if it was only a few free drinks. Smiling gratefully with what he hoped was a measure of warmth and good humour, he brought the glass to his lips. 'Cheers, squire, I don't mind if I do . . .'

As it turned out, if he'd only known it, Frankie had little cause to mourn the loss of his bedroom that Christmas night at The Spotted Cow despite the fact that circumstances had forced him to metaphorically kiss goodbye to his erotic chances with Sharon. By mutual consent, she and Glynis had decided that Sharon should claim her somewhat unconventional raffle prize in the 'prize's' own personal bedroom. And so, giggling and hand in hand, they quickly made their way there.

When they reached the room, which was situated in the staff quarters on the ground floor near the now-deserted kitchens, Glynis gave a mysterious little smile and silently gestured for Sharon to make herself comfortable on the bed, which appeared to be the only available seating space. Then, moving with a kind of serene, unhurried grace from the bedside table to the radiator and the small washbasin, adjusting the lighting and the temperature control, she took a small, unlabelled bottle filled with a slightly pinkish liquid from the vanity cabinet beneath the basin, unscrewed the lid and took a swig before handing it to Sharon with a little shudder of pleasure.

'Fancy a drop?' she asked, eyes shining with mischief. 'It's vodka. It'll get you in the mood. Always works. For me, anyway. Hey . . . I think it's working already . . . Woweee . . .' With a moan of satisfaction, Glynis closed her eyes and stretched her bare arms languorously above her tousled auburn head, breathing deeply and wriggling her hips and bottom delightedly in the skintight dress as the warming, sensual effects of the alcohol reached her ripe, peachy extremities. 'Boy, I needed that,' she breathed, opening her eyes and smiling at Sharon with a girlish twinkle. 'It's absolutely delicious – flavoured with real strawberries, would you believe. My boyfriend brought me a litre of the stuff back from Poland when he was there a few weeks ago, and I decanted it into these empty sauce bottles from the kitchen so the cleaner wouldn't get wind of what it was and polish off the lot. A real dypso, that one. Anyway, this is the last bottle. Go on, have a try. I dare you . . .'

Sharon, game for anything at the best of times and feeling right at that moment in need of a little Polish courage – this being her first sexual liaison with a member of her own sex – needed little if any persuasion. Taking the bottle from Glynis she took a long, satisfying swig before handing it back again and flopping, full-length onto the bed with her eyes closed, licking the last vestiges of it from her lips and smiling gently as the lazy, soporific effects of the alcohol enveloped her long, coltish limbs. Kicking off her high-heeled shoes she yawned and sighed contentedly, then propped herself up on one elbow on the lacy counterpane and looked around her at the small, warm room while Glynis too kicked off her shoes and climbed onto the bed beside her.

The room reminded Sharon very much of the bedroom she'd had at home as a teenager – frilly and ultra-feminine, stuffed with soft toys and pictures of pretty men. She'd been happier at seventeen than at any other time during her highly eventful and rather sad twenty-three years. Her mother was off the bottle at last, she'd landed her first job as a telesales girl for the local rag and had some money of her own at last to buy clothes and make-up. She'd also fallen in love with the boy from the post-room, who was generally regarded by the rest of her peer group as the number one office hunk and something of a catch. Her brief spell of happiness hadn't lasted, of course, but then she hadn't really suspected for a moment that it would. The newspaper went bust and she lost her job, along with the post boy who emigrated with his parents to Australia. Then her mother got pregnant again courtesy of her latest boyfriend, turning to drink once more when the uncouth lout refused to take responsibility for her condition, adding insult to injury by unceremoniously ditching her. Still, the brief ray of sunshine in her otherwise rather bleak life had been good while it lasted.

Soft fingers traced the outline of Sharon's neck, caressing the tender nape and stroking the shiny, pale blonde hairs which had escaped from her backcombed hair-do. 'I get the feeling this is your first time,' Glynis whispered softly in Sharon's ear, her soft breath warming the other woman's skin. 'Am I right?'

With a flutter of excitement, Sharon grinned and turned to face her new lover, nodding and giggling wickedly. 'Yes, awful isn't it? I didn't know I had it in me!' She bit her lip and looked reflective once more. 'It was just that, seeing you up there on stage . . . You looked so sexy, so in control. You had every man in that room in the palm of your hand . . . Me, too. And I wanted some of it . . .' Sharon gazed at Glynis, her eyes burning with an inner fire which made the other woman sit back on her heels and look thoughtful.

'You know,' Glynis said slowly, 'I thought you were a right one when I saw you yesterday with that seedy little boyfriend of yours. All eyes and fanny with nothing between the ears. Know what I mean? But I changed my mind when you came in to dinner tonight. You looked utterly stunning and as sexy as hell in that little designer number. Beautiful, bright-eyed and bushy tailed – like a fashion model straight from the pages of *Cosmo*. And as sharp as nails, too. I thought to myself, there's a lady who knows what she wants and means to get it. I respect that. You seemed tough and yet soft at the same time. I fancied you, Sharon. That's why I gave you the come-on. I'm glad I did . . . How about you? Do you fancy me, too?' she asked hesitantly, her voice a trembling whisper, alive with anticipation and promise.

Actions speak louder than words. Shifting her position on the bed so that she and Glynis were directly facing each other, Sharon smiled softly and, gazing into the other woman's eyes, slowly draped her arms around her lover's neck and bare shoulders. Closing her eyes seductively, Sharon tilted her pretty head and covered Glynis's pouting, already slightly parted lips with her own in a long, lingering kiss which, for both of them, rendered their limbs to jelly and ignited the first, insistent flickerings of arousal in their bellies. Initially tender and rather shy, this delicious first kiss between the two women turned swiftly to one of growing, passionate arousal. Breathing deeply, eyes closed, they began to probe the warm interiors of each others mouths with their tongues, relishing the sweet, feminine taste, similar and yet deliciously different, as their increasingly urgent fingers squeezed and massaged soft, dampening flesh.

Excitingly aware of the scent of expensive perfume and the hammering of their joint hearts as their upper bodies urgently came together in a close, sensual embrace, Sharon almost swooned at the mind-blowing and, to her, previously unknown sensation of another woman's breasts pressing against her own. Somewhat fuller and more developed than Sharon's, Glynis's boobs were lush and beautiful – the delight and envy of all who came in contact with them – and Sharon was far from immune to their twin charms. 'Wouldn't you be more comfortable, babe, if you took that tight dress off?' she murmured cajolingly into Glynis's ear. Pulling away slightly, she feasted her eyes on the gorgeous creamy cleavage which, as if by magic, seemed to have lengthened and deepened along with the gradual descent of Glynis's boned silk bodice as they'd embraced, thereby increasing its shadowy allure and causing Sharon to catch her breath with surprise and delight.

Glynis smiled and pouted, rising to her knees and giving a little shimmy of pleasure which made her semi-revealed breasts shiver and bounce. She was well aware of the effect she was having on the lovely Sharon and was loving every minute of it. 'What a good idea, darling,' she said softly. 'I do so hate feeling restricted by tight clothes. It's so much nicer to be naked, don't you think?'

Sharon's heart skipped a beat and, eyes shining, she ran her tongue over her lips. 'I quite agree. Sexier, too . . .' Almost overcome with emotion, Sharon closed her eyes and gave a long trembling sigh, aware of the small, insistent pulse of arousal deep in her sex. Then, pulling herself together, she continued in a low, seductive whisper: 'Here, let me help you, sweetie.'

With a smile and an encouraging little wink to show that Sharon was on the right lines, Glynis turned her back and sat up straight, whereupon Sharon stroked the soft, bare skin of her neck and shoulders with delicate fingers. Then, finding herself unable to resist the allure of the pale, translucent flesh, she showered her lover with tiny, feathery kisses before slowly lowering the zip at the back of Glynis's dress, revealing a long, delectable gash of still more warm, naked flesh. Catching her breath, her pussy damp and throbbing with anticipation, she allowed the dress to fall with a swish of silk to Glynis's narrow waist, then she placed her soft hands on Glynis's shoulders and gently pulled her round until they were facing each other.

Purring with pride and well aware of her own beauty, Glynis tilted her chin and pushed back her shoulders like a topless photographic model. She seemed to glow from within, fully expecting unquestioning adoration and getting it. Her breasts, though large and rather heavy, were as firm and uptilted as a teenager's, set slightly apart so that her nipples faced coyly away from each other – so bold and brazen and yet apparently so shy – an effect which her various lovers had found stimulating in the extreme. And what nipples! In their fully erect state, deep, dusky pink and engorged with life blood, they were the largest and longest that Sharon had ever seen, even between the pages of the soft-core girlie mags which she and Frankie perused from time to time.

'Come on, darling,' Glynis whispered enticingly, bending forward a little at the waist and cupping her stunning, fleshy breasts in her hands, presenting them to Sharon with a slow, sexy smile and gently tweaking her spectacular nipples to even more generous dimensions. 'Fancy a little suck? Mmmm . . . you do, don't you?'

She gazed into Sharon's eyes, stretching her voluptuous torso and undulating a little which made her bare breasts shiver and bounce and her unfastened dress fall in a pool of bright pink silk to her suspendered thighs. Then, wriggling out of it completely and nudging it carelessly to the floor, she moved closer to Sharon on the bed like a deliciously curvaceous temptress. She was now completely naked save for a minute, shocking-pink G-string – which hardly succeeded in covering her generous pubic mound and left her full, peachy bottom totally bare – a matching pink suspender belt and glossy, smoke-grey seamed stockings which stretched smooth and tight around the pale, firm flesh of her thighs like a sensual second skin. Encircling her tiny waist and accentuating its cover-girl narrowness, which was in divine contrast to the full, feminine dimensions of her hips, Glynis wore a gossamer-fine, twenty-two carat gold chain which glinted expensively in the subdued lamplight as she moved.

'Don't be shy, my beautiful blonde angel. You won first prize, remember? I'm all yours, darling. Every single inch of me . . .'

Eyes like round, blue orbs, their beauty enhanced rather than spoiled by her slightly smudged make-up, Sharon was entranced and exquisitely open to Glynis's tender, loving encouragement and hopelessly moved by the overt eroticism of her words, not to mention the warm insinuation of the Polish vodka. With heart pounding and pussy throbbing, she slipped out of her own clothes as quickly as she could, divesting herself of the soft, pale blue mini-dress and sheer tights. For once she was mindless of the havoc she was wreaking on her glossy, backcombed hairdo as she unfastened her black, half-cup bra and wriggled out of her lacy French knickers. When she had finished, she was bare-arsed naked save for Frankie's 'sapphire' and a pair of long, dangling pearl earrings which, together with her unkempt hair and full, pouting lips, made her resemble nothing so much as a young, Bardoesque sex kitten.

'Christ, darling, what a body,' Glynis breathed, her eyes bright with desire and admiration. 'So slender and tight, like a teenager . . . I know a thousand broads who'd pay a king's ransom to achieve a bod like that. Tell me, angel, do you have a tight little fanny to match?'

Without waiting for an answer, Glynis gave a lusty little shudder and advanced towards Sharon on the bed, enfolding the young, dishevelled blonde in her soft arms so that their bare breasts, so deliciously different and yet so powerfully sensitive, pressed together, flesh against sultry, tingling flesh. Covering the pretty, heavily made-up face with tiny kisses, Glynis advanced on the soft neck and throat, nibbling and licking with voluptuous abandon at the tender, perfumed skin.

Suddenly, with an almost overpowering rush of pure lust, Sharon experienced the mind-blowing sensation of Glynis's big, fleshy nipples grazing with exquisite urgency against her own which, although somewhat smaller and a paler, more delicate pink in colour, were as ripe and engorged with pulsing blood as the other woman's. Overcome with the power of her need, unable to help herself, Sharon pulled away from Glynis, breathing hard and fast, her face a picture of sultry, flushed eroticism as she gazed into her lover's eyes before reaching out with trembling hands and tentatively taking hold of those big, beautiful breasts with their extravagant nipples.

Placing her own hands over Sharon's, squeezing them tight and guiding them with a passionate insistence over and around the firm, heavy flesh of her trembling boobs, Glynis closed her eyes and threw back her head in ecstasy, undulating like an Indian serpent. Then, with a flood of excitement, she opened her eyes wide and swooped down to grab a medium-sized jar from the bedside table. She quickly unscrewed the lid and, with two fingers, scooped out a generous dollop of its contents before proceeding to rub it swiftly and with evident tactile pleasure across her breasts, smearing and smoothing them until the generous, rounded flesh gleamed and wobbled with an almost obscene voluptuousness, coated as it was with a sweet, sinful layer of dark chocolate sauce. Paying particular attention to her big nipples, which each received an extra, delicious blob of chocolate, Glynis licked her fingers, one at a time and, with a naughty giggle of pleasure, peered down to inspect her handiwork. Biting her

186

bottom lip with mischievous schoolgirl glee, she gazed entranced from one to the other whilst crouching seductively on the lacy bedspread, knees slightly apart, revealing a gorgeous portion of silky-haired, scantily clad pussy. Hollowing her back, page-three style, and pushing out her glossy, chocolatey tits to get a better view, she looked like a licentiously wicked blue-movie temptress, or a porno centrespread from one of the raunchier under-the-counter magazines.

Sharon, mouth open and eyes on stalks, knelt in front of this sweet symphony of gooey temptation as though at the feet of a divine Bacchanalian goddess. Never before, she thought with a warm, erotic shiver, had she seen anyone or anything so unashamedly, disgustingly sexual. She felt as though she were a part of some exotically obscene ritual, the like of which she'd never before experienced, and she was loving every gross, over-the-top moment of it with an almost shocking intensity. She felt herself begin to tremble and a fine sheen of sweat broke out between her breasts and thighs, on her smooth forehead and downy upper lip. She swallowed hard, mouth dry, her whole body alive and pulsing to the rhythm of the warm, insistent thud which filled her lower belly and pussy. A slick, musky essence had already begun to seep from her sex, combining with the existing, sultry dampness between her legs and forming a delectable, aromatic cocktail, the heady scent seeming to bathe the small room with erotic promise.

Glynis closed her eyes and sniffed. 'Mmmm . . . delicious,' she murmured, 'Sweeties and cunt juice. Like a Turkish brothel on a summer evening. Come, my beautiful blonde angel,' she whispered, throwing her shoulders back and clasping a big, shiny breast in each hand, holding them out like a pair of luscious sweetmeats. 'Lick my tits. You know you're dying to, and I can't wait to feel your naughty, wet little tongue tickling my nipples . . . Your full, sexy lips all sticky and smeared with gooey chocolate. Wow!' Glynis shuddered extravagantly and narrowed her eyes, her voice low and seductive as she continued her rude invitation; 'It makes my pussy tingle just thinking about it . . .'

Sharon needed no further encouragement. A chocolate fiend at the best of times, the prospect of sucking a quantity of her favourite confection from a pair of firm, sexually aroused breasts, lewdly proffered by their owner – a gorgeous, semi-naked redhead – was a treat not to be refused. With a sigh of relief, she fell on Glynis's chocolate-covered tits like a child let loose in a sweetshop, clutching the soft, slippery flesh in both hands and licking ecstatically at it, eyes closed and eager tongue fully extended.

Watching her through narrowed, lust-filled eyes, Glynis writhed and moaned with pleasure, thrusting her gleaming breasts still further towards Sharon, urging her on with little sighs and whimpers of encouragement. She was delighted and highly aroused by the evident excitement and enthusiasm of the gorgeous blonde who, with flushed cheeks and smears of wet chocolate on her chin and around her mouth, wantonly and with evident pleasure popped first one and then the other succulent nipple into her mouth, rolling it around her tongue and gently nibbling at the turgid flesh as though her very life depended on it.

Catching her breath and holding it momentarily, Glynis felt the first, tentative stirrings of what promised to be a monumental tidal wave of an orgasm. Greedily parting her trembling, stockinged thighs, she pulled aside the tiny, pink silk G-string and allowed the fingers of her right hand to stray distractedly through the soft auburn curls around her swollen pubis, insinuate themselves between her hot, flushed pussy lips and plunge deep inside her dark, throbbing vagina, which opened to receive them like some strangely exotic flower. Thrusting two, three and then four eager fingers inside her welcoming cunt, she stroked and frigged herself by turns, thrilling to the sensation of the hot, tight flesh as it contracted around them. Moaning now with wanton abandon, she undulated her voluptuous hips and bare, trembling bottom which, in the highly aroused state of its owner, was hot, damp and pink-cheeked, like a baby fresh from its afternoon siesta.

At last, with a strangled cry, Glynis ceased gyrating and her body tensed as she was overcome by wave after pulsing wave of pure, physical release. Sharon, aware that the beautiful redhead was lost in the intense grip of climax, released her hold on the juicy boobs, allowing Glynis to fall back, as though in slow motion, against the white lace bedspread and lie there, spreadeagled and completely unabashed, like a sexually sated Botticelli Venus. After a moment or two during which the erotic tension between the two women hung between them like a pussy-scented mist, Glynis opened her eyes, winked and, with a wicked grin, rose slowly to her knees and reached for the chocolate jar.

'Okay, baby, you tickled my pussy so I'll tickle yours . . .' she said in a sexy half-whisper, 'Bend over and let me see that gorgeous, tight little fanny of yours. Come on now, don't be shy . . .' Glynis giggled salaciously and dipped an elegant, varnished forefinger into the sweetie jar, emerging triumphantly with a little sigh of satisfaction and a large, glistening dollop of sinfully dark chocolate sauce.

Sharon felt the blood rush to her face and boobs. Her trembling increased a thousand-fold, tiny beads of hot sweat rose on her flushed skin and her already racing heart beat a wild tattoo within her breast, threatening to send her into a dead faint. Never before had she felt as unremittingly turned on as she did now. This sexually sophisticated woman with her tousled titian curls, abundant curves and wicked grin had achieved a level of arousal within Sharon which few if any men had even managed to come close to, despite her undeniably colourful past. Already practically on the brink of orgasm, despite not yet having been touched, let alone caressed, by this hot-blooded siren beside her on the bed, Sharon's need had reached epic proportions and was almost obscene in terms of its dark, naked urgency. With a swift athleticism which belied the swirling turmoil within her, she rose up onto her hands and knees with her back to Glynis, breasts hanging firm and free like those of a young, fecund animal, slim thighs spread invitingly apart and tight, gleaming bum cheeks thrust brazenly out, wriggling delightfully in their impatience to be rudely plundered.

Glynis, aroused all over again, licked her lips lasciviously and moved closer, gazing at the dusk-pink, shadowy crack between Sharon's arse cheeks which, as they eagerly jiggled and jounced before her, failed to conceal the tiny, rosy bud of her anus. Cupping her big breasts, smeared and glossy still with a combination of what remained of the chocolate sauce and Sharon's saliva, she tweaked her full-blown nipples back to their former firmness so that they jutted extravagantly, her heavy-lidded eyes feasting mesmerically on the stimulating vision of Sharon's wet, swollen pussy lips which pouted back at her whilst exuding the familiar musky scent of female sexual potency. So siren was the reek of sex that Glynis couldn't resist lowering her face to within inches of Sharon's bare genitals, closing her eyes and taking a long, satisfying sniff. 'Mmmm . . .' she moaned, her voice low and trembling with emotion, 'you just can't beat the smell of a randy bitch's cunt. Except, perhaps, when the cunt's chocolate-coated . . .'

Sharon, guessing correctly what was to follow, shivered with anticipation and hollowed her back so that her bare breasts jutted proudly, placing her knees even further apart on the bed so that her arse and pussy thrust up and out in tensed readiness. Then, with a pure, electric thrill which caused her tummy muscles to tense and her legs almost to give way beneath her, she felt the first, chocolatey fingerings against her vulva and outer labial lips as Glynis caressed her cunt with the kind of practised skill which only another woman might possess.

'Like it, baby?' Glynis murmured huskily, dipping her naughty fingers once more into the jar before insinuating them again into Sharon's private parts. 'Mmmm . . .' she whispered soothingly, 'you feel so good against my fingers, darling. All hot and slippery. You smell good, too – pussy juice and chocolate sauce . . . Think I'll bottle it and live off the immoral earnings.' Then, with a sudden firm insistence which took Sharon quite by surprise and caused her to gasp and cry out loud, Glynis slipped no fewer than three rigid fingers through the opening between her swollen inner labial lips and thrust them deep inside her tight cunt before commencing a vigorous though surprisingly tender finger-fuck, her soft thumb stroking feather-like against the swollen nub of Sharon's clitoris.

Sharon, bucking rhythmically against Glynis's fingers, was almost beside herself with intense, erotic glee. Tears of joy sprang to her eyes and she moaned long and low as though in some sort of exquisite, relentless pain. She threw back her blonde, tousled head and bared her teeth, parting her slim legs as far as they'd go without splitting her in two, pushing her arse out with rude, eager deliberation and wiggling it wildly as she concentrated with an almost religious, single-minded devotion on the divine sensations coursing through her naked, sweating body.

Lost in the powerful thrall of her erotic exertions, Glynis felt the warm, ever-strengthening pulse of yet another orgasm begin to build within her. With an unintelligible moan she quickly released her grip on Sharon's cunt, clasped her big, glossy breasts in both hands and rubbed them with an almost rough urgency against Sharon's lewdly proffered arse and wet slit, desperately kissing and nuzzling the firm, white skin of her lover's tensed, quivering belly. Then, scrambling into yet another sexually advantageous position, bare breasts and bottom wobbling delightfully in her haste, she advanced on the hot, aromatic heaven between the sexy blonde's thighs, eyes closed and tongue fully extended, whimpering softly with her mouth full of pussy and breathing deeply through her pretty nose as she licked and sucked on the sweet flesh, drinking in the rich, forbidden fragrance of illicit, chocolatey sex whilst clasping Sharon's hips in a tight grip to still her compulsive undulations.

'Fuck me, you beautiful bitch!' Sharon cried, tears coursing down her cheeks as she finally reached her longed-for climax,

'Eat me alive!' Glynis, excitedly squeezing and finger-fucking her own juicy pussy with no less than four stiff digits, thrust her tongue deep inside Sharon's tight vaginal canal and wiggled it lewdly, thrilling to the sensation of the dark, enveloping flesh as it throbbed and contracted around it. Then, abandoning herself to the hot, relentless waves of her second powerful climax, she wrapped her arms tightly around Sharon's lower body and, moaning with relief, pressed her fevered cheek against the tensed, quivering bum, pink-flushed and damp with sweat.

Naked bodies locked together, as inseparable as copulating animals, Sharon and Glynis dropped slowly to the rumpled bed and, from there, to the carpeted floor where they lay entwined in a motionless, exhausted silence save for the soft whisper of steady, contented breathing.

'Glynis . . . ?' Sharon murmured sleepily after a minute or two, lazily twining a damp, auburn strand of pussy hair around one gentle forefinger, 'I think I could get used to this . . .'

Glynis giggled and kissed Sharon tenderly on the tip of her nose, reaching out a languid arm towards the abandoned divan and tugging the lacy bedspread, together with the quilt, until it fell on top of them both where they lay on the floor in their companionable tangle. 'Sharon, darling?' she murmured back with a tiny, wicked gleam in her smudgy, mascaraed eye, 'You ain't seen nothing yet . . .'

The manager's wife opened the door to her bedroom on the first floor and peered nervously around before tiptoeing out onto the landing and closing it soundlessly behind her. So far so good, she thought, relieved. With a muffled yawn and a surreptitious little shiver she wrapped her diaphanous purple negligee – a Christmas present from her husband – around her ample frame, cast an appraising eye over her bosomy cleavage and made a mental note to organise someone to do a quick check on the central-heating system after breakfast the next day. Then, wobbling slightly on her dainty, high-heeled purple mules with feathery pom-poms – her other Christmas present from her husband – she gingerly descended the shadowy staircase and, with bated breath, made her way to the hotel lounge which, by now, would surely be in darkness.

Those extra-strength painkillers seemed to have done the trick. God bless Dr Wilkinson. She must remember to thank him properly when she next paid him her customary weekly visit after the Christmas break. Her soft, freshly lipsticked lips curved into a little smile at the notion and she quickly put out a hand to stop herself from falling off the frivolous purple heels in her excitement. Roll on next Wednesday . . .

Anyway, she thought, pulling herself together, time to concentrate on the task in hand. After all, she owed it to the poor old sod to try and be nice to him. Especially tonight of all nights. He'd poured everything he had into that Christmas dinner – not to mention down his throat into the bargain, truth be told – and all his hard work seemed to have paid off. You could have knocked her down with a feather when that brassy bit of nonsense won the raffle prize, but never mind, it was all in a good cause (hers and the old man's to be precise) and, besides, it was Christmas.

Puzzled, she stopped in her tracks and gazed at the flood of light escaping from the half-open door to the guests' lounge, her puzzlement slowly turning to something approaching relief at the blessed realisation that she was about to be let off the hook. Tripping resolutely towards the door she pushed it open with the toe of her slipper and, shielding her gloom-accustomed eyes to the glare, the intensity of which would have given Blackpool Illuminations a run for its money, peered inside.

The sights and sounds which greeted her made her smile to herself, albeit with a subtle if barely disguised hint of malice. Every light in the large, low-ceilinged room – wall lights, table lamps, the fluorescent strip over the pool table and the directional spots above the bar – had, for some reason known only to the room's occupants, been left full on. Scattered haphazardly on and around one of the larger coffee tables was a motley selection of bottles – all of them empty. On the floor beside the accompanying sofa lay a teetering pile of some of her husband's more suspect girlie mags, temporarily liberated from the lock-up filing cabinet in his private office. One or two copies lay where they had presumably been cast aside in favour of others, brazen and face-up on the floor, candidly revealing their contents of vast, cellulose-implanted tits and glossy dildoes, flesh-toned and lurid in the exaggerated glare.

And there, right in the midst of the whole, sordid spectacle, was the manager himself, his nerveless arm flung carelessly around the shark-suited shoulders of the little, snake-hipped Italian who'd partnered the aforementioned blonde bimbo, the two of them propping each other up in a grotesque parody of the babes in the wood, wheezing and snoring as though breathing their last. Which is precisely what they would be doing, the manager's wife thought wryly, when she got her hands on the licentious bugger in the morning. Turning on her heel in disgust, she quietly retraced her steps, tiptoeing back to the relative sanctity of her bedroom and illicit dreams of Dr Wilkinson, remembering in the nick of time to lock the door behind her – on the inside, of course.

Chapter Seven

7 a.m. on Boxing Day morning. Large, lazy flakes of snow meandered earthwards in the early morning gloom, softly billowing in the chill breeze, the pale feathers illuminated in the headlights of the inky black Porsche as it pulled into the sweeping drive of High Links Hall and swept smoothly into a vacant parking spot. Switching off the car's music system, thus cutting short the black velvet strains of B.B. King, the driver, insubstantially clad against the cold in T-shirt and jeans, emerged swiftly from the warm interior. Pausing only to grab a small case from the passenger seat, he then made his way on silent feet to the staff entrance at the side of the building.

Crystal woke with a start. Was that a noise or had she been dreaming? Deciding on the latter she peered blearily at the radio alarm on the bedside table. Thank God. There was at least another hour before she'd have to get up and face the day. Just as well, really, bearing in mind the previous night's high jinks in the staff kitchen. Fernando, bless him, had been as good as his word and really done them all proud. So much so that she could barely remember falling into bed at 1 a.m., stuffed to the gills and high as a kite on champagne and vintage port. She considered briefly the wisdom of that last glass of fine old ruby, bearing in mind that she wouldn't actually be off-duty until Boxing Day afternoon. But what the hell! It was Christmas for goodness' sake, and she'd been working like a dog for the last several days. Anyway, she reckoned she deserved the opportunity to get plastered once in a while.

The champagne had been Sheba's fault entirely. Crystal smiled fondly to herself, recalling the sight of the beautiful, statuesque negress standing in the kitchen doorway, face free of make-up and clad in nothing but the scarlet kimono Crystal had lent her, nervously clutching three ice-cold bottles of Bollinger to her satiny breast. To say that Sheba's attitude had been contrite would have been a gross understatement. She was a totally different creature from the furious, fur-coated valkyrie who'd swept into reception the previous day and terrorised poor Bella, and who'd later descended on Crystal in the sanctity of her office, bursting with apoplectic rage at the apparent injustices of the way she'd been treated. This new, reformed Sheba was an altogether more pleasant and amenable proposition. Softly spoken, engagingly witty and even, dare one say, a little shy, she perched girlishly on one of Fernando's spotless work surfaces, long bare legs swinging contentedly, and regaled the pleasantly tipsy off-duty staff with wild stories of life in the fast lane. The staff, in turn, laughed uproariously and gasped with delight at her risqué anecdotes, warming to the rock star's innate charm like moths around a candle flame. Crystal couldn't be entirely sure whether the bitchy little fight in her office had brought about Sheba's transformation, or whether there was some other, unknown cause, but whatever the reason behind this complete personality about-turn, Crystal was eternally grateful for it. For the first time, seeing her as she was now, Crystal had an inkling as to how Sheba had managed to reach such dizzying heights of superstardom.

Crystal yawned and sighed, closing her eyes once more, stretching out her toes to find the warmest spot in the bed and snaking drowsy fingers under her pillow to feel for the cool, reassuring coil of her serpent bangle. Just another half an hour or so should do the trick, she thought dreamily, hovering on the shadowy hinterland between wakefulness and sleep . . .

Isaac Mallory hovered outside the panelled oak door to Crystal's suite, clasping his chilled hands together to stop them from trembling and shifting distractedly from foot to foot as he considered his next move. He'd taken a bit of a risk by coming here at all. Crystal certainly wasn't expecting him. Far from it, in fact – as far as she was concerned he was on the other side of the world in Australia. He couldn't help grinning when he imagined her face when she saw him right there in her bedroom. He only hoped she didn't have heart failure. He hadn't exactly planned for that particular eventuality. In fact, he hadn't exactly planned to be in this country at all over Christmas, but events had overtaken him and the little business venture he'd been keeping warm for the past couple of months had finally come to fruition and, as a result, he'd been compelled to postpone the first few gigs of the Aussie tour in order to accommodate it.

Stalling for time, Isaac held his breath and put his ear to the door, smiling when he heard the steady, even breathing of the woman he cared for most in the world. He imagined her lying there, naked most probably if he knew Crystal, sprawled out under her rumpled quilt, face warm and flushed with sleep and long black hair silky and dishevelled, fanning across her pillow like a raven's wing. He hoped she'd received the present he'd sent her – God knows he'd paid the taxi driver an arm and a leg to deliver it – and wondered whether she'd managed to read between the lines of the cryptic little note which had accompanied it. Maybe she had and maybe she hadn't. And if she had, maybe she was expecting him . . . He'd find out soon enough.

Gingerly he turned the door handle, praying for the door to be unlocked. It was, which possibly suggested that he was right to surmise that she was lying in wait for him. Opening the door as silently as he could manage, cringing as it scuffed disconcertingly across the deep-pile carpet, he entered the room with the stealth of a seasoned burglar and paused for a moment of two to regain his bearings and accustom himself to the velvet darkness. He'd only visited Crystal's suite once or twice before last summer when they'd first become lovers – and then the sunshine had streamed in through the open French windows, bathing the room in warm, coppery light and accentuating the delicate, honey scent of the summer flowers which graced the dressing table and the Chinese inlaid chest at the foot of the big double bed. He remembered one particular afternoon when they'd drawn the floor-length curtains to subdue the light and protect themselves from prying eyes, stripped off their clothes and frolicked like children in the soft, rosy glow which warmed and burnished their naked bodies, adding depth and colour to their already deep tans. He caught his breath at the memory of that afternoon, aware of the faint, sexual stirrings in his groin.

Returning to earth, he gazed slowly around the room, taking in the exotic Mexican drapes and ethnic ephemera, monochromatic in the grey half-light which was beginning to filter through from outside, and finally allowed his eyes to rest on the sleeping woman in the bed. Despite the warm, heady drowsiness of the room she was tightly wrapped in a tangled cocoon of quilt, one arm invisible – masked by the pillow – and the other stretched up above her head, fingers curled like a child's. With a rush of desire he noticed that one of her breasts was free of the bedclothes and lay pale and full against the dark bedclothes, the rosy nipple wine-dark and luscious. Despite the distance between them he could almost smell her – perfume and wine, her favourite shampoo and the familiar, sultry aroma of her skin. He closed his eyes for a moment, drinking in the pure, unmasked essence of the woman asleep, detecting within it a tiny, potent hint of the sharper, feral scent of latent female sexuality.

Looking at her lying there, peaceful in sleep and as innocent as a baby, he suddenly felt like an intruder – uninvited and so far undetected – a feeling which, alarmingly, served to turn him on even more. He shivered, excited and apprehensive at the same time. What if she woke up, saw him standing there in her bedroom and didn't recognise him? She'd be petrified. She might even raise the alarm. That was the last thing he wanted to happen. Gazing once more at her smooth, tranquil face he summoned his courage and squatted down at the foot of the bed, holding his breath as he carefully lifted the corner of the quilt and folded it back so that it revealed her left foot and part of her calf.

At that moment Crystal sighed and turned over onto her back, unconsciously pushing the quilt away from her upper body, which had the delicious effect of baring both her breasts so that they were fully revealed in all their pale, voluptuous splendour to the silent male observer. Shocked at the suddenness of her movement Isaac crouched there, stock-still, eyes like saucers and heart beating wildly in his chest. Ridiculous as it seemed, he was suddenly filled with the irrational fear that the thumping vibration of it would somehow wake her, but the breathtaking sight of those gorgeous creamy globes with their jutting nipples, set slightly apart as she lay on her back, banished his disquiet and replaced it with a growing, boiling need for the thrill of slow seduction followed by rampant possession.

For one brief, uneasy moment, mesmerised by those heart-stopping, naked tits, Isaac considered gently waking her up, thus condensing the agony. But the notion of approaching the situation and the naked, sleeping woman with every last ounce of sensitivity and sexual stealth at his disposal seemed infinitely preferable, not to mention unspeakably more erotic. He waited for a few breathtaking moments until her breathing had resumed its slow even rhythm, then reached out once more and gently stroked the bare toes of her right foot, which had replaced the left one in prominence and was languidly stretched out towards him, with the very tips of his fingers. So far so good, he thought. Crystal didn't stir and the gentle rise and fall of those beautiful naked breasts remained unaltered, Then, heart in mouth and with a tremendous surge of desire, he slowly bent his head, closed his eyes and slipped Crystal's big toe between his softly parted lips and into his mouth, licking all around it with his warm, wet tongue and sucking on it as though on a turgid nipple.

From above him on the bed came the sound of a tiny, soft

whimper, but apart from that Crystal appeared so far to be unmoved by Isaac's tender ministrations. Time, perhaps, for something a little stronger, he thought silently to himself. With a shudder and a silent gulp he wondered how long he could withstand the intense, sweet eroticism of what he was doing to this voluptuous sleeping beauty without being compelled to strip the quilt from her warm naked body and plunge into her without a single, tender preliminary to soften the impact of his sexual plunder.

Gently taking the heel of her right foot in his left hand, he lowered his dark, tousled head once more and ran his tongue from the firm nub of her ankle bone, past her knee, to the middle of her sultry inner thigh, carefully removing the quilt with his right hand as he progressed upwards, almost swooning with pleasure as he caught the familiar musky scent of her soon-to-be-exposed sex . . .

Crystal was dreaming. She was lying, naked, on an exotic, sundrenched beach somewhere in the Seychelles. Tiny, cotton-wool clouds scudded high up across an azure sky, whose colour seemed magically to deepen towards the far horizon. The soft, white sand beneath her was like an enveloping feather mattress and, if she concentrated hard, she could almost imagine that she were up there in the clear sky, spread-eagled on one of those fluffy white clouds, as warm as toast with nothing between her and the golden sun. The only sounds were those of the regal coconut palms, swaying in the light breeze and the soft lapping of the sparkling ocean as it slowly, inevitably, inched its tidal way towards her languid, outstretched legs . . .

Isaac, drunk with the very essence of his comatose quarry which seemed to fill his mind and his senses like an intoxicating honey liqueur, could stand the sweet agony of it no longer. His long limbs, jelly-like with desire, had been rendered almost useless by the power of his heart-thumping anticipation. Despite his efforts to remain silent, his breathing had quickened and become uncomfortably shallow, and it was now clearly audible in the womb-like quiet of Crystal's bedroom. Sweating freely as he was, his tight jeans and T-shirt stuck to his body, making him long to be naked and free of them, a desire made all the more urgent by the increasing length and girth of his rapidly expanding penis.

Quickly rising to his feet, gazing as though transfixed at the dark, shadowy haven between Crystal's softly parted legs, he kicked off his trainers. Then, pulling his T-shirt off over his head and thus disturbing his long dark curls still further so that they clung damply to his cheeks and forehead, he proceeded to unbuckle his wide leather belt, swiftly lowering his Levi's and underpants so that his now-fully-erect penis sprang up and out, pulsing hotly, the ultra-sensitive tip bouncing maddeningly against his flat belly.

With a little thrill of pleasure, Crystal felt the first wet tongues of the ocean caress her bare feet and toes and then, as she lay naked on the soft sand, lazily contemplating the feel of the warm water against her extremities, the tide rose higher still, stroking the inside of her leg and upper thigh and arousing within her desires and warm, billowing emotions normally reserved for mortal, flesh-and-blood lovers . . .

But the hornier she began to feel, the harder it became for Crystal to differentiate between the ocean and the sky, the coconut palms and the sand. Try as she might to hold on to them, the images began to fade and disappear like so much Scotch mist, to be replaced by the cool, grey light of a winter dawn and an urgent, damp throbbing in her sex which, though she was still on the edge of sleep, was beginning to transmit its erotic message through her entire body. Remaining motionless, Crystal slowly regained consciousness, remembering who she was, where she was, what day it was and even, with a sudden rush of pleasure which almost made her cry out loud in her excitement, who it was that was treating her to such a wanton, rude awakening.

Without moving or making the slightest sound, Crystal allowed herself the smallest of smiles, being careful not to alert Isaac to the fact that she was awake, choosing instinctively to maintain the illusion that she was asleep whilst wallowing inwardly in the lewd and luscious sensations which by now were flowing through her in a lusty ocean wave of sexual sensation. Then, still pretending to be asleep, she moaned softly and sighed, pushing the quilt away from her body completely until it fell with a gentle swish of goosedown to the floor, unashamedly revealing her curvy, voluptuous body in all its nakedness and erotic splendour.

As though he himself were in a dream, Isaac climbed onto the bed and knelt between Crystal's parted legs as though at the entrance to some exotic temple. Maddeningly, he found himself unable to control the trembling which assailed his muscular limbs, which was made even more acute by the forbidden nature of what he was about to do in caressing the most intimate parts of this beautiful, naked woman without her conscious awareness, let alone her consent. Eyes blazing and skin flushed with lust, he reached down and grasped his erect cock in his right hand, fondling it vigorously whilst greedily feasting his eyes on the slick, pouting vaginal slit before him, marvelling at the beauty of its dusky oyster folds and tempted almost beyond endurance by its female honey scent – as rich and sinful as a Mediterranean dessert.

With a sigh, he slowly lowered himself onto his haunches, crouching like a jungle cat between Crystal's outstretched legs and letting go of his turgid cock, thus freeing his hands to gently take hold instead of Crystal's firm, curvy hips. Then, lowering his head and closing his eyes in delicious anticipation of the fragrantly sensual oral treat which was to follow, he extended his tongue and tenderly stroked it along the full, pouting length of Crystal's rudely exposed genital lips, from where her bottom cheeks rested on the bed to the tiny, just visible bud of her clitoris. Kissing and nibbling at the soft, rosy flesh he was amazed and delighted to discover that, although apparently still asleep, the woman appeared to be as sexually turned on as he himself undoubtedly was – a fact made all the more indisputable by the copious musky secretions which oozed unchecked from between her pussy lips and the full, engorged nature of the whole, rapidly darkening area between her soft inner thighs.

Overtaken by the urgent sensations in his pulsing groin and a steamy, sexual fever which seemed systematically to be pushing him towards the point where he was in danger of losing control of his mind and senses, Isaac grasped Crystal's hips with an ever-increasing firmness, mindless now of whether or not he'd wake her. Sucking and licking her wet, aromatic cunt like a man possessed, he moaned and grunted deep in his throat, breathing urgently through flared nostrils and forcing as much as he could of his sinuous tongue deep inside her tight vagina.

Crystal, swooning with pleasure at the increasingly lewd attentions of her lover, felt herself to be on the brink of a wild, throbbing climax. No longer wanting, and still less able, to maintain her sleepy charade, she cried out loud with pleasure, threw her arms over her head in pure, erotic ecstasy and, in a single fluid movement, swooped up into a sitting position whilst taking Isaac's curly head in her hands and urging him to rise onto his knees and face her head on. Taking his gorgeous, smiling face – wet with sweat and alive with passion – in both hands, she closed her eyes and brought her trembling lips to his, whereupon they fell into a long, erotic French kiss, tongues entwining and hungrily exploring each other's mouths as voluptuous breasts pressed against firm chest, dark, springy body hair tickling turgid, jutting nipples, Suddenly pulling away, her hands still clasping the back of Isaac's neck, Crystal gazed into his dark eyes, her face breaking into a happy grin, childlike with bubbling excitement and mischief. 'What kept you . . .?' she whispered huskily, 'I expected you hours ago.'

Without waiting for a reply, she took hold of Isaac's broad shoulders, gently urging and manoeuvring him until he lay stretched out on his back on the bed, long legs slightly apart and hands clasped behind his head, thus raising it slightly and affording him a better view of the sensual proceedings. Then, kneeling in front of him she growled like a tiger, flicking back her long, liquorice hair, eyes narrowed with lust, and licked her full, gleaming lips in a deeply lascivious manner which caused Isaac's balls to tighten with anticipation and his heart to hammer even more wildly in his chest. 'I want you, Isaac . . .' she breathed, leaning forward seductively and pressing her upper arms against her gorgeous naked breasts so that they hung suspended, squeezed together, full and gleaming like freshly plucked fruits, the darker nipples, glossy in the half-light, erect and puckered with desire. 'I want to lick you all over,' she continued in a breathy, seductive whisper, 'stroke your nipples, lick your balls, take your gorgeous stiff prick between my lips and . . .'

Halting teasingly in the midst of her horny description of what she planned to do to him, Crystal swiftly and gracefully straddled Isaac's tensed, prone body, her large breasts swaying invitingly as she did so, and lowered her soft mouth to his neck and shoulders. Her long silky hair stroked his skin as she kissed and nuzzled the firm, male flesh, thrilling to the sharp, masculine smell of him. Moving ever lower, she took each tiny, tight nipple in turn into her naughty mouth and nibbled them playfully, running her hands through his dark, curly chest hair, softly stroking his belly and insinuating her tongue into the small, highly sensitive dip of his belly button. Then, using her face and lips alone, she rubbed her slim, aquiline nose against his dense pubic hair, moaning softly as she did so, before moving lower still to gently ease both of his testicles between her lips and into her mouth, licking and wantonly sucking the dark, wrinkled skin of his scrotal sac whilst caressing his rigid penis until he thought he would die with the intense pleasure it afforded him.

After a minute or two of mind-blowing bliss, during which Isaac felt to be on the point of coming, the growing realisation of it making him squirm and moan out loud for Crystal to stop before it was too late, she finally released her oral grasp on his inflamed sex. Isaac, brought back in the nick of time from the sexual precipice, allowed himself an inward sigh of relief, tinged with a *soupçon* of regret at the loss of Crystal's warm, expert lips and fingers against the most private portions of his anatomy. But regret soon turned to fresh waves of lust as the beautiful, smooth-skinned temptress rose above him like an Egyptian sphinx, straight, ebony hair hanging loose and free to her waist, shoulders back and breasts thrust proudly forwards as she squatted above him with the ease and grace of an African native.

'Now for the good bit,' she murmured, her voice lazy and low, laden with erotic promise.

'What, another one?' Isaac gasped, his breathing ragged with emotion and his eyes on fire as he feasted greedily on those glorious boobs, curvy belly, slender thighs stretched wide apart and flushed, gaping pussy lips.

Crystal allowed herself a smile at Isaac's attempt at humour and then, biting her lip in concentration, lowered her wet pussy to Isaac's erect cock and slowly and sensually moved backwards and forwards along its length, hands resting lightly on her hips as she balanced on her heels, sighing with pleasure at the dry, animal warmth of it against her yearning cunt. After a while she began to tremble with exertion and with the sharp, biting need to be penetrated by this powerful, potent prick that she was so cruelly teasing between her strong, sweat-sheened thighs. Breathing quickly, almost out of control, she swiftly changed position so that, while still poised temptingly above Isaac's cock, she rested comfortably on her knees, which were placed one each side of his tense, panting body. Then, raising herself up a little and closing her eyes tight shut, she grasped Isaac's prick in both hands and nudged it insistently against the opening to her pussy. Suddenly, with a grunt of satisfaction, she impaled herself fully on the erect phallus, sinking down on the hot, turgid flesh until it filled the deepest recesses of her sex, whimpering and squealing like a woman possessed.

'I'm going to fuck the arse off you now, you beautiful bastard!' she moaned through gritted teeth, writhing and gyrating her hips and arse to enjoy to the full the sensation of being so completely full of hot, sinewy cock. Then, grabbing hold of Isaac's pelvis with both hands, she raised and lowered her trembling body, sheathing and unsheathing his glistening prick at a powerful, ever-increasing rate, slamming down onto him until she thought she'd split in two whilst crying with passion and the pure, animal joy of being so completely, alarmingly penetrated.

Maddened with lust and on the brink of orgasm, Isaac gazed hotly at his lover through narrowed eyes, totally enthralled and driven almost to distraction by the immense power and potency of her feminine beauty and sexual skill. He gazed entranced at her long, shiny black hair as it whipped wildly about her ecstatic face and body; at the way her big, glistening breasts bounced and jiggled as though with lives of their own; at her long, slender thigh muscles, which pulsed and shone like those of a dancer or a female athlete as she moved above him.

And as he watched her, head thrown back and eyes squeezed tight shut, moaning unintelligibly and breathing rapidly through her open mouth, he felt that, despite the ultimate and undeniable closeness of their bodies, she was somehow lost to him, abandoned and floating free in an erotic universe of her own creation. But then, as though sensing Isaac's momentary disquiet, Crystal powered down onto his cock one last, final time, opening her beautiful, dark eyes as she did so and gazing directly into his with an expression of such intense, unquestioning adoration that his fears melted and vanished like snow in springtime. As she moaned and shouted out loud, trembling uncontrollably as she straddled his body, impaled on his sex as though on a fleshy spit, he felt the muscles of her vagina tense and relax around him with the fluttering rapidity of a butterfly's wings.

As though in loving response to Crystal's heavenly climax, Isaac felt the tightness in his balls achieve epic proportions, precipitating their inevitable flood of hot seed through his penis and into her pulsing, orgasmic vagina in long, rhythmic jets of semen. Isaac too shouted with joy at the mind-blowing reality of his own longed-for sexual release, tensing his body and clenching his fists at his sides until, at long last, the intensity of the sensation subsided and he relaxed completely against the warm, rumpled bed, bathed in sweat and as limp as a rag doll. 'I'm pleased to see you, too . . .' he finally managed to mutter, gazing up with a sleepy smile at the gorgeous, dishevelled goddess crouched above him, grinning down at him with glossy ebony hair awry and partly covering her face as she continued to hold his slowly softening penis a willing captive in the warm embrace of her pussy.

'Thank you for the snake,' she whispered, reaching down and pulling the silver bangle from beneath her pillow, sliding it onto her wrist with a smile of pleasure, 'I love it and I'll wear it always . . . Anyway, buster, enough of all that romantic stuff,' she laughed suddenly, eyes shining with happiness as her mood changed to one of bubbling excitement at the prospect of the day to follow, especially now that it was to be spent with Isaac. 'Let's shower and have some breakfast. I could eat a horse after all that exercise.'

Slowly rising to his elbows, Isaac treated her to a wide smile and a lazy, amused wink. 'Now, where have I heard that before . . .?'

* * *

'Buon giorno, mia cara,' Fernando whispered sleepily, raising himself painfully onto one elbow and kissing the comatose negress tenderly on her one exposed cheek. No response, not even a flicker of recognition. 'Good morning, sweetheart,' the chef repeated, rubbing his eyes and squinting at his stainless steel Rolex, a much-treasured birthday present from his estranged wife. 'Hey, do you know what the time is? Six-thirty already. Time to get my backside into gear and start preparing the breakfasts.' As he spoke, Fernando felt a huge, irresistible yawn well up inside him and as he gave vent to it, his elbow gave way and he flopped back onto the bed, wearily closing his eyes once more, 'Holy mother of God,' he blasphemed softly to himself, swiftly crossing himself to eradicate the inevitable bad luck that such foul language would be sure to elicit. 'I feel as though I've slept for about five minutes, if that . . .' He gave a deep, shuddering sigh and folded his hands across his belly. Why was it, he thought with a stab of regret, that having a good time generally ended in tears the next morning. The Good Lord, in His wisdom, must have had some greater plan in mind when he imbued the humble grape with the ability to intoxicate when fermented and, thus, bring about the symptoms he was currently experiencing. Headache, dry mouth, faint nausea, etc.

Fernando opened his eyes again and turned his head to one side to gaze at the beautiful black superstar, fast asleep and apparently unrousable, beside him in the bed. *His* bed. Fernando's. The ordinary, common or garden chef at High Links Hall. He still couldn't believe his luck in managing to so thoroughly seduce the gorgeous and formidable Sheba in the way that he had. Especially when all that this previously unimaginable feat had seemed to require, it seemed, was a couple of bottles of 1982 Burgundy and the odd honeyed word or two. Well, maybe more than one or two. Come to think of it, he had rather laid it on with a trowel, he remembered with a pang of guilt.

He chose not to dwell on the possibility that the woman had been too drunk to give much of a damn about what was happening to her, still less who it was happening with. Or that, in the absence of someone a little more eligible, Fernando had provided a welcome escape from the trials and tribulations of the previous twenty-four hours with his easy wit, copious supplies of good-quality booze and rampant libido.

Having said all that, however, Sheba had certainly given a pretty good impression of a woman having a bloody good time while they cavorted together, stark bollock naked, in Fernando's small, tidy bedroom in the early hours of Boxing Day morning. What a picture they must have presented, he thought with a lusty chuckle, momentarily forgetting his headache as he began to experience the first, unmistakable stirrings in his groin. Like Puck himself or some other mischievous satyr, making free with a dusky, coal-eyed maiden in the middle of some mythical, Shakespearean forest. The difference in their heights and physical builds hadn't seemed to matter a jot in the full fury of their sexual hunger. In fact, Fernando had found that his own small but well-built, hirsute and rather swarthy frame, when placed in loving contrast with Sheba's immensely long, languid black curves, had been intensely erotic to the point where he'd had to struggle to prevent himself from climaxing too soon and spoiling the fun.

Dreamily, Fernando placed his right hand between his

legs and grasped his erect penis which, generously proportioned at the best of times, even when flaccid, had achieved still more lavish dimensions while he'd been in the process of recalling the greedy excesses of his and Sheba's post-party lovemaking.

'*Madre* . . .' he whispered gruffly under his breath, beginning, slowly at first, to slide his fist along the full, iron-hard length of his throbbing cock, 'that was one crazy fuck . . .' Beginning now to breath more rapidly, he remembered how Sheba had climbed on top of him, naked skin gleaming like black silk, and rammed herself hard onto his hot, pulsing phallus, snarling like a tiger and muttering obscenities at him under her breath, some of which even he hadn't previously been party to. She'd fucked him like a rattlesnake and then, just as he was about to ejaculate into her, egged on by the full force of their joint passion, she'd lazily rolled off him and taken his prick in her mouth, licking and sucking him with such consummate skill and sensitivity that he'd managed to enjoy a further ten minutes or so of delicious sensation before finally being compelled to shoot his load, aiming it directly into her generous mouth and down her throat while she'd gulped greedily, milking him of every last drop of warm emission.

His head filled with mental pictures of their frantic fucking, Fernando turned once more to gaze at the naked, sleeping woman beside him, her silky body obscured by the bedclothes, and he felt himself slowly but surely being overtaken by an insidious flush of renewed desire to possess her. Raising himself once more onto his elbow, eyes glowing with anticipatory lust, he reached out a trembling hand and gently pulled the sheets away from her body until she was finally revealed to him, lying stretched out on her front, as naked and erotic as a Babylonian temple dancer. Biting his lip, he only just managed to stop himself from crying out with pleasure at the glorious sight, which would surely wake her and thus spoil his erotic little plan.

Feasting his eyes on her ebony-black, sleeping form, he drank in the full, majestic power of her beauty, thrilling to the way her full breasts pressed against the bed, bulging voluptuously in gleaming, chocolatey half-moons above her slim ribcage. Continuing their sensual journey along her smooth, satiny back, his eyes dropped to her slender waist and the generous flare of her gorgeous fleshy hips and truly spectacular bottom, which was as full and luscious as a pair of ripe watermelons, beneath which her unbelievably long legs seemed to stretch on forever, her elegant toes hooked casually over the end of the bed.

At each fresh discovery, Fernando felt his penis throb and swell to even greater dimensions until it seemed to leap and pulse in his hand as though with a life of its own. Holding his breath and trembling with nervous anticipation he decided, then and there, to give up the unequal struggle with his conscience. Climbing as carefully as he could onto his hands and knees, being sure not to wake the languid black goddess, the image of whom was filling the very core of him with boiling lust, he shuffled as close to her as he dare, erect penis bouncing eagerly against his hairy belly. Then, as tenderly as he could manage given the reality of his galloping sexual need, he parted her shapely legs, thus revealing an inch or two of her long, dusky slit which, amazingly, seemed already to be damp and slick with seeping love juice. He gazed, entranced, at the slightly parted genital lips, licking his lips hungrily, then almost jumped out of his skin with shock as the subject of his fascination suddenly moaned. The sound seemed to emanate from deep within her and, despite her comatose state, she sensually undulated her long body against the warm sheet, wriggling her gorgeous, curvy arse so that the smooth, glowing flesh jiggled delightfully, raising it up a little from the surface of the bed so that even more of her bare, glowing pussy lips were revealed to him.

When he'd recovered sufficiently from the experience to proceed, Fernando, driven almost to the point of insanity by this new, wholly unexpected turn in the proceedings, climbed gingerly on top of the beautiful negress, straddling her thighs. Then, with a sigh of illicit pleasure, he grabbed his swollen prick and placed the hot, engorged tip of it between her arse cheeks, easing the fiery glans slowly back and forth along her deep, shadowy cleft, holding his breath as he did so for fear of shooting his load there and then, so intense were the sensations coursing through his veins. At one point, maddened with lust, he reached down and parted the big, dusky cheeks to reveal the tiny puckered dimple of her arsehole, considering for one brief, insane moment whether he should risk throwing caution to the winds and plunder her there and then, forcing himself down and into the tight, prick-hugging channel of her most personal and private part. Considering this to be beyond the pale, however, especially given that the owner of the arsehole in question was unable to give her consent to such action, being lost in the arms of Morpheus, he allowed his inflamed member to drop lower and rub instead against her wet, gaping pussy lips.

To Fernando's delight and utter amazement, Sheba moaned again in her sleep, wriggling her bottom and placing her thighs even further apart, thus making it even easier for him to slip inside until his full erection was lovingly ensheathed in the warm, tender grip of aroused womanflesh. Slowly at first, fearful still that she might wake up and bawl him out for taking such obscene advantage of her, he sensually circled his powerful hips and thighs, his fleshy belly rubbing lasciviously against her arse as he felt himself push deeper and deeper inside her velvety cunt. Then, surprised and emboldened by the way she seemed to be moving against him, lewdly raising her arse to greet his giant, pendulous balls, wriggling rudely and rubbing deliciously against his flushed, wrinkled scrotum, he began to piston slowly back and forth inside her, his tempo and lustful anticipation increasing with each wanton wiggle of her voluptuous bottom.

He could smell her now as he began to pump into her with greater and greater abandon. A potent cocktail of Chanel, fresh sweat, clean hair and the musky, feral scent of juiced-up cunt. He almost swooned when she moaned and whimpered once more in her sleep, subconsciously spreading her thighs still further apart and rhythmically jabbing her gleaming, jiggling arse up to meet his strengthening thrusts like a sex-starved she-wolf on heat.

By now, Fernando's mind and senses were reeling with the wild excesses of his great good fortune in having discovered this amazing, rampantly sexual woman. To have been allowed the opportunity to fuck the beautiful, horny creature at all had been enough of a treat in itself, but to fuck her while she was still asleep and yet evidently sufficiently aware of what was happening to her to respond in such an overtly lascivious and randy manner was almost beyond his comprehension. Feverishly clasping her fleshy hips as though his life depended on it, he fucked the stunningly erotic Sheba as he'd never fucked a woman before. The smell of cunt and the slick whisper of squelchy friction as he rode her increased the heat of his flaring passion until, at long last, he ceased his frantic coupling and quickly withdrew his huge, glistening penis so that it flopped wetly against his groin. Then, grunting with the power of his imminent release, he tensed his body and screwed his eyes tight shut, clasping his throbbing prick whilst poised above her sweat-sheened body like a cobra about to strike. Opening his eyes once more and breathing deeply through flared nostrils he watched, fascinated, as gob after milky gob of warm semen spurted from the tip of his jerking member, landing on the smooth, flawless plains of Sheba's perfect body, its pale translucence a stunning contrast to the mahogany silk of her shoulders, back and curvy arse.

After a minute or two during which Fernando, sighing deeply with satisfaction, allowed his breathing to return to normal, a contented peace returned once more to the small room. Allowing himself a wide, lazy smile of sexual fulfilment he carefully dismounted, kneeling on the bed beside the graceful, supine form of the woman he'd just made such passionate love to and gently wiping the spilled semen from her warm skin with a handful of tissues from the box on the floor beside the bed. When he'd finished, he thoughtfully covered her naked, softly breathing body with the bedclothes once more and stood up beside the bed, yawning and stretching, before retrieving his hastily discarded clothes from the night before, crossing jauntily to the other side of the room to fetch a set of fresh underclothes from the top drawer of a small wooden chest.

It was amazing, he thought to himself with a happy chuckle,

what a damn good fuck could do for a man. Even his hangover seemed to have deserted him, annihilated by the heat of his recent passion. Only yesterday he'd been feeling as gloomy as a wet Sunday afternoon, faced with the prospect of spending a working Christmas all on his own without the love of a good woman to warm the cockles of his heart. And then, completely out of the blue, the delectable Sheba – world-famous, not to say notorious, rock star, adored and lusted after by millions – had meandered provocatively into his life, offering him any number of naughty games and shameless sexual shenanigans without so much as a second thought. I mean, it wasn't even as if he was Richard Gere or somebody. That, maybe, he could have understood.

Buttoning his white chef's coat and knotting a small, checked kerchief around his neck he bent over Sheba's sleeping form and kissed her tenderly on her smooth shoulder. 'Farewell, precious,' he whispered softly into her ear. 'Pleasant dreams . . .' Turning and making his way on silent feet to the door, he left the room, closing it quietly behind him and heading with renewed vigour towards the peace and sanctity of his early-morning kitchen, humming softly to himself as he went.

A tall, statuesque figure stood in the entrance to the dining room at High Links, swaying slightly and dressed somewhat inappropriately, bearing in mind the circumstances, in an ankle-length fur coat and Ray Ban shades. After a moment or two during which she peered painfully around the large, gently buzzing room, bright with winter sunshine and fragrant with fresh coffee and warm toast, Sheba made her way rather gingerly, given the height and general unsuitability of her black patent ankle boots, towards the wall table where Crystal and Isaac sat together, companiably enjoying a late, Boxing Day breakfast.

'Any chance of a coffee?' she groaned, dragging a spare chair from the nearest, unoccupied table and plonking herself down on it, wearily resting her elbows on the linen cloth in front of her and placing her black, close-shorn head in her beringed hands. 'Make it strong and black, and laced with painkillers if you have any. Christ! Was that a session last night or wasn't it? Let me tell you, babe, that goddamn chef of yours has a wine cellar like you wouldn't believe. After you'd gone and the rest of the flunkeys had sloped off, he and I sat up 'til 4 a.m. sampling it. So if the eggs are a little overcooked and the toast's a teensy bit singed around the edges . . . Well, don't say I didn't warn you. Anyway, just lead me quietly outside and shoot me, would you? Stand me against a wall and put a bullet through my head, why don't you? Put a poor, reckless broad out of her misery . . .' Sheba groaned again, sinking slowly to the table. Her accent, which only the previous night in Fernando's kitchen had been well modulated and appealingly accented with a subtle though unmistakable hint of Gallic, had mysteriously assumed a hefty dose of its former Texan twang.

To make matters worse, she was feeling distinctly sore around the nether regions. She knew she'd subjected herself to quite a bashing with the little Italian, but nothing she couldn't handle. Hell, she'd eaten guys like Fernando for breakfast before now, so why the mysteriously aching pussy? Somewhere in the far reaches of her consciousness was the vague recollection of something happening to her which hadn't been entirely within her control, but she was damned if she could put her finger on what it was. Shrugging dismissively to herself, she put the matter to the back of her mind.

Reaching across to an adjoining table and filching from it an extra coffee cup and saucer, Crystal poured a generous measure of the fragrant brew into it and pushed it across to the suffering negress, exchanging amused glances with Isaac who, forewarned of Sheba's presence within the establishment, grinned widely and stirred an extra swirl of cream into his own cup.

Sheba, as though in slow motion, winced theatrically as she hoisted herself upright and carefully took the small, porcelain cup between thumb and forefinger. Then she pursed her trembling lips in readiness and tentatively treated her poor, hungover nervous system to its first, reviving caffeine fix of the day. 'Ah!' she sighed, instantly cheered by the dark, aromatic liquid as it slipped smoothly down her throat, barely touching the sides, 'that's a whole heap better. The guy who invented the coffee bean deserves nothing less than the Nobel Prize, and you can tell him I said so.'

Almost choking on his coffee, Isaac began to chuckle. 'For starters, babe, coffee was discovered, not invented, and secondly, the guy who did the deed for which we're all eternally grateful turned up his toes and shuffled off this mortal coil several hundred years ago.'

After a brief pause during which she sat bolt upright and motionless, coffee cup poised midway between saucer and mouth, which was wide open with surprise, Sheba raised her Ray Bans to the top of her head, squinted briefly against the sunlight, and turned to peer blearily in the direction of the disconcertingly familiar male voice. 'Holy shit!' she cried in a piercing falsetto which would have done justice to the high, ear-numbing shriek of an adult screech owl, causing several heads to turn curiously in her direction, many of them raising their eyebrows in recognition of this famous female addition to the High Links guest list. 'Would you goddamn credit it! If it ain't Isaac fucking Mallory!' Momentarily forgetting her hangover, Sheba put down her cup so that it clattered unsteadily on its delicate saucer and reached across to the unsuspecting fellow rock singer, wrapping him in a fluffy bear hug and showering him with big, wet kisses. 'So, Ike, how're you doin'?' she cried, relinquishing her hold on him and settling back in her chair with a vivacity and sparkle which would have seemed impossible a moment or two before. She leaned towards him, her furry elbows resting elegantly on the table in front of her and her hands forming a graceful pyramid beneath her chin, her polished, blood-red talons as bright and shiny as her inky almond cats' eyes.

'More to the point,' she added with a grin, 'what the fuck are you doin' having breakfast in this jumped-up, out of the way excuse for a beauty parlour in the middle of the fuckin' sticks? I'd've thought it was way short of your normal scene, Isaac. What went wrong, babe? You can tell Auntie Sheba.' With an expression which managed to combine mischief with overt eroticism, she leaned across and tickled him playfully under his stubbly chin with the tips of her scarlet-painted nails, a feature which reduced both he and Sheba to hysterical, childish giggles.

'I take it you two have met before.' Crystal, slightly nonplussed, wasn't at all sure she appreciated the barely concealed sexual tension behind the chummy goings-on between her lover and the predatory black tigress in the animal-skin coat. 'Am I right?'

Isaac, instinctively aware of the slight chill which had pervaded Crystal's demeanour since Sheba first started playing her customarily salacious little games with him, patted the latter good-naturedly on the shoulder, being especially careful to give the impression that the whole scene meant nothing to him, and turned to wink suggestively at the vaguely disgruntled Crystal. 'Sheba and I go way back, sweetheart. We did the odd charity gig together back in the early eighties, and last year we both appeared live on *Top of the Pops* on the same night. The audience ratings soared, apparently. Never was too sure which of us was responsible for that . . .' He paused, chuckling wickedly. Sheba shrieked with mock rage and biffed him on the shoulder.

'Anyway,' Isaac continued, recoiling from the blow and turning once more to its deliverer, 'in answer to your question, Sheba, I'm here to spend some much-needed time with my favourite woman here.' With this, he snaked a sinuous arm around Crystal's shoulders and pulled her to him with a covetous leer, planting a generous stage kiss on her forehead. Crystal, instantly placated, smiled happily back at him.

'Well I'll be damned!' Sheba exclaimed, eyes shining with pleasure, a wide smile curving her, full lips. 'Two of my favourite people – well, one and a half, maybe. I only just got acquainted with Crystal – hitched up together like a coupla' love birds. Now, ain't that sweet?' Head solicitously on one side, Sheba treated them both to one of her best maiden aunt smiles, eliciting an oath from Isaac and a raspberry from Crystal before all three of them fell about laughing at the incongruity of it all.

223

'So,' Isaac said at last, regaining his composure, 'what brings you to this "excuse for a beauty parlour in the middle of the sticks", Sheba? And even more to the point, how come you're here all on your own? What happened to that seedy bunch of freeloaders you normally hang out with? Decided enough's enough and done a runner? The healthy regime too much for them, perhaps?'

'Isaac, baby, you may well ask,' Sheba replied, suddenly remembering her headache and clutching her fevered brow whilst taking another, therapeutic swig of now-cold coffee. 'The miserable bunch of suckers didn't even make it here in the first place. Business elsewhere, it would seem. Business, my ass! Some toffee-nosed English fucking viscount or other invited every damn one of them to a week-long orgy at his country seat in Lincolnshire or someplace. On-tap bimbos, hot from some metropolitan whorehouse he makes a point of stopping by at when he's in town, and enough booze and drugs to supply the entire US army for a year. The suave bastard invited me along too, but I told him to go stuff himself. Hell! I'd rather die than spend Christmas with a bunch of bare-assed reprobates, going at it like goddamn rabbits while stuffing coke up their snouts with both fucking hands.'

Sheba paused for a moment, mid-diatribe, sniffing slightly and looking distinctly sorry for herself. 'I mean, I ask you, Ike – would you have gone in my place?'

Isaac, shuffling his feet and gazing silently down at his clasped hands, pretended to look sheepish. Then, slowly looking up, he treated her to one of his sunniest smiles, making it clear that he'd been teasing. 'To be perfectly honest, Sheba, I can't think of anywhere I'd less like to be, especially in the circumstances you've just described. There, does that make you feel happier?' Unbeknown to the two women, the fingers of both his right and his left hands were safely crossed, cunningly concealed beneath the generous folds of the white linen table cloth.

'Phew!' Sheba sighed, 'you really had me going there for a moment. Anyway, to make matters worse, Ike, I arrived here without a stitch of clothing or a cosmetic brush to my name. As Crystal here's my witness.' She glanced resignedly at Crystal who nodded, shrugging her shoulders and raising her eyes heavenwards in silent commiseration. 'Left the whole fuckin' lot outside my front door back in Knightsbridge. Christ! What a goddamn bimbo! I'd almost give Madonna a run for her money, what do you say?'

Isaac drew in his breath and winced as though in pain. 'I'd say, be sure not to come out with slanderous bullshit like that when the lady in question's within earshot, eh? You may end up with more than you bargained for. Get my drift?'

'Reading you loud and clear, pal,' Sheba replied, quaking with mock fear. 'Thanks for the tip. By the way,' she continued, turning to Crystal and taking a somewhat crumpled packet of French cigarettes from the capacious pocket of her fur coat, placing one of them casually between her lips and lighting it with a stainless steel Zippo, 'what time did you say you knock off today?'

'I didn't. But, since you ask, twelve-thirty. I was thinking of taking an early lunch and then sidling off for a mammoth walk across the fields. It's absolutely gorgeous out there. Almost too good to be true – like one of those corny Christmas cards you send your parents with sunshine and snow and cute little robins . . .'

Sheba took a long pull on her cigarette and sniggered. 'Speak for yourself, kid. Last time I sent my parents a Christmas card I was still in knee socks.'

Crystal looked at her and grinned. 'Present company accepted. Anyway, now that Isaac's here, everything's changed a bit . . .' She paused, biting her lip a little awkwardly and looking straight at Isaac. 'Don't s'pose you fancy joining me, do you?'

Before Isaac had a chance to reply, Sheba jabbed her cigarette out in the ashtray and rounded on Crystal with something approaching panic in her voice. 'Hey, wait a minute! What about me? Can't I come, too?' Turning on the full theatricals, at which she was infinitely talented, she grabbed hold of Crystal's arm, raised her Ray Bans to the top of her head once more and gazed beseechingly into the other woman's laughing eyes. 'I mean, I'll be lonely here all on my own.'

Crystal started to reply, grimacing at the towering black patent ankle boots and picturing their owner staggering miserably across the frozen wastes of Somerset in them, when what she'd rather be doing was propping up the bar in some flashy nightclub in town, preferably surrounded by adoring males. 'Well . . .'

Aware of the direction this was leading, Isaac coughed and swiftly intercepted. 'Er, if I might be allowed to get my oar in for a moment, I have a proposal to make.'

'Hey, would you listen to this! Ike's about to propose!' Sheba placed her elbows on the table and leaned provocatively towards Isaac, fluttering her eyelashes and allowing her fur to fall open, thus revealing a scintillating eyeful of cleavage. 'So, babe, which one of us is the lucky lady, huh?'

'Neither of you, sweetie-pie. At least not yet, anyway.' He turned and winked at Crystal, who winked back, unsure of the seriousness of what he'd just said, but thrilled to bits nevertheless that he'd said it at all. 'I think I'd better explain,' Isaac continued. 'Apart from using the postponed Aussie tour to spend a few days with my woman here, I'm in this neck of the woods for another reason, too. There's something I have to check out some time over the next couple of days, so it might as well be this afternoon. It's as good a time as any. The snow's not too thick at the moment so it should be okay for driving. What do you say we make it a threesome and go check it out together?'

Quick as a flash, Sheba's face broke into a wide, happy grin and she sat back in her seat, arms folded with evident satisfaction. 'You can count me in, lover-boy. What about you, Crystal? Still sold on that walk?'

Crystal, who hadn't taken her eyes off Isaac since he'd mentioned the other, as yet unknown reason for his visit, looked pensive. But then, to Isaac's evident relief, she too began to smile. 'Walk be buggered,' she said. 'This sounds like an opportunity not to be missed. What have you been up to since I last saw you, you secretive swine? Hope it's something I'm going to approve of.'

'Oh yes, you'll approve okay, Crystal. But you'll just have to wait and see what the surprise is all about, won't you?' Reaching over, Isaac tickled Crystal under the chin, which made her giggle like a delighted child. 'Meanwhile, lover, you have work to do and I for one would kill for an hour or two in that award-winning pool of yours. As for you, Sheba, I reckon a few hours' sleep should do the trick.

'And so, ladies,' he continued, standing up and stretching

his arms lazily above his head with a contented yawn, 'I'll meet you both here for lunch at twelve-thirty sharp. Okay?'

Nodding mutely, there was little Crystal and Sheba could do except gaze obediently after Isaac's departing form as he ambled from the room, turning several female heads as he went.

'There goes a guy who also could use a few hours' sleep,' Sheba muttered, almost to herself, as she watched him disappear from view. 'Preferably in the arms of yours truly. Not that we'd be doing much sleeping . . . But I suppose we ought to do what the gentleman says,' she added, turning to Crystal with a slightly puzzled grin. 'Agreed?'

Crystal smiled back, polishing off the dregs of her coffee. 'Agreed. But hands off, okay, unless I say so.'

'Spoilsport,' Sheba whispered, leaning over and giving Crystal a tender kiss on her smooth cheek, just to show she was more than willing to play the game by the rules – whatever they may turn out to be . . .

Chapter Eight

The wintry afternoon sunshine crystallised the freshly fallen
snow, making it glitter and sparkle like a king's ransom and
illuminating the few, feathery flakes which continued to fall
from the clear, ice-blue sky. Those which tumbled lazily
against the windscreen of the black Porsche, meandering its
way carefully through the virgin-white country lanes, melted
against the warm glass before being swept away by the
forward motion of the car. From the interior, rising on the
still air and combining with the throaty rumble of the powerful
engine, came the sound of laughter and singing, the voices
joined in a melodic three-part harmony.

> 'I'm dreaming of a white Christmas,
> Just like the ones we used to know,
> Where the treetops glisten, and children listen,
> To hear sleigh bells in the snow . . .'

'Hey, hey, wait a minute, wait a minute! Stop changing
the goddamn subject, will you? Much as I love to sing, it still
doesn't answer my question, Ike. Which is, where in God's
name are you taking us? We've been going for at least half an
hour and we still haven't hit civilisation yet.' Bending her

head to peer through the rear window as they reached a T-junction, Sheba spotted a road sign indicating the city of Bath one way and Bristol the other. Turning right onto the main road, Isaac headed for Bristol.

Sheba smiled, nodding sagely, and curled her spectacularly long legs under her on the narrow back seat, wrapping her huge fur coat more tightly around herself and turning up the generous collar so that it covered her ears. 'So, that's it, is it? We're headed for Bristol. But why? What's so special about Bristol, for Chrissakes? I mean, let's face it, Ike, it ain't the most happening place in the northern hemisphere, now is it?'

'For fuck's sake, Sheba, will you turn the volume down? Or off, preferably! Any more whingeing and I swear I shall be forced to strangle you. It's been almost non-stop since we left High Links!'

Suitably chastened, Sheba pouted and shrank back into her coat. 'Sorry, honey. Just curious, that's all. I mean, it's not too much to ask, is it? All I want to know is . . .'

'Shut it, woman!' Isaac bellowed from the front seat, mildly irritated but more amused than angry at Sheba's child-like desire to wring the truth from him about where they were going. 'Just trust me, will you? I've already told you that this is a many-faceted mystery tour we're on here. In the short term, we're going to have a great Boxing Day, and in the long term, the place we're heading for *may*, just *may*, be to your professional advantage. Now, will you kindly drop the subject?'

'Okay, okay, I get the message!' Sheba yelled back, folding her arms across her chest like a truculent child.

Crystal, snug and warm in the front passenger seat, turned to face the beautiful negress. She was keenly aware of the other woman's unslaked curiosity and smiled at her to show there were no hard feelings. 'I'm just as desperate to know where we're going as you are, Sheba, and I've got a feeling we haven't too much longer to wait before we finally find out.'

Turning round to face forwards once more, she gazed at the sprawling, wintry city-scape spread out before them like an architect's model. From their vantage point, as they drove down into the city itself, she could just see the greyish glimmer of the River Avon as it wound past warehouses and disused factories, through the trendy, recently gentrified waterfront area with its shops and restaurants and on to where it joined the mouth of the River Severn. Giving full vent to her undeniably vivid imagination, she even fancied she could just make out the graceful curves of the Severn Bridge in the far distance, glinting in the sunlight. But, reluctantly, she was forced to put this remarkable, not to say impossible, visual feat down to overexcitement.

Crystal liked Bristol. She preferred it to London, she had to admit. Despite the fact that much of the elegant Georgian architecture which had once graced the city centre had been felled to make way for the ubiquitous roundabouts and one-way systems, within whose confusing confines Crystal had managed to lose herself on more than one occasion, it was still possessed of a warm, characteristic charm all of its own, as well as that particular brand of life and vibrancy peculiar to university cities throughout the whole of Great Britain.

Bristol was a city in which Crystal felt very much at home and she was more than a little intrigued at the notion of Isaac choosing it as the venue for whatever scheme or business venture – she couldn't be sure which – that he was about to unfold before her. She was sorry in a way that she and Isaac weren't alone, but then silently castigated herself for being such a mean cow as to resent Sheba's presence there with them. After all, the rock goddess who only the day before had given such an award-winning performance as the mother of all arch-bitches, had turned out to be a sentimental pussycat at heart, albeit one with a string of neuroses as long as the M5 motorway. Screwed-up she may be, but Sheba was a woman who knew how to let her hair down and have fun – her conduct the previous night had established that – and Crystal knew that the three of them were going to wind up having more than their fair share of jollity and high jinks before the day was through. What she didn't know at this stage, however, was quite how much, or even how the jollity and high jinks would become manifest . . .

'Hey, Isaac, we look to be heading away from all the interesting looking bits,' Sheba called from the back seat, unable to bite her lip a moment longer as she witnessed them leaving the modern, cosmeticised part of the city behind them. 'You know, the shops and restaurants and stuff. Did we take a wrong turn or something? Thrown a right when we should have thrown a left?'

Without taking his eyes off the road, Isaac smiled a smile of resignation and gestured rudely over his shoulder at her. 'Not you again! Who rattled your cage this time? I said trust me, didn't I? So, give me a break and stop asking leading questions. I know exactly where we're going and, what's more, we're almost there. Just around this corner, in fact.'

Ignoring the good-natured banter between Isaac and Sheba, Crystal had been watching her favourite English city unfold past the Porsche's low-slung front-seat passenger window. It was all so quiet and seemingly peaceful on this sunny Boxing Day afternoon. Like a grand old man taking an afternoon snooze after too much cold turkey and bubble and squeak. In fact, it was the most deserted she'd ever seen it. With a little flicker of excitement, she'd noticed straight away when they'd left the main through roads and begun to descend into the less fashionable part of the city, heading towards the river and the old, disused warehouses. On previous afternoons off, strolling around the narrow streets as a refreshing antidote to trailing through crowded shops and department stores on some unfavourable shopping expedition, Crystal had gazed up at the gaunt, brick-fronted buildings crowding in on either side of her and imagined them as they might have been in the past – teeming with life and a kind of raw vigour, ringing with the sound of bells and workman's tools and ripe Bristolian accents as the men and women of the quayside went about their daily business.

This afternoon was no exception. Driving slowly past in style rather than walking by on foot, held a willing captive in the safe, warm cocoon of her lover's Porsche, Crystal still peered in wonder at those tall, imposing facades and tried to imagine, not for the first time, exactly why Isaac had brought them there and what he had it in mind to show them. She watched, ever more intrigued, as Isaac changed smoothly down into second gear and pulled the car off the narrow street and into a cobbled gap between two warehouses, switched off the ignition and turned to look at her, his face wreathed in smiles. Crystal smiled back, eyes bright with excitement. In the split second it had taken for the Porsche to turn off the road Crystal had spotted a large, painted sign fixed high up on one of the buildings. It was rather like an old pub sign;

slightly battered yet welcoming, the somewhat naive illustration of boats and riverside ephemera characteristically faded as though from decades of harsh weathering from the sun and rain, snow and wind. Above the picture itself had been painted the words, *Harbour Music*, in a style in keeping with the general image.

Crystal, hugging herself with glee, hardly dared speak for fear of being wrong in her steadily dawning supposition, 'It's a wonderful sign . . .' she said rather haltingly. 'Where did you get it?'

'Oh, Max and I found it propped up against the wall in the outside lav. Someone had obviously taken it down and put it in there when the old warehouse went bust, so it had been there for some time. Anyway, all we did was clean it up a bit and have the name printed across the top. I managed to find this crazy old artist to do it for us. A guy in his eighties. Lived all his life, man and boy, just around the corner from here. Anyway, glad you like it, I had a feeling you would.'

'Like it?' Crystal said, her voice a little more assured, 'I love it. Who's Max?'

'Max Dupont, sage, wit and general ne'er-do-well; thirty-year-old son of a French father and English mother; lived half his life in Nice and the other half in Camberwell; my esteemed studio manager and at least half if not more of the combined brains behind this whole operation.'

Sheba, who until now had remained silent during the dialogue taking place in the front of the car, pursed her lips in a resounding wolf whistle. 'Amen! Whew, sounds like quite a guy. I think I like him already. When do we get to meet him? Must remember to freshen my lipstick.'

Isaac peered over his shoulder at her and grinned

mischievously. 'Maybe sooner than you think, sweetie. When I told him you were coming he insisted on joining us for dinner, seems he's a fan of yours or something.' He winked conspiratorially at Crystal, who couldn't help experiencing a modest swell of relief that they were to be joined by another male – especially one who, in theory at least, evidently met with Sheba's wholehearted approval.

Sheba narrowed her eyes and growled like a wild cat, then licked her lips with erotic relish, failing to conceal the excitement evident in her flushed cheeks and nervous hands. 'I think I'm beginning to like him even more. Come on, what are we waiting for? Let's go check this place out.'

Inside, Isaac's recording studio was everything Crystal could have hoped for and more besides. Though scrubbed clean, the brick walls lining the large, rectangular space which constituted the ground floor had been left in their natural state, russet-red and unpainted, the mortar patched up in places where it had become crumbly with age, but sound nevertheless. Large iron columns, as straight and substantial as the trunks of elms, stood at measured intervals, holding up huge, heavy crossbeams which, in turn, supported the vast expanse of ceiling. Here and there around the walls were those old-fashioned, lumpen radiators, coiled and heavy like so many boa constrictors, that Crystal remembered so well from her convent schooldays. At any moment she expected to see, out of the corner of her eye, the dusty flutter of black habit as a nun appeared and disappeared again behind one of the columns.

All the ironwork, including the radiators, had been carefully sandblasted and left to gleam dully grey in the subtle light cast by the battery of strategically placed and largely invisible spots, ranged around the walls and ceiling. Also thoughtfully illuminated were the anchors and rusty boathooks, huge cogs and wheels from ancient winches and faded sepia photographs of long-dead sea captains and harbour employees. Men who had decades since turned up their toes and gone to meet that great Admiral of the Fleet in the sky. Crystal smiled up at the characterful, bewhiskered countenance of one such weathered old gentlemen, noting how, despite the age and quality of the print, his eyes twinkled with merry mischief through the curling smoke from his clay pipe, seemingly undimmed by the passing of the years.

Strewn here and there on the concrete floor were ragged Indian rugs, well past their prime, and faded scraps of old carpet. Towards the centre of the floor, pushed up against a pillar, was a huge old chesterfield, draped with what looked like a fishing net, complete with cork floats, its springs long since destroyed by generations of over-enthusiastic use. Next to the chesterfield and filled with coils of heavy cable and a tangle of other assorted electronic equipment was a fine wooden dinghy bearing the name *Lady Minerva*, beautifully carved in a curly decorative script on a small wooden panel near the prow. The boat, which had clearly been lovingly preserved and maintained, was illustrated with delicate pictures of bare-breasted mermaids and slender sea nymphs, sporting playfully in frothy, foam-tipped waves, the paint so faded and worn in places that only the creatures' ethereal smiles were still visible.

Pushed up against one wall and covered with an assortment of magazines, music papers, empty coffee cups and a disembowelled electric guitar was a large, scrubbed-deal table, which Crystal recognised as having been filched from Isaac's kitchen in Camden Town. Along one of the narrower walls of the huge, rectangular space was a large, raised wooden platform, deserted save for half a dozen microphones, headphones, a drum kit and a set of keyboards, surrounded by speakers of varying shapes and sizes and an old mixing desk.

Isaac, monitoring Crystal's reaction to his highly individual establishment, smiled as she made her way quietly and with a certain reverence around the room, leaving no stone unturned as she studied each object, picture and piece of equipment in turn. 'This is just the rehearsal room and general dossing around area,' he said. 'The actual recording studio's through the door over there.' He gestured in the direction of a heavy wooden door. 'It's a fraction of the size of this and completely soundproofed, of course. Max and I managed to pick up a load of excellent recording gear at silly prices from a studio in London that went bust a week or so ago. Sounds a bit morbid, but the daft buggers had totally overreached themselves financially and business these days being the way it is . . . Anyway, they were so desperate for a quick injection of dosh they were practically giving it away. Max and I just happened to be there at the right time. Anyway, to salve our consciences, we've told them they can come down here and use it at cut-price rates whenever they want to and there happens to be a gap in the bookings. Which, please God, won't be that often.'

Beside the door to the studio was another door, slightly open, which seemed to lead on to a kitchen of sorts. At least, Crystal could just see a kettle and the corner of an electric cooker. Isaac spotted her looking at it and added: 'That's the galley. Hardly enough room to swing a cat, hence the name, but fine for heating up the odd can of beans and opening wine bottles. The cooker's handy for lighting fags off.' He laughed and plonked himself down on the chesterfield, stretching his arms across its back. 'You think I'm kidding? Max uses it for that all the time. He managed to flick about two inches of ash into my saucepan of Campbell's condensed the other day.'

Crystal laughed, too. Flicking back her hair she went and sat on his lap, snaking her faded black leather arms around his neck and kissing him playfully on the forehead. 'Well, you're a dark horse, aren't you? This place is astonishing! How long have you had it, and why the hell haven't you mentioned it before? I mean, the fact that you'll be down here in Bristol – at least some of the time – means that maybe we can see a bit more of each other—'

Stopping in mid-sentence, she let out a piercing scream as Isaac grabbed her in a tight bear hug and wrestled with her ancient biker's jacket, struggling to pull it from her shoulders.

'I'm always in the mood to see a bit more of you, darlin', especially some of your more interesting bits!'

Crystal giggled delightedly as Isaac tussled with her on the old sofa, finally managing to relieve her of her jacket and tossing it carelessly over the back and onto the floor before pushing her down, breathless with laughter, against the rusty fishing net and pressing his lips to hers in a long, lingering kiss. 'Welcome,' he whispered, momentarily breaking free and gazing into her sparkling eyes, 'this is the bit I've been looking forward to most. Showing the place to you. Even though I have been a bit quiet about it up until now.' As though in slow motion he lowered his lips to hers once more and they continued kissing and nuzzling each other's faces, tangled together on the sofa like a couple of amorous teenagers.

'Hey, hey! Save the smutty stuff for later, will you? Remember me? Sheba? The friend you brought along for the ride? I'm here too you know.' Emerging from the kitchen, six-foot tall and resplendent in ankle-length fur and ridiculous heels, Sheba strode towards the scrubbed-deal table, brandishing a champagne bottle which she plonked down on top of a pile of *Melody Makers*. 'Got any glasses, Ike? I sure could use a drink. Apart from a couple of square inches of mouldy cheese this was all there was in the fridge, so I guess it'll have to do.'

Lazily disentangling himself from Crystal, Isaac sat up, put his head against the back of the sofa and burst out laughing. 'Christ, Sheba!' he cried through his laughter. 'You have the manners of a goddamn alley cat.' Sheba, uncharacteristically for her, bit her bottom lip and looked vaguely embarrassed. 'But, since you ask,' Isaac continued, 'there aren't any glasses, only mugs, and they're all on a shelf in the kitchen. You can fetch them in you like. Might as well crack open the champers. Now's as good a time as any. I was going to wait until Max got here, but . . .'

Sheba, halting in mid-stride as she made her way to the kitchen, looked surprised and intrigued. 'Max? That name again. This scene gets better and better. I was forgetting Maxie Baby was planning on joining us . . . Hey, a whoresome foursome, eh?' Cackling wickedly Sheba carried on towards the kitchen, rubbing her hands together with glee.

Crystal giggled and, looking at Isaac, raised her eyes to heaven. 'Is Max ready for this?' she asked him, stroking an elegant finger across his stubbly chin.

'More to the point, sweetheart,' Isaac replied, smiling ruefully, 'is Sheba ready for him? The man's a brilliant technician, as well as being an extremely competent musician and no slouch when it comes to business deals, but he's also a complete, no-holds-barred lunatic when he wants to be. When I told him about Sheba he practically had a seizure on the spot. It seems he's been having the most outrageous sexual fantasies about her for years and never dreamed he'd get to meet her in the flesh. I almost needed tranquillizers to calm the guy down when he heard she was coming here this afternoon.'

'Where's Max now?' Crystal asked under her breath as Sheba emerged once more from the kitchen and headed for the table with a clutch of coffee mugs and a lighted cigarette.

'He and I slept here last night, but I left at about six a.m. to come and see you. He told me he was going to go home to shower and change and be back here around five-thirty, having picked up a few things to eat and a couple of bottles of vino collapso on the way.' Isaac paused and looked at his watch. 'It's five now so Sheba shouldn't have too long to wait for her Prince Charming. I'm glad he remembered to switch the heating on before he left. This place is like the Arctic Circle without it.'

'Good afternoon, playmates!' As though on cue the side door flew open, banging back against the brick wall and making the three occupants of the room jump at the unexpected noise, and in walked Max – his top half concealed behind a toppling tower of grocery cartons and carrier bags as he staggered towards the kitchen, the only visible part of him being his skintight, fashionably ripped Levi's and a pair of heavily scuffed Nike trainers which by the look of them had long seen better days.

Pop! The champagne cork ejected from the heavy glass

240

bottle and flew in a graceful, projectile arc across the room, landing at Max's feet and causing him to stop in his tracks. Sheba, half an eye on the Dennis the Menace mug she was slowly filling with chilled bubbly, cast a practised eye over this laden, masculine vision, allowing the bulk of her attention to focus on the alluring bulge between the newcomer's long legs. The faded denim at that particular point of his anatomy was pale and worn with use, throwing the delectable contents in heart-stopping relief.

Carefully placing the champagne bottle back on the table, Sheba ran a lazy tongue over her lips, ran an elegant hand through her tight, closely shorn ebony curls and cunningly allowed the front of her long fur coat to fall open, thus revealing the firm, glossy contours of her scarlet-leather-clad breasts. Resting her bottom seductively against the edge of the table she stretched out her long, slender legs, crossing them at the ankles and slowly flexing her toes in their high, pointed ankle boots as she gazed knowingly at the tall stranger. 'Hiya gorgeous, and good afternoon to you, too . . .' she replied in a low, Gallic-Texan drawl.

At the sound of Sheba's voice, Max Dupont's attention veered fatally away from the bags and cartons he was carrying and they fell with a loud clatter to the ground. As luck would have it, fate was on his side and the box containing the Chablis landed on a scrap of carpet, the bottles mercifully remaining unbroken despite the force of their descent. Apparently unaware of the broken jar of dill pickles at his feet, the vinegar forming a piquant pool on the stone floor, Max stood rooted to the spot and stared at the owner of the voice with silent, unmasked admiration. 'Jesus H. Christ, Isaac,' he breathed without dragging his eyes away from the beautiful rock star, 'I thought you were kidding me when you said she . . .' Lost for words, his voice faded away into nothingness as his gaze travelled the length of Sheba's spectacular body before finally coming to rest on her voluptuous breasts in the skintight scarlet leather.

'Hey,' drawled Sheba, an amused smile hovering about her lips as she basked in the warmth of Max's slow and sensual once-over, 'you look like a guy who could use a drink. Here, be my guest . . .' Pushing her long frame away from the table she shrugged the fur away from her shoulders so that it fell in a sinful, luxurious heap to the floor. Then she picked up the bottle of champagne and slinked towards him on her ridiculous heels, hips swaying hypnotically, fully aware of Max's eyes on her shiny, blood-red crotch in the sprayed-on catsuit.

Crystal and Isaac glanced at each other, astonished at the speed of the proceedings, and then back at Sheba who, having reached the awe-inspired Max, bent to kiss him softly on the cheek before linking an arm through his and, bottle clasped firmly in her free hand, steering him helpless yet uncomplaining towards the door to the recording studio. 'Be a darling and open it for me, would you?' she breathed in a husky, tigerish whisper. 'My hands are a little full.'

Gulping nervously, eyes wide with shock and amazement, Max did as he was told, obediently opening the heavy door as though on automatic pilot and ushering them both through and into the dim, womb-like confines of the small room before closing it quietly behind them. However, before vanishing completely to his inevitable fate, he just had time to treat the two remaining occupants of the rehearsal room to a lewd, throwaway gesture which, unseen by the predatory

Sheba, mercifully reassured Isaac and Crystal that maybe Max hadn't entirely lost control of the situation.

Shaken to the core, the two not altogether unwilling voyeurs stared wordlessly at the closed door for several seconds before catching each other's eye and dissolving into fits of hysterical giggles. 'At least she had the grace to lead him into another room before wrestling him to the floor and ripping off his clothes,' Crystal gasped at last, collapsing exhausted against the back of the sofa and brushing the tears of mirth from her eyes with the back of her hand. 'I mean, bloody hell!' she continued, unable to hide the note of admiration in her voice. 'Talk about a smooth operator. I don't think I've ever seen a woman move in for the kill so fast. I must get her to tell me the sordid secrets of her technique. I could market them and retire tomorrow on the proceeds.'

Crystal paused for a moment, going over the steamy little scene again in her mind. 'I mean, I'm no prude – I'd be more than happy to watch a couple of randy sex maniacs going at it hammer and tongs on the floor at my feet – but I wouldn't mind a few preliminaries before the hard-core fucking. You know, maybe a spot of heavy petting or something? Just to add colour.' The audacity of the thought made Crystal start to giggle all over again and her shoulders began to shake once more with fresh bouts of silent hilarity.

Isaac chuckled wickedly and hugged Crystal to him before rising slowly to his feet and stretching lazily. Then he crouched down and began to gather up the scattered makings of their cosy Boxing Day supper. 'I'm inclined to agree, Crystal. But let me tell you, that woman is notorious for being one hell of a siren. She's got a sex drive like you wouldn't believe. Completely bloody awesome. No man's safe when she's around – every one of us helpless saps is fair prey, a victim to the sensations in the dangly bits between our legs – from roadies and fellow rockers to the man who sweeps up after the show.

Crystal leaned forward on the sofa, chin cupped coquettishly in her hands and elbows resting on her knees, grinning mischievously at Isaac as he crouched there on the floor in front of her, rewrapping a couple of French sticks in their crumpled tissue paper to keep them as fresh as possible until they were ready to be consumed. 'What about you, Isaac?' she said tauntingly. 'Have you ever fallen prey to the dangly bits between your legs where Sheba's concerned?'

Isaac stopped what he was doing and looked up at Crystal, a mysterious little smile curving the corners of his mouth. 'Maybe I have and, there again, maybe I haven't. That's for me to know and you to find out . . .' With that, he reached out both arms and sprang at her like a jungle cat, pinning her to the sofa in a rugby tackle and tickling her mercilessly along her ribcage, causing her to wriggle and squirm like a fish on a hook, helpless with hysterical laughter.

Meanwhile, behind closed doors, warm as toast and simmering nicely in the reddish glow from a single, unobtrusive spot in Isaac's small recording studio, Sheba and Max Dupont stood facing each other, silent save for the beating of their hearts and the gentle whisper of their quickening breath. Neither of them spoke. They didn't need to – their body language and facial expressions, soft and rosy in the flattering half-light, told everything either of them needed to know.

As Sheba lazily and with lust-filled eyes studied the handsome flats and planes of Max's expressive face, gazing deep into his eyes which were shiny and swimming with desire for her, he believed with something approaching panic that she could see through to the very core of his being. Never before had he met a woman capable of seducing him with a mere tilt of the head or arch of an eyebrow, as this woman had done. God knows, he was no slouch where bedding women was concerned. His lust for sexual experience and appreciation of the female form was second to none. With his bouncy, happy-go-lucky charm, twinkling blue eyes which crinkled engagingly at the corners when he smiled – which was most of the time – and unruly mop of blond, shoulder-length curls, he was much sought after by the vast majority of those members of the gentler sex involved in or around the music business. But, after little more than five minutes since she'd first clapped eyes on him, this particular member of the female sex had him well and truly in the palm of her undeniably gentle hand. There was nothing for it, he decided with the deliciously insistent throb in his groin making the crotch of his already skintight jeans tighter still, but to relax and go with the flow . . .

Completing her examination, Sheba gave a throaty chuckle and, resting her backside on the edge of the main mixing desk, raised the champagne bottle to her lips, threw back her head, and took a generous swig. Then, with the guile of an arch temptress, she beckoned for Max to come closer with a smoky, come-hither look. As though at the end of an invisible wire, Max closed the distance between himself and Sheba, astonished at himself for allowing his normally strident free will to be moulded in this way. Without touching him with her hands, the beautiful negress leaned forward and pressed her full lips against his in a voluptuous kiss and, as their lips parted hungrily, Max thrilled to the sensation of the body-warmed, effervescent liquid as it flooded from Sheba's mouth into his own. Gratefully he gulped the champagne down before pressing his eager lips to hers once more and resuming with fresh passion their spine-tingling oral embrace.

Profoundly turned on by this sensual and highly intimate exchange, Max's sexual need and desire for erotic congress with this gorgeous rock goddess spiralled to new heights. He felt as though he were in a dream and would shortly wake up to find himself back in his studio flat which overlooked a small, bijou square in the centre of the city.

For years now he'd been aroused by the strong, earthy image of Sheba, undeniable queen of the female rockers. On the wall above his bed he had two pictures of her, shot by Patrick Lichfield, which he'd filched from an issue of *Esquire Magazine* where they'd run a lengthy, illustrated feature covering her life, loves and spectacular career. In both photographs she was completely naked, tall, dark and statuesque, her nipples and pubic hair cunningly concealed behind strategically placed limbs, which had the uncanny effect of rendering the images even more erotic than they would have been had she been displaying all to the camera. In one of the pictures she stood poised in a tense half-crouch, strong and dangerous, her body glistening like chocolate satin and her even, pure white teeth bared in a tigerish snarl of rage. In the other picture, soft and subtle as though shot through fine gossamer, she lay curled up on her side on a pile of animal skins, her eyes sleepy and half closed and her generous lips parted in a contented pussycat purr.

With a rush of excitement, Max recalled how he'd dwelt on those pictures, fantasising like crazy about the woman in them and yet hardly daring to imagine that one day his erotic reveries might actually become reality. Had he stopped to think about what was happening to him for long enough he'd have been rendered impotent by the sheer, mind-blowing nature of it all. But instead, he allowed himself to move closer still to his beautiful fantasy object, pressing his long, rangey body against her own, which was as warm, fleshy and reassuringly human as that of any woman he'd ever made love to. As he moulded himself to her he felt her soften and melt into him, her stunning, projectile breasts in the tight scarlet leather squeezing and flattening against his chest in a way which made his heart beat alarmingly and his prick become engorged with fresh, pulsing blood.

Exploring her warm mouth and mobile tongue with his own, breathing deeply and rhythmically through his nose as he did so and inhaling with increasing passion the heady scent of womanly musk which rose like an exotic incense from her skin, he broke away suddenly, panting with lust, and slipped the forefinger of his right hand through the small, metallic ring at the neck of Sheba's tight leather catsuit. Standing away a little to afford himself a better view, he watched with narrowed eyes the widening gash of naked skin, glistening darkly in the subdued light and already damp with sweat, as he slowly and with almost painful deliberation lowered the zip as far as it would go, which was to about an inch above the negress's prominent pubis.

Only then did Sheba deign to speak, and this in a husky half-whisper, laden with sinful promise. 'Come on, baby,' she drawled, the large semi-spheres of her naked and partly revealed breasts rising and falling mesmerically as she breathed, and her gorgeous, fleshy lips enunciating each word as though she were indeed intent on hypnotising him, 'strip me naked . . .' Lingering teasingly over the last word, she made it sound like the lewdest, most shocking idea imaginable. A taboo blasphemy, unmentionable within polite circles, with Max a willing victim to its siren invitation.

Tempted almost beyond endurance, he reached out with trembling hands and, as though in slow motion, took hold of both sides of the catsuit and parted them, easing the supple second skin away from her sculpted shoulders until she stood before him, proudly imperious, her bare breasts, full and luscious, jutting extravagantly towards him. Max's heart leaped as he stared at them and his mouth became dry, filled as he was with a mixture of awe and galloping lust at the sight of such wanton, fleshy beauty displayed for him and him alone. Gulping nervously, he reached out and, with the tender forefingers of both hands, lovingly and simultaneously traced the large, outer circles of her glossy, inky black areolae, watching with wonder and ever-quickening pulse as the dusky, wrinkled skin of her big, succulent nipples puckered and swelled at the touch of his fingers as though with a will of their own.

'Suck them,' Sheba ordered, the terseness of her demand tempered by the slow warmth of her voice, husky with sex as she took her breasts in both hands and wantonly offered them to him.

After first taking a deep, reviving breath to still his racing emotions, Max hunkered down until his face was level with her boobs. Then, closing his eyes and wrapping his arms around her proud, naked torso, he rubbed his ecstatic face against the soft, wobbly flesh, moaning softly as he felt the sultry heat and weight of her bare tits against his cheeks. He showered them with tiny, wet butterfly kisses, nuzzling the erect, jutting nipples, loving the turgid warmth of them against his nose and chin. Taking each nipple into his mouth in turn, he licked them wetly with his tongue and sucked on the swollen flesh, sending voluptuous flashes of pure quicksilver from the very tips of her nipples, the exquisite source of her pleasure, way down to the tiny, excited nub of her inflamed clitoris.

Above him, Sheba began to moan and whimper with delight, eyes closed and tiny goose-bumps rising on the surface of her skin at the erotic thrill of standing bare-breasted and unashamed before a complete stranger, trembling uncontrollably at the delicious sensation of Max's stubbly chin rasping against her naked flesh and the soft tendrils of his blond hair tickling her nipples. Then, almost roughly pushing him away from her, she put her hands on his broad shoulders, silently urging him to rise and face her once more. Breathing deeply and gazing steadily into his eyes, her pupils shiny black and fully dilated, she swiftly and with the consummate skill of a high-class call girl unfastened his heavy leather belt and unzipped his tight jeans with a speed and efficiency which nearly took his breath away.

Then, with her naked breasts bouncing and juddering in a way which made Max's penis swell to the extent that the shiny glans poked slyly over the top of his pants, Sheba bent her knees and gracefully lowered herself to the ground until she was kneeling in front of him, her face level with his temptingly semi-revealed genitals. Hungrily licking her lips and quickly tugging down his pants and jeans so that they dropped in a tangle of cotton and faded denim around his ankles, Sheba took Max's erect penis in her hand, cupping his intensely sensitive balls in the other, and with a tender, feather-light touch ran the tip of one long, scarlet-polished fingernail along its pulsing length. She smiled wickedly as Max's cock leapt and throbbed in her hand, his balls tightening and contracting into his groin.

Max closed his eyes and moaned with pleasure, the delicious sensations in his manhood radiating through his entire body like rich, warm waves of treacle. Sheba bit her lip and smiled up at him, an unmistakeable twinkle of mischief in her eyes. Then, taking a deep, trembling breath, she slowly moved forwards until Max could feel her breathing softly against him. Opening his eyes he gazed down at her gorgeous, ecstatic face as she clasped the cheeks of his bare backside in both hands and, closing her eyes and sensually puckering her full lips, placed a voluptuous wet kiss on the very tip of his prick, at the same time extending her kitten tongue and licking away the tiny drop of semen which had gathered there. Holding his thick, turgid cock in both hands, like a child with an over-large lollipop, Sheba nuzzled it playfully with her soft, parted lips and naughty wet tongue, loving the heavy, velvet smoothness of his throbbing shaft, the fine, blue-veined skin taut with arousal.

Moving away for a moment while still holding on to Max's prick, Sheba licked her lips hungrily, eyes narrowed with lust, and growled deep in her throat in a way which was more animal than human. Then, swooping down, she took the full length of him in her mouth, so quickly and smoothly that he was quite taken by surprise, crying out with shock and pleasure, fists clenched at his sides. Rhythmically kneading his arse with her strong fingers and leaving flushed weals in the wake of her lethal, blood-red nails, Sheba drew Max's penis so deeply into her mouth and throat that his pubic hair brushed against her nose and chin. She almost reeled with delight at the pure, earthy masculinity of his scent as it assailed her senses, drawing it deep into her lungs through flared, eager nostrils as she sucked with relish on his phallus.

Sheba squeezed Max's cock expertly with her mouth whilst flicking its rigid length tantalisingly with her tongue. Never before, he thought with a shudder of pleasure, had he been treated to such an awe-inspiring blow job by such a gorgeous, not to mention world-famous, fellatrix. In fact, the very thought of who it was that was sucking him off, bare-breasted, brazen and ripe for fucking, was almost enough to make him shoot his spunk there and then. Just in time, however, he drew in his breath, tensing his tummy muscles to help regain control. Then, reaching down, he clasped Sheba's smooth shoulders in a firm grip, gently easing her away from his cock and encouraging her to stand.

On her feet once more, Sheba slowly began to undulate her hips. As she did so, she gazed knowingly into Max's eyes from under lowered lashes, licking her lips with undisguised, lascivious pleasure and absently playing with her big, dusky nipples, flicking and twiddling them between her fingers, her livid nails a striking contrast to her glossy dark skin. Max watched her, mesmerized by the blatant desire oozing from her every pore, thrilled at the easy skill with which she was so blatantly manipulating his sexual libido, forcing him to face the deep, dark side of his erotic nature.

Trembling now, his breathing fast and fierce with lust, Max took hold of the tight leather catsuit, the top of which had already dropped to around her hips, and ripped it roughly from Sheba's body, yanking it away from her long legs until she had no choice but to quickly step out of it and kick it to one side. Slightly shaken but undeniably turned on by Max's sudden mastery of the situation, Sheba stood proudly before him, completely naked save for a long, incredibly fine gold chain which, glinting expensively against her black, curvy belly, circled her wide hips. A second, slightly shorter length of chain was attached to the main one, linking front and back and passing through her legs, the central section glittering temptingly as it nestled in the dense, glossy black pubic hair covering her prominent vulva before disappearing between the flushed, fleshy lips of her outer labia.

Head on one side, Sheba pouted sexily and watched Max with an expression of lewd invitation as he gazed, intrigued and titillated almost beyond endurance, at this latest, prick-stimulating insight into the habits and sexual mores of this stunning temptress. It was clear to him that with every movement of her body, every step and every wiggle, the tiny chain was designed to stroke and stimulate her in the most sensitive and intimate part of her anatomy. How she could bear the almost constant sexual arousal was anybody's guess, especially given that the chain must pass directly over her clitoris, but Max was in no mood to ponder the intricacies of Sheba's physical fortitude.

Instead, seized by a white-hot flare of burning lust, he grabbed her by the shoulders, turned her roughly round and pushed her down so that she fell spread-eagled on her front over the mixing desk upon which she'd previously been sitting, the hard, shiny controls pressing painfully into her naked breasts and belly. She squealed with surprise and delight, loving the feel of the cold metal against her warm skin, obediently allowing Max to greedily nudge her firm gleaming thighs apart with his knees until they were sufficiently widely stretched for him to feast his eyes on the damp, juicy folds of her bare cunt and her tiny, wrinkled arsehole.

Panting freely now, eyes glittering with anticipation and suppressed emotion, Max kicked aside his jeans and with damp, trembling fingers, unfastened the chain from around Sheba's lewdly proffered hips and arse so that it fell with a tiny metallic jingle to the ground at her feet. Then, grabbing hold of her left hip with one hand and his pulsating prick with the other, he advanced on her rear end, eagerly nudging the shiny red glans against the exposed entrance to her vagina before thrusting forward with a terse grunt, burying himself to the hilt in her tight, slippery warmth. He paused for a moment to relish the feel of her as she tensed and contracted around him before commencing a powerful, steady rhythm of single-minded, rear-entry fucking.

Stretched out in front of him across the expanse of cool metal with her arms flung out in front of her, Sheba was pushed powerfully back and forth with the force of Max's thrusts. As her body flexed and writhed, alive and tingling with the delicious sensations emanating from her cunt, she was exquisitely aware of each and every switch and control as it pressed spitefully into her soft flesh, rasping against her smooth ebony skin and leaving tiny scratches and weals in its wake. She moaned and cried out as her climax approached, tensing her muscles and grabbing hold of the edge of the mixing desk as she pushed out her gleaming arse to meet Max's rhythmic thrusts, feeling the hot, rigid length of his cock as he tantalisingly withdrew it as far as he dare before powering back into her with enough force and passion to take her breath away.

Then, with a loud, feral scream which, despite the soundproofing of the recording studio, must surely have been heard by Crystal and Isaac in the adjoining room, Sheba finally came. Rearing up from the mixing desk, eyes squeezed tight shut, ecstatic face wet with sweat and swollen breasts jouncing and trembling with emotion, she pushed out her arse with great, heaving backward thrusts into Max's tensed groin, spitting herself onto his prick until it was buried in her to the hilt. Max, unable to hold on any longer, groaned long and loud as he too reached his climax, his cock pulsing and flexing as it spurted its semen in rapid, rhythmic gobs into Sheba's orgasmic sex.

Exhausted by the passionate intensity of their frantic lovemaking, the two lovers, sleepy and satisfied, moaned and whimpered together as they curled into each other's nakedness, Max kissing and nuzzling Sheba's neck and shoulders as their damp, sex-warmed bodies slowed and became blissfully still. And there they stayed, lazy and sexually sated as they held each other close, silently allowing their breathing to become slow and steady.

'So, Ike, where do you go from here?' Sheba asked, reclining luxuriously against the pile of cushions and rolled-up carpets which constituted the makeshift seating arrangements in the rehearsal room. Despite the somewhat threadbare nature of her 'throne' and the fact that she was rather minimally though appealingly clad in Max's thoughtfully donated briefs and warm plaid shirt, she looked and acted for all the world like an exotic Roman empress giving an audience to her grateful subjects. Stretching out her long, coltish legs she leaned back, resting a slim arm girlishly behind her head as she took a generous pull on the extravagant reefer before handing it to Max who, squatting adoringly at her feet, accepted it with a wink and a smile. Sheba smiled back, squeezing his shoulder affectionately.

Isaac considered Sheba's query for a moment before replying, thoughtfully toying with a crust of French bread and a corner of garlic pâté on his plate before taking a ruminative swig of Chablis. 'Ah, the million-dollar question . . .

'Obviously the Steel Dinosaurs will continue to do their stuff. It'd be madness to knock them on the head right now, especially given the revenue the band pulls in and the kind of following its got. God knows, Max and I are going to need all the loot we can get our hands on just to keep this show on the road.' Isaac paused with a small sigh, gesturing around the room with a shrug and a wry smile. 'Anyway,' he continued, 'while we're still on top, and particularly now I've got this place, I'd love to play around a bit with the stuff we knock out. You know, create something a little more adventurous, maybe appeal to an even wider audience. The wham-bam-thankyou-ma'am material's all well and good – I mean, it's paid our wages over the last goodness knows how many years – but I've got a real yen to rock the boat a bit musically. I think I owe it to myself to give it a try at least. For the benefit of the rest of the band too, especially now that Barney's left us to play at being a country boy in the wilds of North Wales.'

Sprawled on the floor between Isaac's long legs, Crystal smiled to herself, nursing her drink and munching on a tortilla chip as her imagination dwelt on an image of pretty

Polly, High Links' erstwhile receptionist, who'd gone off to join Barney in his rural Welsh idyll. They'd made a good pair, the two of them, and she couldn't help but hope that they'd continue to make a go of it – especially now that Polly was expecting a baby. Her 'Christmas card' to Crystal, which was a hastily scrawled note on the back of a colour photograph of the two of them, arms around each other and standing in front of their tiny stone cottage with a couple of sheep at their feet, had been full of happiness and hope for the future.

Isaac reached forward to take the spliff which Max was offering to him, taking a hit before continuing: 'Anyway, for the time being most of my plans involve putting this place on the map. I know Bristol isn't exactly London, but it's a big enough centre to count for something and there's enough going on for bands to want to record here. That's my theory, at least.' He took another drag on the joint, drawing the smoke deep into his lungs and closing his eyes as he rested his head against the back of the sofa, enjoying the heady, marijuana-induced sensations which began to fill his head and limbs. After a moment or two he pulled himself back to Earth, reaching down and handing the joint to Crystal. 'Meanwhile, I want to see this place booked up twenty-four hours a day, seven days a week, and no messing.'

'Sock it to me, Mr Businessman! That sounds like real fighting talk,' Sheba drawled, eyes narrowed lazily as she gazed unblinking at Isaac. 'You can sure count me in, babe. Me and the boys'll be your first customers.' Leaning forward to take the joint from Crystal, Max having declined the offer, she took a long hit, closing her eyes luxuriously before peering once more at Isaac, this time through a blue, billowing haze of expelled smoke which failed to disguise the expression of calculated interest in her dark eyes.

Sheba's scrutiny of him failed to be lost on Isaac. As he'd told Crystal, the two of them went back a long way. But what he'd failed to point out, for obvious reasons, were the handful of occasions when their relationship had transcended the purely professional. Looking at Sheba now, watching him with those black, shiny cats eyes, full of mischief and sensual promise, and those full, pouting lips of whose expertise in certain directions he was only too well aware, he experienced a definite stirring in his groin which, try as he might to dispel it, just wouldn't go away.

Rising slowly to his feet, Max yawned and stretched his arms above his head. 'Jesus Christ, I could use some fresh air. Anyone fancy joining me?' He gazed uncaring at the jumble of empty cartons and paper bags which had once contained a variety of exotic pâtés and cheeses. Picking up a half-empty glass of wine he raised it to his lips and took a swig before swaying a little on his pins and looking enquiringly at the three remaining revellers.

'Think I will,' Crystal replied somewhat fuzzily, rising unsteadily to her feet and pulling on her black leather biker's jacket before linking an arm companiably through Max's, as comfortable with him as though she'd known him all her life instead of just a few hours. 'Lead the way, Sir Galahad!' Giggling riotously, the two of them weaved their way to the lobby and the outside door and disappeared into the night-time city, determined to walk off their lightheadedness, slamming the door noisily behind them amid fresh gales of hysterical titters.

Listening to their friends' laughter dwindle away to nothing outside, Isaac and Sheba looked at each other across the few feet which separated them, their minds clearly on other things. They had no need to speak. They both knew what the other was thinking. Isaac, lazy and laid-back, lounged languidly along the full length of the sofa and treated himself to another, slow hit of marijuana. His attraction to Sheba, profound at the best of times, had been massaged and amplified still further by the wine and drugs he'd consumed, as well as by the easy conviviality of the evening the four of them had spent together. To his eyes at this moment, Sheba's raw sexuality and pure animal magnetism had achieved new heights of potency and he wasn't at all sure that he'd be able, still less willing, to refuse her if she came on to him. And, right now, it looked very much as though she might do just that.

Isaac had been turned on more than he cared to admit by the way she'd poleaxed Max in the way that she had. Goodness knows, it took some kind of a woman to have that particular customer eating out of her hand with such apparently effortless ease. Max Dupont was a noted philanderer and unrepentant womaniser. As far as he was concerned, women were little more than attractive playthings, agreeable adjuncts to one's daily existence with whom it was unwise to attach oneself too enthusiastically and to whom one should never, ever make promises. Even during the relatively short time they'd known each other, Isaac had been forced to lend a comforting shoulder and an avuncular ear to any number of disappointed young women who'd made the mistake of taking Max's attentions too seriously.

Swinging his legs to the floor, Isaac stretched across and offered the glowing remains of the reefer to Sheba, who took it from him, looking knowingly into his eyes in that uncanny way she had, as though reading his mind. Isaac began to feel strangely exposed, as though his emotions and possible sexual motives were written across his forehead, and his pulse quickened with excitement. He was sure now what was likely to follow. The question was, should he throw caution to the wind and approach her, or should he wait for Sheba to weave her inevitable magic around him? Knowing his quarry of old, he was well aware that one false move could spell disaster. Where erotic fun and games were concerned, Sheba was a woman for whom maintaining control of the situation for as long as possible before seeming to willingly surrender herself was of utmost importance to her own enjoyment of the proceedings.

'Boy, it sure is hot in here. Mind if I take something off?' Her voice was low and drowsy as, like a serpent uncoiling from her pile of strewn cushions and rugs on the ground, Sheba rose to her feet and stretched her long body with an easy, provocative grace, standing on tiptoes with the effortlessness of a dancer. She raised her arms above her head so that the tails of her over-large, borrowed shirt rose along with them, revealing a tantalising glimpse of the twin half-moons of her gleaming bottom cheeks. She turned and looked at Isaac, a knowing smile curving her full lips as she studied his face for the inevitable dawning of his realisation that she was no longer wearing knickers. She'd craftily discarded them some time before in readiness for this moment, which she'd known deep in her gut would present itself, ripe and ready for her to utilise in her own inimitable way.

Isaac's heart missed a beat and his cock leaped with anticipation at the sight of Sheba's bare bottom, which she was so wantonly and with evident relish displaying to him.

He swallowed hard, eyes glowing now with excitement and pleasure, and settled back to meet head-on whatever it was that this gorgeous temptress had in mind for him.

Turning to face Isaac as he sprawled, entranced, on the sofa, Sheba slowly and sensually undid the buttons of her shirt, taking her time as inch by tantalising inch of her gleaming black torso was revealed to him. Unfastening the final button, she raised her head and gazed defiantly into his eyes, her own narrowed and smoky with desire, and ran a sensual tongue over her generous lips before throwing back her shoulders and shrugging free of the shirt, allowing it to fall to the ground. Standing before him, naked and proud, Sheba began slowly to caress her stunning breasts, voluptuously heavy and yet as firm and uptilted as a teenager's. Coyly watching Isaac's reaction to her rude display from under lowered lashes, she drew in her breath, pulling in her tummy muscles and thrusting out her boobs as she ran her hands over her smooth belly and curvy hips. Gently parting her long legs, she slowly twined her glossy pubic hair around her fingers before insinuating them between her prominent labial lips and into her pussy.

Flushed and panting now with lust, Isaac watched the stunningly beautiful rock goddess as she began to masturbate lewdly and with a complete lack of self-consciousness in front of him. He'd seen her naked before, a condition in which she seemed to revel, exploiting it fully and delightfully with the innocence of a child. And yet every time, the sight of her seemed to strike him afresh, hitting him clean between the eyes with an explosive combination of straightforward lust and frank amazement at the beauty of her unclothed body and her complete lack of shame or reticence in displaying it.

As Sheba's mobile fingers worked their magic inside her pussy, she began to moan and writhe, head thrown back and eyes ecstatically closed as she trembled uncontrollably with the onset of her climax. Spreading her legs further apart and rhythmically swaying her hips, she pinched the swollen buds of her prominent, jutting nipples with the fingers of her free hand, an action which made her cry out at the sharp, exquisite pleasure it afforded her. Suddenly, with an uninhibited scream of joy, her body convulsed as she became lost to the delicious, advancing tremors of a powerful orgasm, at the summation of which her body ceased its passionate, shamanic dance, becoming still and languidly fluid once more.

Gleaming with fresh sweat and ripe with the scent of rampant sex, the steamy, aphrodisiac aroma of the sated and freshly orgasmic woman lingered in the warm room, assailing Isaac's nostrils and driving him to fresh peaks of throbbing passion. Somewhat shakily he stood up, half-crazed with lust as a result of the scene he'd just been encouraged to witness and feeling himself to be losing control of his habitually strong reserve. Pushed almost to the limit of his sexual endurance, he was unsure of how best to relieve the hot, insistent pounding in his sex, which was driving him almost insane with boiling need, and of how to react to the indomitable female spirit of the woman standing proud and brazenly naked before him.

For a brief, uncomfortable moment an image of Crystal swam across his fevered mind. Crystal who loved him, trusted him, wouldn't imagine for even a minute that he'd sink so low as to fall prey to Sheba's charms the instant she'd turned her back. Maybe he should put an end to this scene straight away. After all, neither of them had any idea how long

261

Crystal and Max would be gone. But, on the other hand . . .

At last, with a swell of relief, he was gratefully aware that the problem was about to be resolved. Sheba, taking matters into her own hands as always, advanced upon him, naked breasts and hips swaying hypnotically and lips parted in a sexy, somewhat amused smile. At the same time, Isaac's noble resolve to nip this thing in the bud deserted him completely and irreversibly. Sheba's eyes, which were darkly luminous, glowed with sinful intent as they devoured his tensed body, seeming to undress him, layer by heart-stopping layer. Taking what he understood to be an unambiguous hint, Isaac began frantically to loosen his clothing, tugging his T-shirt out of the top of his tight jeans and fumbling with his fly as Sheba stood little more than a foot in front of him, casually playing with her breasts and nipples and gazing at his efforts with a sultry pout.

Slowly shaking her head she clicked her tongue with apparent disapproval and began to chuckle with amusement, the deep, husky sound emanating from deep within her. 'Hey, cool it, honey,' she drawled sensually, 'You'll bust a goddamn blood vessel if you carry on like that. Why not let Auntie Sheba do it for you, huh? Just relax, babe, and enjoy the ride . . .'

Raising his arms obediently, Isaac allowed Sheba to pull his T-shirt off over his head before pausing to run her greedy hands through his dark chest hair. Closing her eyes with undisguised pleasure she moaned softly, pressing her sculpted, mahogany cheek against his firm flesh, inhaling his fresh, masculine aroma and gently kissing each of his nipples in turn, squeezing her lips around them and giving them a spine-tingling little suck as she did so, which caused Isaac's balls to contract exquisitely against his groin. Then, turning her attention to other, more vital matters, Sheba dropped, animal-like, to her haunches and proceeded to unfasten the front of his straining jeans, unzipping them with her strong white teeth and displaying a level of skill and oral tenacity which left Isaac spellbound with admiration. Surprised and delighted, he drew in his breath, pulse racing dangerously and eyes glowing with pent-up sexual tension as his jeans and pants dropped to the ground.

Nimbly stepping out of the discarded garments and kicking them across the room, Isaac was more aware than ever, now that he was fully naked, of the trembling in his limbs and the way his thick, swollen prick bounced crazily against his belly. With a low groan, he advanced on Sheba like a starving man, wrapping his arms around her in a powerful hug, thrilling to the feel of her soft pubic hair against his hot cock and the way her big breasts squeezed and flattened against his chest, her erect nipples grazing agonisingly against his own. Covering her beautiful, sweat-sheened face and elegant throat with quick, urgent kisses he began to steer her backwards, their entwined bodies moving together as he attempted to direct them both, as one, towards the waiting sofa.

When they reached the sofa they fell blindly onto it in a tangle of flailing limbs, each of them seemingly intent on embracing and kissing as much and as many parts of each other as they possibly could. Then, breaking free from a long, passionate kiss, Sheba drew sharply away, staring wildly into Isaac's eyes, her own glittering with a feverish intensity which quite alarmed him. 'Lie on your back,' she hissed, her voice trembling with emotion. 'I'm going to fuck you . . .' She almost spat the last two words, making them sound grossly obscene and strangely malevolent, their malign resonance lingering in the air between them. Isaac, taken aback by the apparent severity of Sheba's need, nevertheless did as he was told.

Once she had him exactly where she wanted him Sheba climbed swiftly and athletically on top of Isaac, straddling his lean haunches and positioning her gaping pussy directly in line with his prick, which she eagerly grabbed hold of, nudging its dry, velvet head against her wetness. Then, grabbing hold of his shoulders in a tight grip she gazed at him for a moment, her entire countenance alive with an expression of imminent victory, before plunging down and forward, stabbing herself onto him over and over again in a hard, almost violent rhythm, muttering and cursing volubly in her advanced state of passion. With each downward thrust her heavy breasts brushed against his face and after the first few times, maddened by the feel of his lips tickling and nuzzling her turgid nipples as he reared up to meet them, she chose to intensify the sensation by swooping forward and rubbing her tits lewdly against his face with her free hand.

At last, Isaac felt the warm tidal wave of spunk rise inexorably within him and he knew with a certainty borne of experience that he'd reached the point of no return and was powerless to stop himself from climaxing. With a yell of triumph, he threw back his head and shot his seed deep within her while, at the same time, Sheba's gorgeous body tensed and shuddered with the onset of her own, deliciously powerful second spend . . .

Half an hour later, cool and pink-cheeked from their walk and chuckling together at some shared joke, Max and Crystal arrived back at the studio. 'Ah, how sweet . . .' Crystal whispered, tiptoeing up to the sleeping couple, mercifully dressed once more and curled up together on Sheba's former throne of rugs and cushions. 'God knows what they got up to while we were out, but it obviously got the better of them . . .' Giggling good-naturedly, she slipped off her leather jacket and draped it over them for extra warmth, carefully so as not to wake them.

Max, creeping up behind Crystal, wrapped his arms around her supple body, taking generous handfuls of her breasts through her thin sweater and nudging aside her long hair with his nose while kissing her neck. 'Quite fortuitous, really. I mean, them being asleep . . .' he muttered through her hair, his voice thick with desire.

Crystal allowed her head to fall back against his shoulder and she closed her eyes dreamily, feeling a warm pulse of desire rise within her, which increased when she felt Max's hardness pressing urgently between her bottom cheeks. 'Mmm . . .' she sighed, beginning to rub sensually against him, 'you could well be right about that. Now, where were we . . .?'

Chapter Nine

'And so, my dear, there you have it. Six months in the South of France, all expenses paid and earning one and a half times as much as you have been here at High Links.' Tapping her dainty foot appreciatively to the sound of the well-known Beatles song issuing from the discreet speakers secreted in all four corners of the ballroom at High Links, Sadie St George nestled comfortably into the crook of Claude Pettifer-Jones' solicitous arm, the latter resplendent in white dinner jacket and bow tie.

'By all accounts, Crystal dear, *Le Soleil*'s quite a place. An exclusive, ultra-modern health club in the very heart of the Côte d'Azur with some of the best exercise and work-out facilities in the whole of Europe, and more available treatments and therapies than most of us have had hot dinners.' Sadie brushed an imaginary piece of fluff from the skirt of her floor-length, turquoise satin dress, graciously accepting a dainty canapé from a passing waitress before continuing. 'Anyway, dear, I'm frightfully envious. I only wish I were the one selected to manage the place for six months, but Viscount Summerfield, bless his heart, absolutely insisted it be you. His aim, it seems, is for *Le Soleil* to eventually become the flagship for his entire business empire, taking some of the pressure off poor old High Links. He feels, quite rightly, that it needs a younger, more energetic spirit than mine to help the club achieve such dizzy heights.

'And after all, who am I to argue?' Sadie shrugged, taking a ladylike bite from her canapé, which she held delicately between the thumb and forefinger of one elegantly black-gloved hand. 'Besides,' she added, popping a flaky crumb which had transferred itself to her lavishly lipsticked lower lip back into her mouth, 'I can't help agreeing with the man. Not to mention the fact that I've got quite enough on my hands with High Links to look after – especially now that dear Claude has kindly agreed to visit me here whenever he can manage to do so.' Tilting her head coquettishly, Sadie peered up at the handsome face of the stately, grey-haired gentleman photographer sitting beside her, treating him to one of her winning smiles and patting him reassuringly on the knee.

Crystal smiled at the handsome, middle-aged couple sitting opposite her, hoping against hope, not for the first time since Claude's arrival, that Sadie had at last met her match in this gentlemanly man-about-town. Maybe, at long last, she'd stop making sheep's eyes at every single male under the age of thirty who became employed at High Links, freeing the field for some of the younger female staff members to get a crack of the whip from time to time.

Crystal glanced across the crowded ballroom, which was buzzing with staff and guests who were staying over to witness the dawning of the new year in true festive style. She caught Isaac's eye as he and Max stood on the small stage, testing for sound the few pieces of musical equipment which they'd humped up there earlier in the day, ready for a duo he and Sheba were planning to stage later that evening. Isaac grinned and winked at her and she smiled back, swallowing the lump which had formed in her throat.

In her heart of hearts, Crystal knew that Viscount Summerfield's offer was one which she really couldn't refuse. She wouldn't get another one like that in a hurry and she had a strong enough streak of ambition to understand the difference a move like this could make to her career. Who knows, one day she may have a place like High Links or *Le Soleil* of her own . . .

The one and only fly in the ointment was Isaac and their blossoming relationship. When in God's name would they ever get to see each other if she moved to the South of France for six months? Despite his vehement assurances to the contrary when she'd mentioned Sadie's sudden revelation to him earlier, she couldn't help feeling that he'd meet someone else while she was away and, romantically, Crystal would be well and truly back to square one.

Her career or Isaac? Isaac or her career? She'd tossed the problem over and over in her mind since that morning when she'd first been summoned to Sadie's office and given the news, but she knew now what the answer had to be. She was damn sure Isaac wouldn't hesitate to further his career given the opportunity, even if it meant a few months away from her, so why should it be so different for Crystal? Maybe she was worrying unnecessarily about his abandoning her for another woman. Surely she could find it within herself to trust him, couldn't she . . .?

Crystal looked at Sadie and grinned, 'What can I say,

Sadie? It's almost too good to be true. When do I leave?'

Sadie's eyes opened wide with delight and she clapped her hands, giving a little squeal of pleasure and leaning forward to press Crystal to her ample bosom, causing the recipient of the somewhat over-enthusiastic caress to gulp with surprise. If Crystal didn't know any better, she'd have sworn that the old bird was only too happy to get her out of the way.

'Good girl!' Sadie cried. 'I'm so glad you've decided to accept. You won't regret your decision, I just know it.' A faraway look came into her eyes as she continued: 'Just think of all those famous film stars and rich movie moguls you'll end up rubbing shoulders with. The *crème de la crème* of the entertainment industry.' Then, bubbling over with excitement at the thought: 'Not to mention all those hunky French playboys with more money than they know what to do with! Crystal, my dear, this will be the making of you.' Sadie hugged herself with glee and Crystal, unable to prevent the other woman's contagious excitement from spilling over into her own mood, laughed out loud with delight at Sadie's preposterous, extravagantly romantic notions.

Claude Pettifer-Jones, who until now had chosen to remain silent, merely regarding the exchange between the two women with an amused smile, turned now to Crystal with a broad grin. 'Sadie's right, Crystal. You'll have a whale of a time in France. Cannes really is a fabulous place, especially for a beautiful young woman like yourself. All sorts of opportunities will open up for you, so long as you keep a steady head on your shoulders and don't allow yourself to be taken in by any sweet-talking sharks with empty promises and dodgy bank accounts.'

'Not much chance of that, Claude,' Crystal laughed, touched by his compliment. 'I've learned to recognise that type at a hundred paces! But thanks for the tip, anyway.

'Now,' she said, rising to take her leave of them, 'I'd better go and mingle with the guests before you fire me anyway for neglecting my duties. See you a bit later.' With that, Crystal left Sadie and Claude, making her way to a group of revellers in party hats who appeared to be in need of some fresh glasses.

Skirting the bar and narrowly avoiding being pinched on the bottom by the trainee wine waiter, whom she grinned at saucily, slapping his wrist for good measure, she thought she spotted Frankie de Rosa. Smartly kitted out in his best off-duty togs, including a paisley silk cravat and an expensive camelhair coat thrown nonchalantly over his shoulders, Frankie sported a giant Churchill cigar and was flanked on each side by a pair of gorgeous, scantily-clad bimbos, the like of whom Crystal had seldom set eyes on outside the covers of *Playboy* or other similar rags. Bloody hell, she thought to herself, it's obvious he's had a good Christmas. He looked like the proverbial dog with two tails, unsure of which one to wag first. She was constantly astonished at how, every time she set eyes on him, the man resembled more and more a mafioso boss. It was uncanny, really.

One of Frankie's women Crystal recognised as Sharon Neavis, the ex-Steel Dinosaur chick who'd transferred her romantic alliance to Frankie when her drummer boyfriend had done the dirty on her once too often. The other woman Crystal had never clapped eyes on before, but by the way she was snuggling up to Frankie, pressing her semi-revealed boobs against his camelhair arm, it was obvious they knew each other intimately. In fact, the way the sultry redhead was gazing knowingly at Sharon, who was hanging decoratively on Frankie's other arm, Crystal would be prepared to hazard a guess that the two women had also enjoyed more than a passing acquaintance.

Crystal shook her head with resignation. She couldn't help smiling at the absurdity of life and all its puzzling little idiosyncrasies, especially where the relationships between men and women were concerned. Never mind, she thought, without the occasional whiff of intrigue life would hardly be worth living. Grabbing a glass of wine from a passing waiter she decided to go and spread a bit of New Year cheer in the kitchen, where Fernando was busy putting the finishing touches to the gargantuan cold buffet he'd been slaving over since the early hours of that morning.

'Right, my gorgeous twin cherubs, what can I get you both?' Frankie de Rosa leered salaciously at his two female companions, glassy-eyed from the one-too-many celebratory drinks he'd already consumed that evening with his working partner, Nick Knack, and attempting none-too-successfully to peer down the front of Glynis's plunging, black velvet neckline. 'Speaking for myself, I think a glass of bubbly would be in order. What with it being New Year's Eve, and all that.'

'Why not make it a bottle, sweetie? Then we can all have a glass,' breathed Glynis seductively, squeezing her generous milky cleavage with ever-increasing intimacy against Frankie's expensive sleeve. 'Besides, Sharon and I have something to tell you which might just call for a little celebration, don't you agree, darling?' She winked at Sharon, who nodded eagerly and gazed with baby-blue, wide-eyed adoration into Frankie's slightly bloodshot orbs.

'You've got it, girls,' Frankie said, voice shaking with excitement. 'Your wish is my command. I'll just be two ticks, and then I'm all yours,' he added with a low, suggestive growl. Really, he thought, these two babes had the sexual appetites of a couple of Mae Wests on speed. They'd end up being the death of him with all those kinky sex-games they seemed constantly to want to inflict on his poor, overworked body. A lesser man would have given up the ghost long ago, but not him. Frankie de Rosa, thank the Lord, was made of sterner stuff than most of the poncey, limp-wristed Brits the girls had previously had to make do with. In fact, he prided himself on the fact that his staying power when it came to humping bits of skirt was second to none.

Goodness only knew, though, what the randy-arsed pair had in mind for him now. A three-way fuck whilst hanging suspended from the crystal-drop chandelier which hung in the centre of the ballroom, he shouldn't wonder. That would start tongues wagging, he thought with a chuckle. Anyway, doubtless he'd find out what they were after soon enough.

'You are naughty,' Sharon said with a giggle when he'd gone, 'making him think we're about to suggest something rude to him, rather than what we're really going to tell him.' Sharon bit her lip in disbelief at Glynis's audacity.

'Not naughty, you silly sausage, just devious,' said Glynis, stroking away a stray blonde curl from Sharon's cheek which had escaped from her exotic hairdo. 'I mean, if our little business venture's going to work at all we're going to have to learn every trick in the book, just in order to survive.

'Just think,' she added, a dreamy, faraway look in her eyes, 'our own little pad, lots of plush and pink velvet, and a ton of gold-embossed visiting cards, one for every grateful client to remind him of his visit. "Gabriel Neavis Associates, a partner for every occasion" – how does that sound?'

'Absolutely bloody marvellous . . .' Sharon, picking up on Glynis's obvious enthusiasm for the 'dating agency' idea they'd spawned between them, began to believe for the first time that it might actually happen. A thrill of pleasure ran through her at the thought of having money of her own at last. To be able to go to all those swanky restaurants in Piccadilly – the ones she normally only saw when she walked past them in the rain – and blow a hundred pounds on a slap-up dinner which would keep her going for a week whilst thumbing her nose at the snobby waiters who, given the choice, would rather not have to give her the time of day let alone serve her. To be free at last to swan into Harrods or Harvey Nicols and splash out on an expensive little present to herself – something utterly useless and ridiculously frivolous to make up for all those times she'd waited in vain for the bunch of flowers or box of chocs which had never come . . .

It was a shame about Frankie, though. He was a nice guy and he'd shown her more respect and consideration than all the other wallies she'd previously hitched up with put together. But at the end of the day he was still a man and men, on the whole, meant trouble. They didn't possess an ounce of decency between them. They were just as likely to piss off and leave you up shit creek without a by your leave as they were to whisper sweet, empty nothings in your ear when they fancied getting their end away. On the whole, Sharon decided, she was better off without them – except on a purely professional level, of course . . . As Glynis had so rightly pointed out, a girl had to look after herself in this life, and since most men kept their brains in their dicks, those few precious square inches could prove to be an absolute goldmine for any woman with an ounce of business acumen.

Taking Glynis's hand in her own she gave it an intimate little squeeze. Yes, there was no doubt about it, Sharon thought, women were altogether a more agreeable proposition as far as emotional sensitivity and mutual trust were concerned. In fact, in a great many ways, really. Sharon's heart skipped a beat when she saw the glint of mischief in Glynis's eyes, imagining how she'd look naked, soft and warm, when they were in bed together later. All in all, things had turned out very nicely for Sharon Neavis this Christmas. Very nicely indeed . . .

'. . . I can make you mine, taste your lips of wine
any time, night or day,
Only trouble is, gee wiz, I'm dreaming my life away . . .'

Crystal sniffed, wiping away a stray tear as she stood in the doorway, clutching a glass of wine and watching Isaac and Sheba perform one of her favourite ballads. They looked good together, the two of them, bathed in a subtle rosy glow up there on the small stage, standing close together and gazing into each other's eyes from time to time as they sang. They sounded good too, knowing from previous experience, having sung together before, how best to complement each other's voices – Isaac's clear strength overlaid with Sheba's smoky blues – in a way which sent emotional shivers up and down Crystal's spine as she listened to them sing.

She must have had one too many glasses of vino, Crystal thought wryly, wiping away yet another tear. She was behaving like a silly kid, jilted at a teenage party. Suddenly she jumped and almost spilled her wine as a pair of warm, sinuous arms snaked around her waist, the hands clasping together over her belly with an easy familiarity as a soft, masculine voice murmured in her ear, 'I've been waving at you for hours from over the other side of the room and you didn't even see me. Whatever you're thinking about, it must be important.'

Crystal smiled gratefully and closed her eyes, leaning back into Max's strong, male frame, putting her free hand over his and giving it a squeeze. 'Not really. I was just wondering what we'd all be doing in a couple of months' time. You, me, Isaac . . .'

Max tightened his grip on Crystal, pressing into her supple body so that she could feel his warmth and hardness against her buttocks, his soft, winey breath caressing her neck. 'Hey, hey, why the tears? If it's Sheba you're worried about, I can tell you here and now that she doesn't stand a cat's chance where Isaac's concerned. He wouldn't touch her with a bargepole. At least,' he added hastily, remembering the cosy little Boxing Day scene he and Crystal had walked in on at the studio, 'not for very long anyway. I mean, she's a terrific broad – a walking sex manual really, more than a living woman – but she'd drive him stark staring bonkers within the space of a fortnight. She's as nutty as a fruitcake, that one. And here speaks a guy who's had the raving hots for her since he was in short pants. Metaphorically speaking, of course.'

Crystal giggled.

'Believe me,' he continued, 'women like Sheba are great as fantasy fodder for weak-kneed jerks like me to drool over, but they come with a bloody great price on their heads, and our Isaac's more aware than most of that fact.'

Crystal sighed, rubbing her cheek against Max's so that he could smell her sleek, shiny hair and the subtle scent of her perfume. 'It's not really Sheba I'm worried about, Max. It's just all the changes that are happening around the place at the moment . . .'

'Isaac told me about the job in Cannes,' Max whispered, pulling Crystal round to face him. 'Have you accepted it?'

Crystal smiled at him and nodded, slowly putting her arms around him and nuzzling his nose with her own.

'Great! You'll love it,' he said, taking her face in his hands and planting a kiss on her forehead. 'We all need a change of scene from time to time – even you. I've a good mind to have a holiday down there next summer and come and see you. Besides, just think for a moment of six months' worth of sun, sea, sand and sex. Makes the mind boggle just to think about it. Especially the sex . . .

'Anyway, that's quite enough about the future,' Max murmured huskily, his face inches from Crystal's as his eyes gazed into hers. 'Let's think about what's going to happen right now. Your place or mine . . .'

At that moment, the sound of Big Ben striking midnight resonated from the speakers in all four corners of the room, heralding in the New Year, and every person present at High Links Hall that night joined forces with streamers, party poppers and shouts of joyful greeting until the whole place resounded with laughter, happiness and hope for the coming year.

Only two people were conspicuous by their absence. Crystal and Max had disappeared in search of a little privacy, hell-bent on a party game or two of their own.

Headline Delta Erotic Survey

In order to provide the kind of books you like to read - and to qualify for a free erotic novel of the Editor's choice - we would appreciate it if you would complete the following survey and send your answers, together with any further comments, to:

> Headline Book Publishing
> FREEPOST (WD 4984)
> London
> NW1 0YR

1. Are you male or female?
2. Age? Under 20 / 20 to 30 / 30 to 40 / 40 to 50 / 50 to 60 / 60 to 70 / over
3. At what age did you leave full-time education?
4. Where do you live? (Main geographical area)
5. Are you a regular erotic book buyer / a regular book buyer in general / both?
6. How much approximately do you spend a year on erotic books / on books in general?
7. How did you come by this book?
7a. If you bought it, did you purchase from: a national bookchain / a high street store / a newsagent / a motorway station / an airport / a railway station / other........
8. Do you find erotic books easy / hard to come by?
8a. Do you find Headline Delta erotic books easy / hard to come by?
9. Which are the best / worst erotic books you have ever read?
9a. Which are the best / worst Headline Delta erotic books you have ever read?
10. Within the erotic genre there are many periods, subjects and literary styles. Which of the following do you prefer:
10a. (period) historical / Victorian / C20th / contemporary / future?
10b. (subject) nuns / whores & whorehouses / Continental frolics / s&m / vampires / modern realism / escapist fantasy / science fiction?

10c. (styles) hardboiled / humorous / hardcore / ironic /
      romantic / realistic?
10d. Are there any other ingredients that particularly appeal
      to you?
11.   We try to create a cover appearance that is suitable for
      each title. Do you consider them to be successful?
12.   Would you prefer them to be less explicit / more
      explicit?
13.   We would be interested to hear of your other reading
      habits. What other types of books do you read?
14.   Who are your favourite authors?
15.   Which newspapers do you read?
16.   Which magazines?
17.   Do you have any other comments or suggestions to
      make?

If you would like to receive a free erotic novel of the Editor's
choice (available only to UK residents), together with an up-
to-date listing of Headline Delta titles, please supply your
name and address. Please allow 28 days for delivery.

Name..

Address...

....

....

A selection of Erotica
from Headline

SCANDAL IN PARADISE	Anonymous	£4.99	☐
UNDER ORDERS	Nick Aymes	£4.99	☐
RECKLESS LIAISONS	Anonymous	£4.99	☐
GROUPIES II	Johnny Angelo	£4.99	☐
TOTAL ABANDON	Anonymous	£4.99	☐
AMOUR ENCORE	Marie-Claire Villefranche	£4.99	☐
COMPULSION	Maria Caprio	£4.99	☐
INDECENT	Felice Ash	£4.99	☐
AMATEUR DAYS	Becky Bell	£4.99	☐
EROS IN SPRINGTIME	Anonymous	£4.99	☐
GOOD VIBRATIONS	Jeff Charles	£4.99	☐
CITIZEN JULIETTE	Louise Aragon	£4.99	☐

All Headline books are available at your local bookshop or newsagent, or can be ordered direct from the publisher. Just tick the titles you want and fill in the form below. Prices and availability subject to change without notice.

Headline Book Publishing, Cash Sales Department, Bookpoint, 39 Milton Park, Abingdon, OXON, OX14 4TD, UK. If you have a credit card you may order by telephone – 0235 400400.

Please enclose a cheque or postal order made payable to Bookpoint Ltd to the value of the cover price and allow the following for postage and packing:
UK & BFPO: £1.00 for the first book, 50p for the second book and 30p for each additional book ordered up to a maximum charge of £3.00.
OVERSEAS & EIRE: £2.00 for the first book, £1.00 for the second book and 50p for each additional book.

Name ....

Address ....

....

....

If you would prefer to pay by credit card, please complete:
Please debit my Visa/Access/Diner's Card/American Express (delete as applicable) card no:

Signature .... Expiry Date ....